Edward Cary

George William Curtis

Edward Cary

George William Curtis

ISBN/EAN: 9783743441927

Manufactured in Europe, USA, Canada, Australia, Japa

Cover: Foto ©Raphael Reischuk / pixelio.de

Manufactured and distributed by brebook publishing software (www.brebook.com)

Edward Cary

George William Curtis

American Men of Letters

GEORGE WILLIAM CURTIS

American Men of Letters

GEORGE WILLIAM CURTIS

BY

EDWARD CARY

BOSTON AND NEW YORK
HOUGHTON MIFFLIN COMPANY
The Riverside Press Cambridge

TO

MRS. FRANCIS GEORGE SHAW

THIS LIFE OF OUR DEAR FRIEND

IS WITH RESPECT AND AFFECTION

DEDICATED

BY THE AUTHOR

CONTENTS.

CONTENTS.

Note. The portrait of Mr. Curtis which forms the frontispiece of this volume is reproduced by permission from a photograph made by the F. Gutekunst Co., of Philadelphia.

GEORGE WILLIAM CURTIS.

CHAPTER I.

FAMILY AND YOUTH.

The "Elizabeth and Ann" sailed from the port of London on the 6th of May, 1635, for New England. In Hotten's "List of Emigrants to America"[1] the names and ages of her seven "passingers" are given, and it is stated that they "brought certificates from the Ministers where their abodes were, and from the Justices of Peace, of their conformitie to the orders and discipline of the Church of England, and y^t they are no subsidy men." It is added that they had taken the oaths of allegiance and supremacy. Of these names the last is that of Henry Curtis, and his age is given as twenty-seven. This was the founder of

---

[1] "(Regi)ster of the names of all ye Passingers wch Passed from ye Port of London for on whole year Endinge X mas 1635.

6 May 1635.

Theis under-written names are to be transported to New England, imbarqued in the Elizabeth and Ann, Roger Coop (Cooper) Mr. the p-ties have brought Cert: from the Ministers where their abodes were and from the Justices of Peace of their conformitie to the orders and discipline of the Church of England and yt they are no subsidy men. They have taken the oaths of alleg: and Suprem : "

the family [1] of which George William Curtis was a descendant in the sixth generation. Henry Curtis [2] settled at Watertown, in Massachusetts, having had five " lots " granted to him, and having bought two. Later he removed to Sudbury, where his eldest son, Ephraim, was born in 1642, he having married Mary Guy, the daughter of Nicholas Guy, a carpenter who had emigrated from Upton Gray, near Southampton, England. Ephraim appears in the colonial history of his time as a man of energy, courage, and a strong will. In 1675, when he was thirty-three years old, it is recorded of him that, because he was " noted for his intimate

[1] The genealogy of Mr. Curtis, as traced by his son, is as follows : —

CURTIS.	BURRILL.
Henry–Mary Guy	George
1608–1678	1630–1683
Ephraim	John–Lois **Ivory**
1642–1734	1651–1703
John–Rebekah Waite	Ebenezer–Martha **Farrington**
1707–1797	1676–1761
John–Elizabeth **Hayward**	Ebenezer–Mary **Mansfield**
1731–1768	1701–1778
David–Susanna Stone	James–Elizabeth Rawson
1763–1813	1743–1825
George–Mary Elizabeth Burrill	**James–Sally** Arnold
1796–1856	**1772–1820**
George William	Mary Elizabeth
1824–1892	1798–1826

[2] James Savage, in his *Genealogical Dictionary of the First Settlers of New England, showing Three Generations,* notes (vol. i. p. 485): " Curtis, Henry, Watertown 1636, an orig. propr. of Sudbury, m. Mary, d. of Nicholas Guy, had Ephraim, b. 31 Mar., 1643; John, 1644 ; & Joseph, 1647; nam. in their gr.mo's will 1666 ; & d. 8 May 1678."

knowledge of the country, his quickness of comprehension and cool courage, and his large acquaintance with the Indians, whose language he spoke fluently," the court sent him as an interpreter with an embassy which started from Cambridge, July 28, with an escort of twenty men under Captains Edward Hutchinson and Thomas Wheeler. On the 2d of August they were attacked from ambush. Eight of the little force were killed and five were wounded. The remainder took refuge in a house in Brookfield, and Ephraim Curtis, with a companion, was sent toward the nearest post to report their plight and secure relief. He returned before leaving the town, having learned that the Indians were in force and intended a night attack. A second time he " readily assented to adventure forth again on that service " alone, his companion having been killed meanwhile. Again he was forced to return. " But towards morning," says Captain Wheeler, " said Ephraim adventured forth for the third time, and was fain to creep on his hands and knees for some space of ground, that he might not be discerned by the enemy. But by God's mercy, he escaped their hands and got safely to Marlborough, tho' very much spent and ready to faint by reason of want of sleep before he left us, and his sore travel night and day in the hot season till he got thither." For his gallant services in this year he was made a lieutenant, accredited as in the " direct service " of the council, paid the sum of " 2£," and given the right to gather the corn of "our enemies, the Indians that are fled." Later in the year the English were withdrawn from Worcester, the place was burned, and Lieutenant Curtis returned to Sudbury.

He had been the first settler of Worcester. Indeed, he was so emphatically the first, and was so solidly settled, that when a committee of the General Court visited the place to lay out a town there, they found Ephraim Curtis established, and so resolved to assert his rights that it took extended legal proceedings, all of which are recorded in the quaint language of the time, to dislodge him. Nor was this finally accomplished until there had been made over to him other lands, which seem, by the description of them, to have been compensation in ample measure for those which his enterprise had laid hold upon. I have said this much of the life of Ephraim Curtis, because he is the only one of the earliest members of the family of whom there is a clear record, and because it makes plain the nature of the stock from which George William Curtis was derived. It was not the usual Puritan or Pilgrim type, but apparently that of the smaller gentry of England, whose " conformitie to the orders and discipline of the Church of England" was duly acknowledged, and who were "no subsidy men." The men of this class had independence and self-reliance in plenty ; were full of resource, quick of wit, eager to seize every opportunity ; resolute, even daring ; faithful to duty, —

good as friends, formidable as foes. It was a good stock. In the life of George William Curtis some of these qualities will reappear; and if they are not generally associated with his name by his contemporaries, it is because in part they were rendered less prominent by the radiance of gentler and rarer qualities; but, as will I hope be seen, the better of them were not absent, and in the phrase of the physiologist " persisted," and were very strong.

One other figure in the Curtis family attracts attention, — that of John Curtis, the eldest son of Ephraim. He was born (1707) in Worcester, and up to the outbreak of the Revolution was an active and noted citizen, — selectman, surveyor of the highways, captain in the French and Indian War. He was also a tavern-keeper and a leading member of the church, and his house was much frequented by the clergymen of the day. But he was a sturdy and open loyalist. In 1774 he signed a protest against what he regarded as the revolutionary action of the town, whereupon the town, premising that he was one of those on whom it had " Conferred many favours and Consequently might expect their Kindest and best Services," resolved that he and his fellow-signers be " Deemed unworthy of holding any Town office of Profit or Honour until they have made satisfaction for this offence to the acceptance of the town which ought to be made as public as their Protest was." He declined at this time to make any retraction, and in the next year he was declared a public enemy, disarmed, and forbidden to leave the town. But in 1777 he seems to have made his peace, as it was voted to receive him and others "into the Town's favour, and that further prosecution against them as enemies of the United States of America shall cease, they paying the costs that has arisen already by means of their being prosecuted as Enemies to the United States, agreeable to their petition." Here was a strain of practical independence in the Curtis blood not inconsistent with a disposition to make the best of facts that could not be changed. .

The great-grandson of this John Curtis was George Curtis, the father of George William. He was born in Worcester in 1796, but removed to Providence, R. I. There he married Mary Elizabeth Burrill, daughter of James Burrill, Jr., who was Chief Justice of Rhode Island, and at one time a member of the United States Senate from that State, an opponent of the Missouri Compromise, and a man of marked ability and high character. Of this marriage were born James Burrill Curtis, in 1822, and George William Curtis, February 24, 1824. Mrs. Curtis died in 1826 when George was but two years old. In 1835 Mr. Curtis married, as his second wife, a daughter of Samuel W. Bridgham, of Providence. Of Mr. Curtis his eldest son (now living in England) writes that he was of "high integrity, sound, practical judgment, and excellent business talents, together with political and literary taste. He was popular among his associates — leading business and professional men —

in Providence and New York. He was most affectionate and beloved in his family, and extremely
kind and indulgent to his children, though sharp
and severe in his demands as to manners and
morals. He valued truthfulness and honesty above
all other qualities, and his example and influence
in these respects early impressed both George and
me very deeply. In a letter of 1860 George, replying to a question of mine about his religious views,
writes thus (the italics are George's) : ' I believe
in God, who is love ; that all men are brothers ;
and that the only essential duty of every man is
to be *honest*, by which I understand his absolute
following of his conscience when duly enlightened.
I do *not* believe that God is anxious that men
should believe this or that theory of the Godhead,
or of the Divine Government, but that they should
live purely, justly, and lovingly.' These, I take it,
were the essential articles of his creed to the end ;
and, whatever may be thought of them, at least
the paramount value, or his estimation, of honesty
and practical goodness, is conspicuous."

To this instructive glimpse of the influence of
the father I am happily able to add one equally instructive, from the same source, as to the influence
of the second mother. Mr. J. B. Curtis writes
of her : " She was a woman of much good sense
and practical energy, of strong and generous sympathies, and of high public spirit and piety ; and
she added to these things literary cultivation de-
cidedly above the average. She wrote with ease,

whether in letters or other compositions, a full, graceful, flowing, delightful English style. She once wrote to us in high girlish spirits that she believed she loved her ready-made children the best. Certainly she made herself to a very unusual degree our intimate friend and companion, becoming mother and sister (we never had an actual sister) in one; and she was thus able to encourage in George and me, in the most genial and natural way, everything that was good."

From the age of six to that of eleven, George, with his elder brother, attended the school of C. W. Greene at Jamaica Plain, near Boston; but on his father's second marriage he was brought again to Providence and placed in school there, until he was fifteen, when (1839) his father removed to New York. Of the school days at Jamaica Plain I know nothing save that they left pleasant and tender memories, and furnished some of the detail for the earlier chapters of "Trumps." There is in "Sea from Shore," one of the chapters of "Prue and I," a picture of the Providence wharves that is worth citing for its delightful local color, and its suggestion of the influence of the seaside town and of the sensitiveness of the boyish mind: —

"My earliest remembrances are of a long range of old, half-dilapidated stores; red-brick stores with steep wooden roofs and stone window-frames and door-frames, which stood upon docks built as if for immense trade with all quarters of the globe.

"Generally there were only a few sloops moored

to the tremendous posts, which I fancied could easily hold fast a Spanish Armada in a tropical hurricane. But sometimes a great ship, an East Indiaman, with rusty, seamed, blistered sides and dingy sails, came slowly moving up the harbor, with an air of indolent self-importance and consciousness of superiority, which inspired me with profound respect. If the ship had ever chanced to run down a row-boat, or a sloop, or any specimen of smaller craft, I should only have wondered at the temerity of any floating thing in crossing the path of such supreme majesty. The ship was leisurely chained and cabled to the old dock, and then came the disemboweling. Long after the confusion of unloading was over, and the ship lay as if all voyages were ended, I dared to creep timorously along the edge of the dock, and, at great risk of falling in the black water of its huge shadow, I placed my hand upon the hot hulk, and so established a mystic and exquisite connection with Pacific Islands; with palm groves and all the passionate beauties they embower; with jungles, Bengal tigers, pepper, and the crushed feet of Chinese fairies. I touched Asia, the Cape of Good Hope, and the Happy Islands. I would not believe that the heat I felt was of our Northern sun; to my finer sympathy, it burned with equatorial fervor.

"The freight was piled in the old stores. I believe that many of them remain, but they have lost their character. When I knew them, not only was I younger, but partial decay had overtaken the town ; at least the bulk of its India trade had drifted to New York and Boston. But the appliances remained. There was no throng of busy traffickers; and after school, in the afternoon, I strolled by and gazed into the solemn interiors.

" Silence reigned within, — silence, dimness, and piles of foreign treasures. Vast coils of cable, like tame boa-constrictors, served as seats for men with large stomachs and heavy watch-seals, and nankeen trousers, who sat looking out of the door toward the ships, with little other sign of life than an occasional low talking, as if in their sleep. Huge hogsheads, perspiring brown sugar, and oozing slow molasses, as if nothing tropical could keep within bounds, but must continuously expand and exude and overflow, stood against the walls, and had an architectural significance, for they darkly reminded me of Egyptian prints, and in the duskiness of the low-vaulted store seemed cyclopean columns incomplete. Strange festoons and heaps of bags; square piles of boxes cased in mats, bales of airy summer stuffs which even in winter scoffed at cold, and shamed it by audacious assumption of eternal sun ; little specimen boxes of precious dyes, that even now shine through my memory like old Venetian schools unpainted, — these were all there in rich confusion.

" The stores had a twilight of dimness; the air was spicy with mingled odors. I liked to look suddenly in from the glare of sunlight outside, and then the cool sweet dimness was like the palpable breath of the far-off island groves; and if only some parrot or macaw hung within would flaunt with glistening plumage in his cage, and, as the gay hue flashed in a chance sunbeam, call in his hard, shrill voice, as if thrusting sharp sounds upon a glistening wire from out that grateful gloom, then the enchantment was complete, and without moving I was circumnavigating the globe.

"From the old stores and the docks slowly crumbling, touched, I knew not why or how, by the pensive air of past prosperity, I rambled out of town on those well-remembered afternoons to the fields that lay upon hillsides over the harbor, and there sat looking out to sea, fancying some distant sail, proceeding to the glorious ends of the earth, to be my type and image, who would so sail, stately and successful, to all the glorious ports of the Future."

These are passages both of memory and imagination, and date fifteen years later than the life to which they relate. But the memories of a man of thirty are not dim, and the imagination owns the spell of memory when it plays upon the time of boyhood. I take the picture to be a true one.

In these early days, and until Curtis was twenty-five years old, there was one person whose influence, strong and continuous and intimate, was always remembered as "a great debt," — his brother Burrill. During this quarter of a century, and for more than a third of Mr. Curtis's life, they were constantly together, occupying the same room at home, at school, at Brook Farm, at Concord, and during much of the journeying abroad. He is the model from which was drawn the portrait of "Our Cousin the Curate" in "Prue and I." It does not concern me or my readers to know how far the story embraced in that sketch is based on the brothers' experience, but it will throw light on the springtime of Mr. Curtis's life, when the sap coursed free and strong and the force and direction of aftergrowth were being determined, to cite here a few passages from the sketch : —

"There is no subject which does not seem to lead naturally to our Cousin the Curate. As the soft air steals in and envelops everything in the world, so that the trees and the hills and the rivers, the cities, the crops, and the sea, are made remote and delicate and beautiful by its pure baptism, so over all the events of our little lives, comforting, refining, and elevating, falls like a benediction the remembrance of our cousin the curate.

"He was my only early companion. He had no brother, I had none, and we became brothers to each other. He was always beautiful. His face was symmetrical and delicate ; his figure was slight and graceful. He looked as the sons of kings ought to look, — as I am sure Philip Sidney looked when he was a boy. His eyes were blue, and as you looked at them they seemed to let you gaze out into a June heaven. The blood ran close to the skin, and his complexion had the rich transparency of light. There was nothing gross or heavy in his expression or texture; his soul seemed to have mastered his body. But he had strong passions, for his delicacy was positive, not negative; it was not weakness, but intensity.

"Often, when I returned panting and restless from some frolic which had wasted almost all the night, I was rebuked as I entered the room in which he lay peacefully sleeping. There was something holy in the profound repose of his beauty; and as I stood looking at him, how many a time the tears have dropped from my hot eyes upon his face, while I vowed to make myself worthy of such a companion! for I felt my heart owning its allegiance to that strong and imperial nature.

"My cousin was loved by the boys, but the girls worshiped him. His mind, large in grasp and subtle in perception, naturally commanded his companions, while the lustre of his character allured those who could not understand him. The asceticism occasionally showed itself a vein of hardness, or rather of severity, in his treatment of others. He did what he thought it his duty to do, but he forgot that few could see the right so closely as he, and very few of those few could so calmly obey the least command of conscience. I confess I was a little afraid of him, for I think I never could be severe.

"In the long winter evenings I often read to Prue the story of some old father of the church, or some quaint poem of George Herbert's; and every Christmas Eve I read to her Milton's 'Hymn on the

Nativity.' Yet when the saint seems to us **most** saintly, or the poem most **pathetic** or **sublime**, we find ourselves talking **of** our cousin the curate. I have **not** seen him **for many years**; but when we parted, **his** head had the intellectual symmetry of Milton's, without the Puritanic stoop, and with the stately grace of a cavalier."

CHAPTER II.

WITH the evidence afforded in the passages quoted in the last chapter, written some six years after parting with his brother in Europe, of the place that brother held in his heart and life, I venture to give some notes by Mr. Burrill Curtis of their life together from 1835, when they returned from school to Providence, to 1846, when they sailed for Europe : —

"Not long after (1835), another powerful influence reached us, which prevailed in our lives for seven or eight years. This was the influence of R. W. Emerson. It was then first beginning to extend itself in New England, and not only the United States, but Great Britain also, have since become indebted to it. He was the sympathizing leader and moderating patron, so to speak, of that ferment and stir after all kinds of reform which, according to his own account, had taken possession of so many men and women around him from about the year 1820 onward. His large endowment of cheerful humor, of intellectual acuteness, and of sober common-sense did not prevent his holding persistently aloft, in an exceptional degree, the torch of the ideal in everything ; and though his thought was usually characterized by profundity, comprehensiveness, and severe balance, — albeit it was often too fine-spun and mystical, — he was so sanguine, and so optimistically enamored of his ideals, as not unfrequently to overlook the exorbitancy and impracticability of some of them. He was an ardent apostle of ' liberty ' even to the apparent obeying of one's ' whims ; ' but he was an equally ardent and strenuous apostle of ' law ' in its highest or most stringent senses. Nature's law (which includes the moral law) ordains liberty, it is true, but it ordains the ' regulation ' of liberty also; and while Emerson stands on the one hand stoutly for freedom, independence, self-reliance, heroism, — nay, even inconsistency and nonconformity, — he stands on the other hand as piously and immovably, like a rapt saint, for obedience to natural and moral law. Our coming into contact with this New England ' movement ' (called in our time ' Transcendentalism '), and especially with its leader and moderator, proved to be the cardinal event of our youth; and I cannot but think that the seed then sown took such deep root as to flower continuously in our later years, and make us both the confirmed ' Independents ' that we were and are, whilst fully conscious at the same time of the obligation of living in all possible harmony with our fellows.

" I still recall the impressions produced by Emerson's delivery of his address on the ' Over-Soul ' in Mr. Hartshorn's semicircular school - room in

Providence, our native town. He seemed to speak as an inhabitant of heaven, and with the inspiration and authority of a prophet. Although a large part of the matter of that discourse, when reduced to its lowest terms, does not greatly differ from the commonplaces of piety and religion, yet its form and its tone were so fresh and vivid that they made the matter also seem to be uttered for the first time, and to be a direct outcome from the inmost source of the highest truth. We heard Emerson lecture frequently, and made his personal acquaintance. My enthusiastic admiration of him and his writings soon mounted to a high and intense 'hero-worship,' which, when it subsided, seems to have left me ever since incapable of attaching myself as a follower to any other man. How far George shared such feelings, if at all, I cannot precisely say; but he so far shared my enthusiastic admiration as to be led a willing captive to Emerson's attractions, and to the incidental attractions of the movement of which he was the head; and Emerson always continued to command from us both the sincerest reverence and homage.

" I do not remember that George ever committed himself to any important extravagance of 're-form.' I, for my part, was at first carried away into personal experiments of disusing money and animal food; but I was soon convinced of my errors and abandoned them. Comparatively unimportant vagaries about dress we both partook of. The 'movement' affected and modified our aims and ideas in various respects as individuals, but did not enlist us as permanent and well-drilled soldiers in social schemes and causes. It awakened our interest in the reforming ideas of others around us ; but neither the anti-slavery cause (which afterwards aroused in George an heroic zeal and devotion), nor the temperance cause, nor any other, however apparently important, then secured from us anything more than a reasonable speculative consideration. We were intent mainly, not on reforming others, or reforming society at large, but on the ordering of our own individual lives."

In 1839, when George was fifteen, his father removed from Providence to New York, and became connected with the Bank of Commerce, first as cashier and afterwards as president. His home was on the north side of Washington Place, then the centre of the most desirable residence quarter of the city. It is a pleasure to note that the fine old house has remained for more than half a century in the Curtis family, and is one of the few in which has been amassed a fund of those associations, glad or sad, but with the lapse of time always and uniquely sweet, which make a house, in a far deeper than the technical sense, " real " estate. Mr. George Curtis, by his personal qualities, tastes, and attainments, as by his business relations and ability, became naturally a member of what was in truth, if not by its own claim, the best society of the city of that time, and in this society both he and his wife were fitted to get and to give the best.

They were members, first, of Dr. Orville Dewey's Unitarian congregation, and afterwards of that of Dr. Bellows. Young Curtis was surrounded by influences that awakened and developed in him the remarkable social gifts which afterwards distinguished him, and trained his active and adventurous mind in healthy ways. I do not learn much of the details of his life at this time, further than that he devoted a good deal of time to study at home, partly under the guidance of tutors, partly under that of his father and mother, and that there was a brief experience in the counting-room of a German importing and shipping house, which was abandoned, for what reason I cannot say, but with happy result.

Mr. Burrill Curtis writes : " As I, while at college, had fallen so much under the influence of the New England 'Transcendental Movement' as to have been led by it into a practical vagary about money and its use, it was probably something of a relief to our father that, a while after my having come to my senses, George and I proposed nothing worse than to become boarders, and boarders only, with the Community at Brook Farm." This was in 1842, and about two years were passed by the brothers at West Roxbury, — for George, the years from eighteen to twenty. As he and his brother were " boarders, and boarders only," it is hardly worth while to describe here the purposes of the founders of this peculiar home. Mr. Emerson, in his " Historic Notes of Life and Letters in New England," sums them up sufficiently : —

"The founders of Brook Farm should have this praise, that they made what all people try to make, an agreeable place to live in. All comers, even the most fastidious, found it the pleasantest of residences. It is certain that freedom from household routine, variety of character and talent, variety of work, variety of means of thought and instruction, art, music, poetry, reading, masquerade, did not permit sluggishness or despondency, broke up routine. There is agreement in the testimony that it was, to most of the associates, education ; to many the most important period of their life, the birth of valued friendships, their first acquaintance with the riches of conversation, their training in behavior. The art of letter-writing, it is said, was immensely cultivated ; letters were always flying, not only from house to house, but from room to room. It was a perpetual picnic, a French Revolution in small, an Age of Reason in a patty-pan."

Unfortunately, Mr. Emerson, like many smaller men, was not wholly free from the temptation of phrase-making, and the last sentence is more amusing than clear. So far as I can trace the influence of the life at Brook Farm on young Curtis, he escaped pretty well the element of the " French Revolution " and the " Age of Reason," unquestionably made close and valuable friendships, and had (as well as contributed) his full share of the " picnic." I find that he studied, with apparently much application, German, agricultural chemistry, and music, the last with great zest under the instruction of Mr.

John Dwight. In June, 1843, his second year, he wrote to his father : —

"My life is summery enough. We breakfast at six and from seven to twelve I am at work. After dinner, these fair days permit no homage but to their beauty, and I am fain to woo their smiles in the shades and sunlights of the woods. A festal life for one before whom the great sea stretches which must be sailed; yet this summer air teaches life-navigation, and I listen to the flowing streams, and to the cool rush of the winds among the trees, with an increase of that hope which is the only pole-star of life."

This expresses, I should say, the spirit of the youth. It was essentially earnest in its main motive, and was not inconsistent with the utmost delight in the pleasures that presented themselves, or that were to be had for the seeking. He had a most pleasing voice, and a face and form of exquisite beauty, and I read of his singing lingering in the memory of his companions thirty years later, and of equally vivid recollections of his personal charm. One chronicler recalls a "masquerade picnic in the woods," — "We were thrown into convulsions of laughter at the sight of G. W. C. dressed as Fanny Elssler, making courtesies and pirouetting down the path;" and another occasion when he "led the quadrille as Hamlet, and looked 'the Dane' to the life."

A lady who was a resident at Brook Farm, and whose friendship then formed lasted through the life of Curtis, furnishes some notes as to that time that confirm the impression I have indicated. She recalls one "bright May morning" when, going from the "Eyrie" to the "Hive" for breakfast, she approached the "gate through which George Bradford and the fascinating Hawthorne" were wont to drive the cows. The gate was "held wide open by our handsome young man, Charles A. Dana, who did himself proud at such honors, not having the certain reserve and diffidence that many of our Brook Farm men had. . . . With C. A. D. were two young men who, as I remember them, looked like young Greek gods. 'These must be the Curtises,' I thought, 'two wonderfully charming young men' of whom Mr. Ripley had spoken.

"Burrill, the elder, with a typical Greek face and long hair falling to his shoulders in irregular curls, I remember as most unconscious of himself, interested in all about him, talking of the Greek philosophers as if he had just come from one of Socrates' walks, carrying the high philosophy into his daily life; helping the young people with hard arithmetic lessons; trimming the lamps daily at the Eyrie, where the brothers came to live (my sister saw George assisting him one day, and occasionally, she says, he turned his face with a disgusted expression, trying to puff away the disagreeable odor); never losing control of himself, with the kindest manner to every person. He and George seemed very companionable and fond of each other.

"George, though only eighteen, — one year older

than I, — seemed much older, like a man of twenty-five possibly, with a peculiar elegance, if I may so express it; great and admirable attention, as I recollect, when listening to any one; courteous recognition of others' convictions and even prejudices; and never a personal animosity of any kind, — a certain remoteness of manner, however, that I think prevented persons from becoming acquainted with him as easily as with Burrill.

"George and Mr. Bradford, on cold, stormy washing days in winter, used to wrap themselves as warmly as possible, and insisted on hanging out the clothes for the women, — a chivalry equal to that of Walter Raleigh throwing down his cloak before the Queen Elizabeth."

This lady speaks also of the part taken by George Curtis in the gayeties of the place, and the charm he lent them. I find in one of his own letters, written a few years after leaving Roxbury, a reminiscence of Brook Farm that shows the impression made by some of the characters there. He speaks of "the solemn sphynx, Alcott, dispensing his great discourse on one of his visitations with L——, his solemn shadow, to Brook Farm, when he held a talk in the dreary Morton House one glorious June evening. It was as stately and inhuman as if there had been no stars shining, and Carrie S. and I slipped out of one of the long windows and went to walk. It is a great pity that Mr. Alcott is too old to learn that the condition of the Kingdom is, not the being a grave philosopher, but a little child. Yet he always has about him the grandeur you would predict of his brow and eye, the solitary old sphynx grandeur of the desert."

I add the following reference, in a letter to his father, to Webster and his oration at Bunker Hill in June, 1843, partly because a good sign of what a boy of nineteen has in him is what he finds in others, and partly because these extracts show the fine and fruitful sympathy between young Curtis and his father : —

" I was sorry not to see you on the day we watched eagerly the coming of the 'Sons of New England from New York,' when they were marching to the Common to form. The day was a fine one to me. Finest of all, that I saw and heard Daniel Webster. We struggled through the crowd, and stood only a rod or two in front of him, saw him plainly, heard him distinctly. It was a noble spectacle. As far on one side as the eye could reach up the hill was a silent multitude, out of whose midst, solemnly and lonely against the sky, rose the monument. On the other stood this man solemn and lonely also, the strength of Olympian Jove in his figure and mein, yet a wild, lonely spectacle. Too great for party, not yet great enough for quiet independence. Not the calm dignity of a soul self-centred who rules the world, but the restless grandeur of a Titan storming heaven. His mouth curled, his eye flashed, as if among that mass he was king, but the higher crown could not be seen upon him. Though by no means satisfying my idea of a great man, he is certainly a strong man, — Hercules, if not Apollo."

Brook Farm was notoriously the home of reformers. A lad as warm-hearted, eager, and imaginative as Curtis might easily have been unsettled and warped by them. That he was not is shown in the following passages from still another letter to his father, in which that keen guardian of sanity, a sense of humor, shines lightly : —

" DEAR FATHER, — Will you send me $20 to pay for a coat which I have had made in Boston ? You will smile at such a request after my unmitigated condemnation of coats and resolute tunic-wearing in Providence last summer; yet had you taken apartments in my mind since then, and closely observed all changes and growths that occurred, you would see how natural it is. The stern protest, which distinguishes the birth of reform, against society, the church, and all things but the sovereign *I*, gradually gives way to that other better state of affirmation and reception which, deserting the faith not a whit, leads an outward life in beautiful harmony with all men and things ! ' What was done before,' says Fénelon, ' to gratify the lusts and vanities of the man is now done for the glory of God.' No wise man is long a reformer, for Wisdom sees plainly that growth is steady, sure, and neither condemns nor rejects what is, or has been. Reform is organized distrust. It says to the universe fresh from God's hand, ' You are a miserable business ; lo ! I will **make you fairer !** ' and so deputes some

Fourier or Robert Owen to improve the bungling work of the Creator." After a couple of pages of this elaborate badinage, the youngster concludes: " From such brief hints, possibly some time to be expanded as more light flows in, you may get dim glimpses at my position, and so perhaps not altogether smiling, send me $20."

The importance of the Brook Farm episode in Curtis's life may very easily be exaggerated, and I think has been so in the minds of some who have written of him. The fame, not to say the notoriety, of the place and the persons associated with it made a strong impression, though a vague one; and it is almost unavoidable that any one even indirectly engaged in the " movement " should have borne a more or less distinct mark of it in the public mind, and not wholly to his advantage, since it suggests a strain of " queerness." I very well recall the conviction of a man of strong nature, in general sympathy with Mr. Curtis in his mature years, who accounted for the views of the latter on the rights of women by the theory that " there must be a screw loose somewhere in a man who graduated from that lunatic school at Brook Farm." It is true that Mr. Ripley, the very father of the scheme, became one of the broadest, sanest, and most just of literary critics; that Mr. Dana, who was a very active coadjutor of Mr. Ripley, became a famous journalist, whose acute and trained scholarship was coupled with qualities not at all suggestive of fanaticism,

and whose aims were the opposite of visionary or
utopian. Unquestionably Curtis was influenced
strongly by the experience of those two years; he
must have been a very dull boy had he not been;
and what that influence was, in part, is described
in the lines of Uhland's Song, of which he was
fond : —

> " What morning dreams reveal to me
> The evening makes forever true."

There was much in the generous confidence, the
courageous hope, the high aspiration, and the fine
assertion of the right and duty of individuality
of the leaders at Brook Farm with which Curtis
remained in intimate sympathy all his life; and
he had no less true appreciation of it, but one all
the more true, because he saw the comical side of
the experience and enjoyed it.

In one of the Easy Chair essays, Mr. Curtis
wrote of Brook Farm *à propos* of a passage in
Hawthorne's " Note-Book : " " The society at Brook
Farm was composed of every kind of person.
There were the ripest scholars, men and women
of the most æsthetic culture and accomplishment,
young farmers, seamstresses, mechanics, preachers,
the industrious, the lazy, the conceited, the sentimental. But they associated in such a spirit, and
under such conditions, that, with some extravagance, the best of everybody appeared, and there
was a kind of high *esprit de corps*, at least in
the earlier or golden age of the colony. There
was plenty of steady, essential, hard work, for the

founding of an earthly paradise upon a New England farm is no pastime. But with the best intention, and much practical knowledge and industry and devotion, there was in the nature of the case an inevitable lack of method, and economical failure was almost a foregone conclusion. But there were never such witty potato patches, and such sparkling corn-fields before or since. The weeds were scratched out of the ground to the music of Tennyson or Browning, and the nooning was an hour as gay and bright as any brilliant midnight at Ambrose's.

" Compared with other efforts upon which time and money and industry are lavished, measured by Colorado and Nevada speculations, by California gold-washing, by oil-boring and the stock exchange, Brook Farm was certainly a very reasonable and practical enterprise, worthy of the hope and aid of generous men and women. The friendships that were formed there were enduring. The devotion to noble endeavor, the sympathy with what is most useful to men, the kind patience and constant charity that were fostered there, have been no more lost than grain dropped upon the field. . . . The spirit that was concentrated at Brook Farm is diffused, but not lost. As an organized effort, after many downward changes, it failed; but those who remember the Hive, the Eyrie, the Cottage, when Margaret Fuller came and talked, radiant with bright humor, — when Emerson and Parker and Hedge joined the circle for a night or day; when those who may not be named publicly brought beauty and wit and social sympathy to the feast; when the practical possibilities of life seemed fairer, and life and character were touched ineffaceably with good influence, — cherish a pleasant vision which no fate can harm, and remember with ceaseless gratitude the blithe days at Brook Farm."

After Brook Farm there was an interval at home in New York which was crowded with work and pleasure. The latter came chiefly from music and the social circle in which the family moved. In November, 1843, he writes from New York to a very dear friend, with whom the relations formed at Brook Farm continued through life: " I have heard fine music since I have been here, — Ole Bull, Castillan, etc., etc." After describing some of his social occupations, he adds : " My days I pass in my room reading Goethe's ' Wilhelm Meister ' and Novalis. With Burrill I read ' Agricultural Chemistry ' and ' Practical Agriculture.' Next week, with mother, we shall begin the Epistles and Gospels. Apart from these, more strictly, studies, I am reading Shakespeare, Beaumont and Fletcher, Massinger, Ford, and smaller poets."

Thus the winter passed in the old home. In the spring of 1844 the brothers, George being then just passed twenty, went to Concord, " for the better furtherance," as the elder writes, " of our main and original end, — the desire to unite in our own persons the freedom of a country life with moderate outdoor manual occupation, and with intellectual cultivation and pursuits.

"At Concord we first took up our residence in the family of an elderly farmer, recommended by Mr. Emerson. We gave up half the day (except in haytime, when we gave the whole day) to sharing the farm work indiscriminately with the farm laborers. The rest of the day we devoted to other pursuits, or to social intercourse or correspondence; and we had a flat-bottomed rowing-boat built for us, in which we spent very many afternoons on the pretty little river. For our second season we removed to another farm and farmer's house, nearer Mr. Emerson and Walden Pond, where we occupied only a single room, making our own beds and living in the very simplest and most primitive style. A small piece of ground, which we hired of the farmer, we cultivated for ourselves, raising vegetables only and selling the superfluous produce, and distributing our time much as before."

Here was a very different life from that of Brook Farm. Both had in common healthy, outdoor occupation which built up Curtis's constitution, and helped make possible the arduous and incessant labor of later years, and both had the charm and advantage of dwelling with nature in a lovely land. But the "picnic" and the "masquerade" of Brook Farm had given place to afternoons in the woods or on the water; and the social intercourse was simpler, graver, less exciting, though not less stimulating, and more formative. "Have

I told you of our club," he writes to his father, — " Mr. Alcott, Mr. Emerson, Mr. Hawthorne, Ellery Channing, Henry Thoreau, George Bradford, Burrill and I, some known to you? We meet on Monday eves in Mr. Emerson's library, and there discuss

"' Fate, freewill, foreknowledge absolute.' "

Some half dozen years later, in an article on Emerson written for the " Homes of American Authors," Mr. Curtis gives a reminiscence of this club: "I went, the first Monday evening, very much as Ixion may have gone to his banquet. The philosophers sat dignified and erect. There was a constrained but very amiable silence, which had the impertinence of a tacit inquiry, seeming to ask, ' Who will now proceed to say the finest thing that has ever been said?' It was quite involuntary and unavoidable, for the members lacked that fluent social genius without which a club is impossible. I vaguely remember that the Orphic Alcott invaded the Sahara of silence with a solemn ' saying,' to which, after due pause, the honorable member for Blackberry Pastures[1] responded by some keen and graphic observation, — while the Olympian host,[2] anxious that so much good material should be spun into something, beamed smiling encouragement upon all parties. But the conversation became more and more staccato. Miles Coverdale,[3] a statue of night and silence, sat, a little removed, under a portrait of Dante, gazing

---

[1] Thoreau.   [2] Emerson.   [3] Hawthorne.

imperturbably upon the group; and as he sat in
the shadow, his dark eyes and hair and suit of
sables made him, in that society, the black thread
of mystery which he weaved into his stories, while
the shifting presence of the Brook Farmer [1] played
like heat-lightning around the room."

Mr. Curtis's writings contain many references
to these happy, fruitful years at Concord : glimpses
of the temper and growth of his mind at the time
will be had from the following extracts from letters to his father in the autumn of 1844 : —

"I have recently been reading J. Q. Adams's
address to his constituents in 1842, and Dr. Channing's tracts upon slavery. These and my own
observation of the course of the South, especially
within a year, indicate very plainly that at last the
country will divide upon Slavery. This will not
be the result of Northern agitation, but of the
perpetual attempt of the South to extend its limits
and thereby prolong the institution, and therefore
to continue the reserved power which now always
confirms its attitude towards the North. This attempt, which now is plainly seen, which now forms
one of the two great topics upon which the parties
— indeed, upon which the North and the South
differ — will not be tolerated in its success by the
conscience of Northern men. They must then
take the stand that will join the issue."

Then follows an ingenious argument as to the
clause in the Constitution giving representation to

[1] Bradford.

the South for its slaves as " persons," though held
by the masters as " property," and as to the inevitable revolt of the North against the unfairness
of this agreement, and the arrogance and extravagance of the Southern claims regarding it.

" The conduct of the South outrages the moral
sentiments and the letter of the laws, and, to the
remonstrance of the North, at one time challenges
it with intent to dissolve the Union, and at another fiercely brandishes the threat against the
North. While the wise statesman calmly illus-
trates its treachery and actual violation of the
compact, let him firmly say that we can submit
no longer to be accomplices in this angel-abhorred
guilt. We do not deny that the articles of Union
bind that community upon us, and therefore must
insist upon amendments. Quite willing not to in-
terfere politically in the matter within your borders, we cannot, we will not, aid you in so monstrous a sin.

" How nobly might Mr. Webster, a man too
great that we should ever despair, crown his fame
in hearts which would fain welcome him, but cannot yet, by assuming this position!

" But if the strongest statesmen will not advance
in this matter, there must come men from different
pursuits than politics to press the question on. It
is idle to think or to hope that it will not be asked.
Mr. Choate and Mr. Bates and the courtly Mr.
Winthrop and colleagues will be reserved at home
for graceful times of peace and public ease, while

men that cannot speak fluently at mass meetings
will go and demand justice of the South. They
will say: ' We will unite with you as citizens, not
as robbers and unjust.' Dear father, write me
how these things are. I trust all nobility and gen-
erosity has not fled out of politics, and left them
bells and baubles for foolish men to wear."

The father seems to have pointed out in reply
the value of the Union, and the hope that slavery
would yet be abolished without disunion. To
which the son responded : —

" I read your last letter with pleasure, dear
father, for I did not know if mine would touch
an interest that was very prominent in your mind.
It is most true that slavery will be abolished
finally by the force of public opinion. But the
North begins to groan already. While it recognizes the comity of nations and the solemn bond,
it begins to speak of the separation with plain
words. It may not be expedient just now, but
then when will it be ? The old conviction that
no law, no arrangement, no gain, can permit such
direct participation as is provided by the Constitution, will at last distinctly demand some change,
and, even if the demand be postponed an hundred
years, the South will not be ready. What gains
the South by separation ? It will take Texas to
its bosom and possibly conquer Mexico, but no
State can endure the unalterable disapprobation of
the world. It would yield to the heat of universal
censure like wax. It becomes a very grave ques-

tion to every man. In the event of a disunion,
the North might enjoy less commerce and a thousand decreased political advantages, but, as unto
an individual who sacrifices to Justice, there would
be no real loss, but an eternal gain. Nor could it
tighten the bonds. Men complain that the anti-
slavery movement has had that effect upon the
slaves. But it is very transitory, if it be so. It
is the winking of eyes upon which light suddenly
flows, — a moment and they will be strong and
clear in the sun. It is not credible that a stroke
for freedom ever served to perpetuate slavery,
because it is an indication of that spirit, alive
and in action, to which alone slavery will yield. I
have not now the inclination to pursue the theme
further, though it has wide and inviting relations."

This is not a weak statement for a young man
of twenty. Disunion as a remedy became clearly
enough futile and unnecessary to his riper and
better informed judgment, but the conception of
the evil demanding a remedy was sound and firmly
defined, and remained through the gallant struggle
he was afterwards to make.

In another letter he discusses the question of
the tariff, then a very urgent one. Remembering
that his father was a protectionist, and had publicly defended protection, the letter is a pleasing
proof at once of the son's independence and of
his confidence in the fair - mindedness of his father, — no slight element in the education of the
former : —

"Just now I am sad, as I close Webster's speeches (the old), which have occupied me some days, to reflect how narrow are our sympathies. Born an American, I am by that fact heir to certain responsibilities. But also I am born an inhabitant of the world. I owe to my country the duty of a citizen, but I cannot surrender to that my duty as a man. My obligations are imperative towards Englishmen and Frenchmen. If I am bound, so far as lies in me, to see that my land is well governed, I must not forget that no government is essentially good for that land which is selfish and small. My country is well governed when the world is. All my obligations as a man include those of a citizen. I have no right to protect American labor at the expense of foreign. What does it matter to me or to God whether Lowell or Manchester be ruined? Extend this into politics and it places us upon a wide, universal platform. It does not suffer any American feeling or British feeling. While I confess that the British laborers starve, I do not do very well to refuse to take what they make; I must pull down my restrictive laws. I must say to the whole world, ' He who makes the best cloth shall have the best pay.' Then come English and all manner of foreign goods into the market and spoil our trade. But there is plainly but one way of paying for all imports, and that is by exports. Sugar and rice, potatoes and grain, must pay for all this, and there will be no more goods than I give an equivalent for.

Then if there be not enough, let our own manufacturers turn to. Besides, commerce rests upon natural laws and not upon human will. If America is not a productive garden for some other land, no tariff will make her so. But suppose that our philanthropic, not national, government, is established, then the world becomes the subject of a wonderful organized moral power. Or, again, America cannot stand upon such a basis of humanity, and sinks, what then? The nation who conquers us has pressed a sharp thorn in the side of its selfish ambition. Into the heart of selfish Europe — Russia, England, France or whatever nation — is transferred a body of men who are obeying eternal laws and not state laws, or state laws only so far as they are eternal.

" We ask, in our political relations, Will it benefit the state? — very seldom, Is it right? But the state is not necessarily benefited because it has a full treasury, and armies and navies, and commerce and trade, any more than a man is benefited by fine houses and parks. Let us make a maxim in politics, that what is good for America is good for the other nations, — for all, because it is universal and unselfish. I have a right to wear fine linen, and use Paris handkerchiefs, if I choose to pay for them at their prices, and you have no right to make me buy yours by making theirs dearer. I see no necessity that American manufacturers should flourish if they cannot do so without thrusting our neighbor out of the market.

I will have no fear that God has given us a land
that cannot support itself against the world in the
noblest, freest manner, or, if I see it cannot, I shall
also see that it is no proper home.

" ' Be not forced from your integrity ' — so says
the wise statesman, who is then a student of the
divine government — 'by the dishonesty of others.'
The citizens of the republic, who are willing to be
men of the world also, will be content to sleep on
hard beds and forego luxuries if such means be
necessary to preserve the law they cherish. Now
we are arrayed against each other. The great aim
is, which state shall be highest, strongest, wealth-
iest, — which shall thrust down the other and rise
beyond it, — not which shall lift the other and then
nobly rise beyond. The laws of nature are as simple for the mass as for the man. The life of a
state should be as sound and unincumbered as of
the individual. If we are not ready for such a
state, let us at least say nothing of the older governments in their disparagement. We are not the
experimenters upon the free order of society that
the world has flattered us into the belief that we
are."

CHAPTER III.

EUROPEAN TRAVEL.

In the autumn of 1845 Mr. Curtis returned to his father's house in New York, and there passed the winter. His thoughts were turning toward Europe, though he spoke of them only as "budding hopes." In a letter to one of his old friends of the Brook Farm days, he describes his time as given to "reading Italian three hours and German about two, going to my room at nine, and coming down to dinner at four." The evenings were devoted to society, and very frequently to music, at home and elsewhere. In the spring he returned for a while to Concord, — "the soft, sunny spring in the silent Concord meadows, where I sat in the great cool barn through the long, still golden afternoons and read the history of Rome." By summer his plans were completed, and in a note to his father in June, 1846, he submitted a proposition that the latter should provide a letter of credit for ten thousand francs, "not that I shall expect to spend that sum in two years, but because it is well to have a generous background to our picture."

He sailed from New York early in August on the packet-ship Nebraska for Marseilles, the " magic voyage over the summer sea " lasting forty-six days. The first winter was spent in Rome, the second in Berlin, the third in Paris, the fourth on the Nile and in Palestine. He kept a very full diary for the first two years, which I have been permitted to consult, and from which some extracts will serve to show the manner of the impressions made by this wholly new experience, which was in some ways the richest of his life.

During his journeying in Europe, he wrote pretty regularly to the " Courier and Enquirer," of which Mr. Henry J. Raymond was then the managing editor, and to the " Tribune." These letters were devoted mostly to public affairs and public men. They are good " newspaper work," with no rhetoric or nonsense about them, — clear, straightforward, careful reporting of the higher sort. They show keenness of observation, sound, shrewd judgment of men and things, and a breadth and penetration which were remarkable in so young and entirely inexperienced a writer. It will be recalled that when he reached Italy Pius IX. was the idol of the Liberals, and was stirring all Europe with hope or dismay, as the case might be, by professions and by proofs of confidence in the people. His sojourn in Germany covered the troublous times of 1847 and 1848, and his stay in Paris some of the most trying experiences of the second French Republic, so that there was much to excite the generous sympathy of a young American, which in his case was certainly not lacking, and much also to test the coolness of judgment and the practical sense of a journalist, and these also were not wanting. Although these letters were necessarily ephemeral, I think the writing of them was a fortunate thing for Mr. Curtis. They imposed on him, with his standard of duty, the discipline of regular and systematic observation and statement, and gave him the opportunity of practice in writing, with just enough responsibility to steady his energies, and without the temptations which the attempt at " literature " presents to a youthful author. The letters, of course, vanished promptly; he never even kept a collection of them, and they are not likely to be known even to the few survivors among his friends of that period. But it was with satisfaction that I hunted down a considerable number of them in the yellow files of the old journals, — so strangely meagre and limited as they now seem, — and found them distinctly better than most of the work of the same sort, and showing evidence of the qualities that were to make of the writer one of the strongest journalists of his time, and one whose influence was to be great, and in important directions decisive.

The first distinct impression of the strange life about him came from the observances of the Catholic religion, so remote from anything with which he had been familiar at home.

" Late in the evening," he wrote at Genoa, " a funeral procession of priests glided swiftly, silently by us, bearing flashing torches, but themselves shrouded in their long, straight black robes, and a pointed black veil or bag hanging from their broad sable hats to the breast, so that they seemed shapes moulded of the darkness. It was dreary and mournful, their rapid motion and entire blackness. How is the sweeping black of the Christian a more hopeful emblem than the inverted torch of the splendid old Grecian Pagans? The faint echo of their tread had scarcely died before a loud singing arrested us in one of the narrow by-streets, and, turning up, we found a group of people of every age kneeling and standing and singing before a shrine of the Virgin at the street corner, dimly lighted by a lantern, and a few withered flowers lying before it. The vesper song was of a few long-drawling notes sung in unison, and sounded so forlorn and heartless and hopeless in the desolate streets, which looked like caverns fit for midnight assassinations, that it made my heart ache. It seemed as if all elasticity must be gone from lives which could be fed by such means and men as this evening has shown us, and yet the people seem less serious and more contented than similar classes in America. As we returned to our hotel, the echo of the vesper hymns came floating out of the desolate, narrow streets on every side, — wild and wailing and foreign. To-night, more than ever, I felt how far away I was from home."

In Florence, where he spent a month, the notes in his diary disclose a similar vein of reflection. " The old buildings, and the sense of pictures all around, and the fine statues which meet your eye as you walk in any quarter, make this southern city and its inhabitants superficial motes upon the antique grandeur. I have not met a man in the street who did not look sharp and mean and stupid. There is no fine air about them which could possibly suggest that their ancestry were once the kings of the world; the women have nothing romantic or interesting in their faces or mien; and one feels very soon that these are the purveyors, and persons of convenience, in places to which all that is best and noblest must be sympathetically drawn. In America there is the charm of universal harmony: the people, in character and form and feature, correspond with the state of every art; the congregation and the worship are as impressive as the temple; the wise shrewdness of the merchants and the general aspect of action harmonize with the universal absence and postponement of art. Here the churches seem withdrawn farther away into the cold depths of antiquity, because the worship is so tawdry and trivial, not in itself, but because the men who lead it appear to feel it no more than their gorgeous robes. One can imagine sometimes a yearning in the broad, lofty spaces of these buildings, which are themselves the stately children of genius and religion, to feel their heights and depths once thrill with the shock of an equal worship. And yet, if one would be harmoniously satisfied, he may well be so in one of them, where, with music and incense and the dazzling splendor of robes of flowered gold, the Catholic service is performed. And that is the way it should be contemplated. The forms which are used are of a birth as religious and sincere as the temples themselves, and there is no need of regarding the priests as men at all."

As he journeyed towards Rome, the charms of Italy took closer possession of him. "Italy," he writes after a week in that city, "is no fable, and the wonderful depth of purity in the air and blue in the sky has hung upon my eyes all this glorious day. Sometimes the sky is an intensely blue and distant arch, and sometimes it melts in the sunlight, and lies pale and rare and delicate upon the eye, so that one feels that he is breathing the sky and moving through it. I looked from a lofty balcony at the Vatican upon broad gardens, intensely green with evergreen palms and orange-trees, in which gleamed the golden fruit and the rich, rounding tufts of Italian pines; and the solemn shaft of cypress stood over fountains which sported rainbows into the air, which was silver-clear, transparent, and on which the outline of the hills and foliage was drawn like a flame against the sky at night. Into the air rose floating the dome of St. Peter's, which is not a nucleus of the city, like the Duomo at Florence, but a crown more imposing as one is farther removed."

In Rome again, it was the church that first impressed him strongly. Of the music at St. Peter's, he writes : —

"Then from the high choir at the opposite side of the church and far over our heads came swimming down the tremulous delicacy of the 'nuns' chant,' like voices from heaven. The sound pervaded the dim air of the church like a radiance too subtle to be seen, but warming and ennobling the soul with a sense of celestial splendor. It was also of the extremest melancholy—a hymn so sad that all the bright days and hopes of life seemed then no more than the few keen stars at night and as powerless as they upon the darkness. It was a service all incense and music, upon which daylight seemed not bold enough to obtrude, and exhaling a worship like the delicatest fragrance of flowers."

He mentions the Pope, whom he saw quite frequently, always with sympathy, as in the following description of the festival of the Eve of St. John's:—

"Last night at the Pope's Palace upon the Piazza Cavallo upon the Quirinăl Hill, we saw a rare and beautiful spectacle. It was the Eve of St. John's festival, whose name the Pope bears. Therefore at dusk crowds began to assemble upon the hill, which in front of the palace is very spacious, looking toward the west over the city and its crown of St. Peter's dome, and surrounded only with stately palaces. In the centre of the hill is a simple, ample fountain whose water rises from a broad vase into which it falls again, dripping enough over the edge to girt the urn with a shining silver fringe. Over this fountain an Egyptian obelisk points steadily upward in the blue air, at whose base two noble figures of Grecian youths restrain two rear-

ing horses, the work, it is said, of Phidias and Prax-
iteles. The spire, its centre, its sides and its pros-
pect are all worthy, and here in the early evening
after the Ave Maria the people assembled. Colored fires flashed upon the palaces from an altar of
Liberty, emblematic of the spirit which rules the
country and which the people hail and celebrate on
every occasion. The clouds were heavy and a flash
of lightning swept at intervals a broad light over
all; a slight shower passed, at which thousands of
umbrellas made a smooth billowy surface for the
human sea. But when the procession approached
with torches and music, the rain ceased, the umbrellas fell, the torches crowded into the crowd;
from the people rang a long, heaven-piercing shout,
from the balconies and palaces streamed fires of
various splendor until a new day shone steadily
over the multitude, touching the statues into life,
and in the midst of it, the doors of an upper balcony were thrown open and, preceded by the cross,
which always precedes him on public occasions,
and by four huge wax torches, the Pope came forward above the ringing shouts and in the steady
splendor and bowed his head to the railing of the
balcony. Then came a moment of stillness; the
crowd was hushed as a sleeping child, and the Pope
raised his hands, breathed a short prayer, and
turning to the crowd gave his blessing and retired.
Then came the shouts again and the music and
new rockets and candles — until in a few moments
all was still again, but it was a sight rare and im-

pressive. The vast crowd drawn alone by reverence and respect to their chief—and he responding to their call with no appeal to passion or pride, but with a prayer and his blessing. In no other country could that be seen. In no other country could the vast sentiment inspired by a mass of people obeying a noble instinct be so sublimely crowned. It was perfect. It was a scene for the Arcadia of a poet — or the paradise of a wise Christian."

Here is a trace of a different sentiment : —

"Saturday, October 31, 1846. To-day I went to the graves of Shelley and Keats, who lie in a green, sequestered spot under the walls of old Rome, where the sunlight lingers long and where in the sweet society of roses whose bloom does not wither, they sleep always a summer sleep. Shakespeare sang long ago Shelley's epitaph : —

> ' Nothing of him that doth fade,
> But doth suffer a sea change
> Into something rich and strange.'

And Keats sighed his upon his death bed : —

> ' Here lies one whose name was writ in water.'

Fate is no less delicate than stern, which brought Keats from his cold north to lie in an Italian grave, and which, sucking the sweet breath of Shelley in a stormy night at sea, laid his ashes and unburned heart in the spot whose beauty, he said, might make one in love with death. Yet, by these graves too, one feels the grimness of fate which strikes so suddenly into silence the lips which heaven seems to yearn to pass in music. The sun was setting as we came away, after one of the aerially soft days with which our imaginations endow Italy. The rich golden flood streamed through the arches of the Coliseum, but could not unbend the stern gravity of its decay. It looked cold and still, the image of the destiny which consumes it."

And here is a note made on the eve of his departure from Rome.

"Thus far I find that my European life has taught me a cosmopolitanism which I could never have learned at home. I have read very few books this winter and have been very little at home, but I have been unsphered in the society of so many persons and I have begun to realize how good every sphere is, although so different from my own. When we are children we fancy the horizon is the end of the world, but the man who lives just beyond the edge sees grand mountains and seas of which we do not dream, and if we are wedded to our quiet groves and streams by long years of intimacy and habit, when by chance we pass the boundary, we shall not enjoy the magnificence, and so lose the various splendor of the world."

Leaving Rome in mid-April, Curtis passed a month or more in Naples and its neighborhood, another in Florence, a third in Venice, a few weeks' leisurely wandering in northern Italy, and crossing the Alps from Como, settled in Berlin for the winter. The next spring opened at the close of April with a week in "Saxon Switzerland" on foot, and the summer was given to journeyings through Austria and Hungary, back to the Rhine, again crossing the Alps and recrossing to the Geneva country; then by a wide détour into Germany, Paris was reached, where the winter of 1848–49 was passed. I have, perhaps, given enough from the diary to show the spirit of this experience. It was a varied one, with much intense enjoyment, numerous interesting acquaintances, some valuable friends won and to be kept, and a steady mental development of which the diary shows mostly the soberer side. The record he made, and which, I think, he had some intention of publishing, is singularly void of personal allusions either to himself or to his companions. It gives nothing as to the comfort or discomfort of the inns, and little as to the conveyances. A larger part is given to the scenery than to any other one thing, and it is plain how much he was gaining in that deep and rich knowledge of nature that counted so greatly in his subsequent work. He saw many pictures, knew many artists of various races, and had obviously a keen enjoyment of their works. But though, in a very important sense, he was by mental gift a true artist, I do not think he ever got far, or ever cared to get very far, into the mysteries of the craft. The subject, the sentiment and the general impression of the color and form remained with him, but of the processes and their details, of the elements of the war that was then raging still between the Romanticists and the Classicists, or the one on which the pre-Raphaelites were entering, I find no hint. He must have encountered these things in the society with which he was intimate, but I imagine that they left him indifferent. Nor is there much sign of the studies in which he really engaged with energy and must have pursued with some system. He seems to have been at this time, as he was in later life, the very reverse of what we usually understand by a man of books, still more of a bookish man. In his diary he very rarely quotes poetry, and in the homes of Dante and Petrarch, of Goethe, of Voltaire, their names come only incidentally to his pen. The places as they were, the landscape in which they were set, the life he found in them are what he describes. The people did interest him greatly as persons, as races, as political communities. He was in Italy, in Germany, and in Austria at the time when the ferments which reached their height in 1848 were general. He saw the Milanese " rise " and saw them again when their hopes were crushed. He was in Hungary on the eve of the outbreak that brought Kossuth, later, to the United States. . All these events awakened interest of the keenest, and sympathy, but it was a very calm judgment that he passed upon them. He was always struck by the contrast between the moods and manners he saw and those to which he was used at home. The theatrical element, and the rhetorical, while they amused him, made him distrustful. In Europe, as at Brook Farm, he never lacked the saving sense of humor, and the sobriety, the saneness of his general view were remarkable. There was no cynical affectation in it, not a trace of indifference, nor any pride, personal or national, but always the quiet appreciation of the extent and complexity of anything like a national movement, and of the need of breadth and steadiness and common sense.

CHAPTER IV.

THE LITERARY FIELD.

MR. CURTIS's literary career began in 1851, on his return from Europe and the East, with the publication of the Howadji books. It was a period of marked mental activity in the United States, when reputations that were to become world-wide were still making, and when only two or three of the now widely famed writers had yet achieved an established name at home, and only one, the veteran Washington Irving, could be said to be much known abroad. The habitat of what there was of American literature was geographically very limited. Nearly all the writers of the day were New Englanders by residence, or, as was Mr. Curtis, by descent. A smaller group of very active minds centred in New York, and there were scattered workers here and there along the Atlantic Coast. But the intellectual life of the country, so far as it was expressed in books, or even in newspapers, was still east of the Alleghanies and on the eastern edge of the slope. The magazine as we know it, the roomy and hospitable, stimulating and nourishing home of writing of every sort, inviting the writer who has anything

worth saying to address all the readers of the
land — and of other lands — worth having, did not
exist, though the "North American Review" in
Boston and the "Knickerbocker" and "Harper's"
in New York had made notable and valuable begin-
nings. Within what now seems the restricted society of the opening of the second half of the century
there was, as I have said, marked mental activity
in a considerable variety of directions, much of it
wayward, eager, curious, some of it grotesque,
much of it shallow, affected, and of no importance,
but much of it also serious, pure, lofty, and, as
the event has proved, of lasting influence. Curiously enough in this confused and unformed society of writers the most conspicuous and eminent,
though certainly not the most representative, was
Washington Irving, as completely a man of letters,
and yet distinctly of his own time, as Addison.
He was the Dean of the American literary body,
being, in 1851, sixty-eight, with the "Knickerbocker's History of New York," one of the most
characteristic of his works, more than forty years
in the past and the "Sketch Book" and "Brace-
bridge Hall" but ten years nearer. Substantially
all his work was done, and the "Life of Washington" and "Wolfert's Roost" alone awaited
publication. It is a pleasant thing to note that
nearly forty years later Mr. Curtis's Monograph on
Irving became one of the most valued publications
of the Grolier Club of New York, and remains
a graceful and affectionate tribute to qualities of

mind and character, some of which the writer richly shared with the beloved subject of the Essay. It may be added that Mr. Curtis's correspondence discloses a personal intercourse with Irving of a sympathetic if not intimate nature which must have had its influence.

At this time, Hawthorne was in the prime of manhood, forty-seven years of age, but was known chiefly as a writer of sketches of singular and subtle charm. The two volumes of " Twice-told Tales " had been published in 1837 and 1845, and the " Mosses from an Old Manse " in 1846. " The Scarlet Letter " had appeared the year before, but the author was still a self-distrustful, almost gloomy half-recluse, hardly comprehending the position which that most original of American books has assured to him. With Hawthorne, Mr. Curtis had had a certain degree of friendly relation at Brook Farm and at Concord, and I like to think that his remote and slightly cynical attitude of mind was felt as a counterpoise to the " transcendental " tendencies of the other companions of that period, and may have counted in maintaining the sanity of spirit with which the youth came from those stimulating but not entirely wholesome associations. The purely literary influence of Hawthorne it is not easy to trace, especially in Mr. Curtis's earlier work. But I cannot doubt that the sobriety, lucidity and restraint of expression in a writer of such powerful and penetrating imagination, united with the early personal intercourse, aided in the development of that later style which in the "Easy Chair" and in portions of "Prue and I" was to become not less delightful than that of the tenant of the "Old Manse." Of other novelists and essayists Fenimore Cooper, the most prolific and widely known, was just passing away; Miss Sedgwick and Mrs. Sigourney, greatly read, though not destined to a lasting fame, had closed their literary labors; Herman Melville, R. H. Dana, Jr., Donald G. Mitchell, Bayard Taylor, were of Mr. Curtis's own age, or nearly so, and some of them of his own circle. Nathaniel P. Willis, in literature, as in life, claiming the function of *arbiter elegantiarum*, and so far recognized as such that I find a correspondent naïvely flattering Curtis with the opinion that he may attain to Willis's level, was then at the height of his vogue.

More brilliant, and with a larger number whose fame was to be permanent among the writers of that day, were the poets. Bryant at the age of fifty-seven was the oldest, and had already achieved the hold on the future which was sustained if not strengthened by his later work. In 1851, he was most prominent as a journalist of deep conviction and of rare vigor and purity of style. Emerson's poetry was accepted, with his prose, as an expression of lofty and often mystical thought, and was as yet more the object of a limited cult than the general delight that it has since become. Whittier's reputation also was high with a somewhat limited class, but had not gained general recognition. Longfellow was already the most read and most widely loved of American poets. Lowell, but five years the senior of Curtis, was at the height of the peculiar popularity won by the "Fable for Critics" and, in a different vein, "The Biglow Papers." He had fairly thrown down the gauntlet in the long fight with slavery, and, incredible as it now seems, had perceptibly clouded his prospects of advancement with those who were supposed to distribute the prizes of literary effort. Curtis, who was to become one of his closest friends, and who was later to join him in the memorable contest with slavery, was as yet but an admirer of his varied but irregularly developed genius. Holmes, who at twenty-two, had given the country one of the most spirited of patriotic poems, "Old Ironsides," was known chiefly as a Harvard professor, with a rare gift for "occasional" verse. The sisters, Alice and Phœbe Cary, published their first volume of poems in the same year with the "Nile Notes." Buchanan Read and Stoddard had each one volume of poems to his credit. John G. Saxe's little volume, revealing one of the brightest and lightest of American humorists in verse, was published in 1850.

It remains to mention that in history, Prescott was the only writer who had achieved very much. His "Ferdinand and Isabella," "Conquest of Mexico," and "Conquest of Peru," were, at that time, the chief American histories. Bancroft had issued but three volumes of his great work. Hildreth's

was in course of publication. Motley was hardly
decided as to his own course and was known only
as the author of "Morton's Hope," and "Merry
Mount," which one hardly thinks of now in connection with his name.

It is not easy in these closing days of the century, when Mr. Curtis's name is more or less
closely associated with the group of New England
writers whose names are so generally honored and
whose work has become an integral part and a
large part of the intellectual inheritance of educated Americans, clearly to imagine how different
from that which we now recognize was the influence they were able to exert upon him at the opening of his career. It is worth while to dwell with
some emphasis upon the fact that he was himself
one of the builders of American literature, and that
when he began to write, the conditions by which he
was surrounded were such as necessarily to throw
him upon his own resources. What he brought to
the structure was his own material, fashioned by
himself. It was not and could not be borrowed
from those who had gone before him, and if it was
a worthy and a substantial contribution, as, without exaggerating its importance, I believe that it
was, it must be remembered that what there was of
it was original. I think that it was so in style as
well as in matter, and it is in the hope of bringing
that fact more definitely to the minds of my readers
that I have given this brief, but I hope fairly accurate, review of the literary field in 1851.

On the other hand, given a mind of native vigor and of genuine sensitiveness, given healthy aspirations toward mental achievement, given a point of view of rational independence and a character of sound substance and of firm as well as fine texture, and it was a good thing to begin near the beginning, to be of the pioneers, to share in youth the common and powerful impulse of a young literary society, to be more conscious of the immensity of the future than of that of the past, and to feel that what one shall succeed in accomplishing may have a steadily widening influence upon the maturing national mind. These were the advantages of one whose work was begun in the middle of the nineteenth century in our country. Mr. Curtis felt them, and I think he made the most of them.

CHAPTER V.

Mr. Curtis returned from Europe in 1850 with a definite resolve to undertake the career of an author. His first work, "Nile Notes of a Howadji," was published the following spring, when he had just entered his twenty-seventh year. "To-day," he wrote from Providence to a friend in Cambridge, "will bring me the Nile Notes as a book, I suppose, — but I cannot have the proper emotions. It seems all very natural, very much as it seems to a young papa, who beholds a redness in a white blanket, and is told that it is his heir; or perhaps even more as a sensible tree feels when it sees one of its fruits fallen separate upon the ground — My hand trembles (as I speak of no emotion) for this moment my book is placed in my hand — even as I wrote 'ground' it arrived. You will surely have received it before you read this. Ah! speak it fair! my first born, my only child!"

The book was very kindly received by the newspapers, though the notices of it which I have come upon do not make that fact very conclusive as to its merit, for most of them are curiously flat and perfunctory. More significant was the sale of an edition of twenty-five hundred copies within the first half year. The author himself said, in April, in his straightforward way: " The Nile Notes I cannot hesitate to call successful, but not a great hit." John Dwight, in the " Commonwealth " of Boston, spoke in a tone at once flattering and discriminating. E. P. Whipple, one of the oracles of the day, declares of it that he had " never before felt the East." In referring to some pleasant opinions he had heard, Mr. Curtis wrote : " In his letter Mons. Aubépine (Hawthorne) tells another twice-told tale. But how sweeter so ! How like Fame, when a famous man applauds and says, ' I see now that you are forever an author ! ' " Bentley of London published the book under the title of " Nile Notes of a Traveler," apparently afraid to trust the English reader with the Arabic equivalent, Howadji. For this edition the publisher paid the sum of five guineas, — a curiously early example of the necessity for international copyright. It was explained that if the book "took " it would immediately be printed for a shilling for all the railway stations, while Bentley printed it for ten shillings and sixpence. The English press was extremely cordial. The London " Daily News," the " Weekly News " (a wholly different paper) the "Athenæum," the " Literary Gazette " and the " Spectator " all noticed the book, and nearly all with praise. " Leigh Hunt," wrote Curtis, " speaks of it in his 22d March number. He likes it and praises it, but in an amusing way. He says something about the Author's meaning to outdo Long-fellow's Hyperion!! and of traces of D'Israeli, Emerson, Eothen, and I know not how many more. But he so evidently likes it that the most morbidly vain author would be more amused than annoyed at his notice."

The book did not escape censure. "May an immoral Howadji," wrote the author to a friend, "dine with you on Wednesday?" This was the smile that would hide pain. Mr. Curtis was deeply wounded by some of the comments on his work. His letters of this date, though full of expressions of grateful surprise at the praise bestowed upon him, and of simple-hearted, modest joy at his success, contain other expressions of hot and passionate indignation for those who had impugned the purity of his purpose. The anger was natural; with regard to some, it was just; but on the whole, it was undue. That Mr. Curtis's mind in youth as in his riper age was pure, no one who knew him could doubt. It did not necessarily follow that those who did not and could not see as he saw, were not pure. It was the forever-recurring dispute that art provokes from generation to generation. Mr. Curtis was, in a great part of his nature, in some of the most attractive and engaging manifestations of his nature, an artist. Without offense and with immaculate devotion, he made some of his studies from life. When his pictures came from his easel, he did not find it requisite to drape completely the beauty he had recognized and rejoiced in. One of his best loved artists in the long, happy days in the Venetian galleries, before he crossed the Mediterranean to Cairo, was Correggio. It never occurred to him, the boy fresh-hearted from the cool walks of the Concord Academe, that the women of Correggio were shocking to look upon. If one cares to re-read, forty years after, the chapters through which dance Kusheek Arnem and the dove Xenobi, and remember that they flowed from the pen, almost untried, of a youth of twenty-six, he will find readily what lay open to criticism on the score of taste and might honestly be disapproved as the too vivid presentation of a sensuous scene. But if he do not also find a grave and noble feeling under the rich play of color, a sense of the pathos and the tragedy that make the sombre background of a scene at once so alluring and so disquieting, if there shall not remain with him the impression of singular elevation and breadth of view in this young writer, then, while we may not dismiss him with the contempt the young writer showed for some of his critics, we may be permitted at least to differ from him.

On this particular point, I shall let Mr. Curtis speak for himself, in the following manly letter to his father written a few days after the publication of the book : —

PROVIDENCE, March 15, '51.

MY DEAR FATHER, — When I received ——'s first letter I was amused but not surprised. But when he wrote that you were so shocked with my book, I was extremely grieved, and so must always be — yet always with a conscience void of offense. My aim in the book was such that I was unwilling you should see the manuscript because I knew that we should differ so essentially that your displeasure might only be prolonged. But when I saw that Mr. Raymond, whom you regard so highly and who has no personal feeling for me, had selected the exceptional chapter for the Magazine, I supposed that I had overrated the nervousness of the general mind, and that the edict which cannot but seem to me contemptible — of immorality, or whatever it is — would not be passed.

I am sorry that I was not at home for two reasons, and glad for a good many that I was away — I was sorry that I had not ordered a copy sent to you immediately, which, however, I had not done for any one — having only made a list of sundry persons connected with journals and one or two friends in distant parts of the country. Then I was sorry that my absence seemed to indicate that I had run away from a bad impression. However, that is nothing, — I want to say precisely how the thing is — and am very sorry that —— should talk about obfuscated moral sense.

When I was in Egypt I felt that the picture of impressions there had never been painted. Travelers have been either theorists and philosophers or young men with more money than brains, or professional travelers. In no book of any of them was the essentially *sensuous*, luxurious, languid and sense-satisfied spirit of Eastern life as it appears to the traveller represented. I aimed to do that. Here and in every newspaper notice (some dozen) that I have seen I find that I have achieved that success, and I find the same thing in all this outcry of immorality or indecency, or whatever it is, and which comes from New York alone. Now, the moral condemnation of ladies and gentlemen who would sell any daughter to any man, for a sufficient fortune, I do not very highly esteem — and that is the character of some, who, I hear, are most eloquent against my book. The moral sense of New York in general is so vitiated that I care for it in general no more than for such particular condemnations. My only sorrow is that you should necessarily condemn the book, and I am sorry, because it ought not to be condemned! The dancing girls occupy no more space in the book than they occupied in the voyage, and they must always occupy a large space because they are the life and the most characteristically Eastern life of the river. You of course will feel that the whole thing might be omitted, but it would not be the same book, it would not be my book, and it would not in that case give the true picture of the Egyptian life.

It is only the affected and self-conscious exaggeration of the moral sense that could be so alarmed — I am angrier than I am vexed. The very brilliance of the coloring shows that it is *not* prurient, but poetic.

However, there is no end of such talk. I have written, dear father, that you may know that I deplore your disappointment, while I feel that it was unavoidable. Had I written a book to please you, I would not have published it because it would not have pleased myself; and while I confess certain expressions are too broad and might well be altered, the essential spirit of the book is precisely what I wish it. I would not have it toned down, for I toned it up intentionally. My objections are not moral but literary.

The feeling that you have is, I am sure, more personal to me than real to yourself. If the book had been anybody's else, I doubt if you could have been shocked. But with your natural interest in me and equally natural desire that I should favorably impress every one, you were necessarily grieved by what was suspicious to them, not regarding if it *ought* to be, but simply if it *was* so to them.

I never could regret having written the book. If I should differ in my nature and character a score of years hence, I shall be no more sorry than I am that I once wore frocks, — and I can say so absolutely because, as I began, my conscience is void of offense. This outcry seems simply ludicrous.

Your affectionate son,
GEORGE WILLIAM CURTIS.

The "Nile Notes" and the "Howadji in Syria" which followed in the next year, were the first product of a mind of extraordinary sensitiveness, of much strength, released rather suddenly from associations and habits of thought which, sustained with entire sincerity, had exercised a restraint of which the writer may have become aware only when freed from it. There may be detected a touch of half-humorous, half-deliberate defiance of the men and the manners Mr. Curtis had left in the little circle of New England transcendentalists. " When the Persian Poet Hafiz," says the Preface to the " Nile Notes," " was asked by the Philosopher Zenda what he was good for, he replied ; ' Of what use is a flower ? ' ' A flower is good to smell,' said the Philosopher. ' And I am good to smell it,' said the poet." The function of a poet, promenading a sensitive and irresponsible soul through the lotus-fields of Egyptian experience and observation, finding in the enjoyment of languorous odors not merely the excuse but the justification of his occupation, was certainly as far removed as well could be from the lofty and severe ideals of life in which Mr. Curtis had been nurtured. It is not difficult to imagine the dismay it must have caused some of his older companions to be asked to take him at his word, and it is not surprising that in the pages of the Howadji books they found only too much evidence that his word was at once sincere, and accurate, and that he had really descended from their cold heights to wander as long as he could with Hafiz in the flower-carpeted vales.

As the rôle he had announced was novel, the

style he assumed in it was novel also. It was essentially artificial, the style of the stage he had constructed for himself and had boldly furnished with an elaborate set of conventions, which he summoned his readers to accept, if they cared to understand the piece. The offer, indeed, was, with gay haughtiness, *à laisser ou à prendre.* The writer would abate no jot of his terms. From the moment that "in a gold and purple December sunset" he walked down to the boat bound for the Nile to the moment when he reached Cairo again "while the sun was wreaking all his glory upon the West," the demand upon our imagination is constant. We must read as we would watch and listen to an opera, granting completely the assumptions of the composer. This done, there are melody and harmony, passion and sensuous delight, and — to him who will take it — aspiration toward beauty and deep and varied beauty. But the conditions must be observed.

The note of invitation and of warning is sounded on the first page.

" To our new eyes everything was picture. Vainly the broad road was crowded with Muslim artisans, home returning from their work. To the mere Muslim observer they were carpenters, masons, laborers and tradesmen of all kinds. We passed many a meditating Cairene, to whom there was nothing but the monotony of an old story in that evening and on that road. But we saw all the pageantry of oriental romance quietly donkey-ing into Cairo. Camels too, swaying and waving like huge phantoms of the twilight, horses with strange gay trappings, curbed by tawny, turbaned equestrians, the peaked toe of the red slipper resting in the shovel stirrup. It was a fair festal evening. The whole world was masquerading, and so well that it seemed reality.

" I saw Fadladeen with a gorgeous turban and a gay sash. His chibouque, wound with colored silk and gold threads, was borne behind him by a black slave. Fat and funny was Fadladeen as of old, and though Fermorz was not by, it was clear to see in the languid droop of his eye, that choice Arabian verses were sung in the twilight of his mind.

" Yet was Venus still the evening star ; for behind him, closely veiled, came Lalla Rookh. She was wrapped in a vast black silken bag, that bulged like a balloon over her donkey. But a star-suffused evening cloud was that bulky blackness, as her twin eyes shone forth liquidly lustrous."

No one, of course, will pretend that this is a natural tone in which to write or talk, and the young writer himself must have been free from any such pretension, but if it was an artificial style, it was not an empty one. The scenes he had witnessed, the associations by which they were surrounded, the thought they had aroused, were intensely interesting, animating, absorbing. The style was a sincere and faithful attempt to clothe fitly what he had to say, to adapt the costumes and

the stage setting to the curious subject matter of
the piece. If what was to be said was of sufficient
substance, the plan of presentation was logical and
should justify itself, as in fact it does. One who
would seek a suggestive picture of travel on the
Nile and in Syria a half century since, before the
comforts of modern travel had opened the river
and the desert to those beneficiaries and victims
of Cook whose purpose is not strong enough to dis-
pense with such comforts, can find none more truly
informing than in Curtis's books, delightfully free
as, for the most part, they are, of information.
The plan, it will be noted, was peculiarly elastic.
The writer sets out to tell you that which he saw
or experienced, and his thoughts, in the way that
seemed to him most suitable. He reserves to himself the guidance of the way. He gives you no
clue. He promises no definite destination. He
lays out no task of which you shall have a right to
exact the completion ; you shall have what history
he may choose to give you, and in such remote and
fanciful relations as may occur to him ; you may
see the people as he saw them, with the eye of the
poet and the artist, with flashes of philosophic insight and merry glances of humor, but you shall
not complain of the picture as lacking in detail or
in breadth, as too sober or too light. It is the picture as it lies in his memory, as his imagination
and sympathy have developed and colored it. It
does not satisfy the reader? *Allons !* " Of what
use is a flower? "

The result naturally is that while you get from these books much, very much of Egypt and Syria, of the Nile and the desert, of Damascus and Jerusalem and Esne, of the land of the mighty past and of the squalid and tragic present, of Cleopatra and of Khadra and of the Ghazeeyah, you get still more and constantly of the writer, and therein lies the charm which still holds many readers. For now, after the face of the land he visited is greatly changed, and no one may again see, traversing his itinerary, what was then to be seen; though the questions of that time, with which he occasionally deals vigorously and acutely, are not the questions of our day and will henceforth engage only the historians, there remains, in the soft rich light of these old volumes, a portrait of the young Curtis. Those of us who knew him, if only by his work, in his ripe and beautiful maturity, in that splendid afternoon of his life when the sun so near its sudden setting seemed still the sun of midday, will always find in this portrait a mournful but deep enjoyment. It is that of a noble youth, delighting in life, in its novelty, its richness, and its opportunities, not unmindful of its duties or of its tragedy, of its infinite incitements and its relentless limitations, but keenly sensitive to its beauty, and mingling a genuinely earnest sense of its graver side with the ready enjoyment of its lighter aspects natural to the buoyancy of healthy spirits.

It is interesting also to trace in these volumes, unique among Mr. Curtis's writings, as they are

in their subject matter, and written in a style that
was never afterward, — save in brief portions of
" Prue and I " — in any great degree maintained,
the qualities that proved lasting in his work. The
two that impress me most strongly were those that
contributed most to his extreme charm as an orator, the picturesqueness of his impressions and the
rhythm of his expression. These are the more
noticeable because they had not yet been subdued
by study and reflection and labor. By picturesqueness of impression I would not suggest a view sensitive to " bits " and readily catching the subject
of a sketch, but rather the sensitiveness to effects,
a breadth of vision which took in what lay before it, not in detail or by a continuous analytic
effort, but as a whole. Curtis was an ardent
lover of nature ; none of all our writers with whom
the love of nature is a characteristic trait was
more devoted or happier. His delight in it, from
his earliest to his latest years, was deep, unfailing,
as fresh and joyous in the latest as in the earliest.
But I find little trace of a minute knowledge of
nature in his writing and recall little in his talk.
He does not betray the intimate acquaintance with
facts or the acute interest in them that Lowell discloses on every one of so many pages. He easily
might have been, though I do not know that he
was, ignorant of the names or relations of the flowers and unable to tell more than the very general
characteristics of the trees that gave him such exquisite pleasure. There was little of the naturalist

in him. It was, if I may venture to say so, the generic beauty of nature that appealed to him — the landscape, not its features, the glory of the day or night, the sweep of the horizon, the mood of the sea, the sky, the valleys or hills or groves that lay about him. " The palm-grove," he writes, " is always enchanted. If it stretch inland too alluringly, and you run ashore to stand under the bending boughs, to share the peace of the doves swinging in the golden twilight, yet you will never reach the grove. You will gain the trees, but it is not the grove you fancied — that golden gloom will never be gained — it is an endless El Dorado gleaming along the shores. The separate columnar trunks ray out in foliage above, but there is no shade of a grove, no privacy of a wood, except, indeed, at sunset, — ' A privacy of glorious light.' " It was the grove and not the trees that would satisfy him, and throughout his later work as in these first books, the reader feels the curious charm of the completeness and strength of his integral impressions. His vision disclosed pictures, not objects, and with whatever care and skill and patient workmanship he wrought them, it was not objects but pictures that he presented.

The second quality that I have noted, the rhythm of his expression, is clearly allied to the first. Curtis seems to me to have been, in an important sense, born an orator. Even the words of these first pages read as if they had been thought aloud, as if their cadence had been realized to the ear in the sound of his own rare voice. Often they come to the mind like the singing of the solitary and unconscious singer. His passionate and constant delight in music shaped his phrases and marshaled his sentences. There are plentiful instances of excess in this indulgence in the oriental books, before his taste had been trained and his judgment enlightened, but the excess is incidental — accidental even — and the sense remains to the reader of a pure, sincere and constant joy in the music of his own expression. I merely remark here these characteristics, which in more and more highly developed form, are found in all his work, and lent to it, in his maturity, much of the charm that won his host of readers and hearers, and of the completeness and force that held them.

CHAPTER VI.

Before he had completed "Nile Notes" Curtis had made his venture in the lecturing field. The first lecture seems to have been given in his native city of Providence, whence I find him inquiring about the next "Assembly" — not a Legislative gathering — at Boston, and announcing that though he must "repeat" his "lecture" on the "26th February" "he firmly intends to come back for the Fancy Ball." In the spring, Horace Greeley having gone to Europe, he went "on" the "Tribune" where, April 14th, he writes that he is "already in labor with the critiques upon the Academy Exhibition." His work was varied, what in newspaper parlance is known as "general utility," the art notices, music, reading manuscript and foreign papers, writing paragraphs and now and then a "leader," described by one of his companions in the office as "clever, agreeable, bright, never violent or ugly." Some of the gentlemen on whose work he passed judgment were not so lenient. "The artists," he writes, in June '51, "are angry with me, some of them. R—— thinks I am malicious — Ye Gods! — and considers what I say of

Hicks impolitic! Well, I shall invite Dogberry to comprehend these vagrom men, — I give it up." The companion quoted above thinks that Curtis was "not a hard or very steady worker at that time. He took the world easy and amused himself a good deal." Curtis's own impression was quite different. When urged to buy a share in the Tribune property and permanently unite himself with the enterprise, he declined. " I shrink," he wrote, " from the utter slavery of such a life. I have no moment of day or night properly my own. If I hear a concert, or a lecture, if I go, as to-night, to the Cooper Commemoration, it is all to be written out — every bit of experience must be grist to this imperious mill. I fear that every personal and more interesting ambition or intent must be sacrificed to this incessant employment." And again, " H—— is terribly lazy, which to me — who await foreign papers at the office until 2 A. M. and then reel, drunk with sleep, homeward to correct Syrian proofs, which startle me with the languid, sunny repose they recall — is the unpardonable sin."

In the summer of 1851 came a long respite. "Soon," he writes in July, " I shall spread sheeny vans for flight — Niagara, Sharon, Berkshire, Nahant, Newport and general bliss *ad infinitum.*" These journeyings were the occasion of a series of letters to the " Tribune," afterward published under the title of "Lotus Eating," linking them thus to the Howadji books. The little volume was illustrated with pleasant woodcuts from sketches by his warm friend Kensett, and was quite as successful as anything of the kind could be. There is much still to enjoy in its notes of a life that has quite passed away, and though the little volume was essentially ephemeral, in form and purpose, it gives clear signs of the two tendencies of the writer which were to be embodied in " The Potiphar Papers " published the next year, and in " Prue and I " four years later. It bears marks also of the weariness with which Curtis's mind necessarily reacted from the rather feverish social life in which he had plunged, and which overtaxed his strength, on which large demands were made by his really laborious pursuit of his profession, and shows still other marks of varied personal experiences, which deeply affected him at the time and contributed to the development of his character.

In the autumn he went to Providence to complete the preparation of the Howadji in Syria. Among his letters from there, I find one to his father, commenting on Judge Curtis's charge to the grand jury of the United States Court on the crime of treason ; the treason consisting in resisting the return of fugitive slaves. It is so clear-cut and firm in its reasoning that I quote it as showing in what direction his mind moved on the question. Referring to the Judge's declaration of the uniform and absolute authority of law, Curtis writes : —

" He forgot that the inherent human weakness which makes laws necessary also affects the essential character of those laws, and that there may be a legal organization of society worse than social chaos. The very oath by which we bind ourselves, as officers of the human law, is the direct recognition of a higher and more solemn obligation, and the point where the citizen merges in the man he did not consider, apparently, a point for his notice ; yet that is the essential point of the difficulty. Nobody denies the obligations of the law, but laws may be irretrievably bad, as in the case of the Roman Emperors, as now in Italy under the Austrian rule ; and by no obligation is a man bound to regard them. In fact this pro-fugitive slave law movement and the doctrine of law at all hazards, is, in politics, the same damnation that the infallibility of the Romish church is in religion, and wherever, as with us, the tendency of the times is to individual and private judgment, the cause of the wrong is just as much lost in politics as it is in Religion.

" All these things, which good order and common sense and patriotism require to be discussed publicly by our judges and legislators, they all shirk, and, emphasizing the obvious, cry Victory ! Thus William Goddard said to me : ' What a fine charge ' — ' Yes,' I said, ' but there is something more.' "

For the next few years Mr. Curtis led a varied life. He formed a more or less close connection with the house of Harper and Brothers, who had published his books ; wrote sketches and social notes for the Magazine, of which Henry J. Raymond

was then the editor, and for the Weekly, in which
he started the department of the Lounger ; became
an associate, but subordinate editor of " Putnam's
Magazine," to which he was a regular contributor ;
gave a good many lectures, mostly on books, and
went often and much into society, the gayeties as
well as the richer fruits of which he enjoyed with
great zest. The work for the Harper periodicals
was of many sorts. In part it was slight comment
on the pictures, the plays, the players and singers
of the day, on the incidents of the life of New
York, more interesting in some ways than now and
much more easily grasped. Some of it was, however, serious enough, and from time to time the
notes on men and events in Europe showed a firm
touch and a clear intelligent vision. In the social
articles, under the light and rather sentimental
surface treatment, there was a strong tone of morality. In one of his longer paragraphs, he wrote
of Thackeray : " He seems to be the one of all
authors who takes life precisely as he finds it. If
he finds it sad, he makes it sad : if gay, gay. You
discover in him the flexible adaptability of Horace,
but with a deep and consuming sadness which the
Roman never knew, and which in the Englishman
seems to be almost sentimentality." This I imagine describes pretty nearly the Thackeray that
Mr. Curtis deeply loved and admired, and to whom
he yielded the tribute of more or less conscious
imitation. The sadness in the younger man was
not so real, the seeming sentimentality was rather

more obvious, but was a passing indulgence for a
mind not yet sufficiently settled to be as earnest and
genuine as it could and was to be, not yet having
found the object that could be pursued resolutely
enough to prevent the influence of Thackeray's
manner, rather than of Thackeray's purpose.

In these days Mr. Curtis wrote verse and a considerable amount of it. He even contemplated "a
volume of poems with Ticknor," and he delivered
a number of "poems" at college commencements.
These are not, so far as I have been able to find
them, of a high order. They were smooth enough,
and in passages they were what was then known as
"elegant," fashioned on the model of the Queen
Anne poets, but they seem so foreign to the character of his mind as it afterward developed most
strongly, that I should never recognize one of
them as his from internal evidence. He had no
fondness for the work and no pride in it. " I 'm
not a poet," he wrote, " and I wish they would n't
ask. But as that is the worst excuse for not writing verse, I consent." In this as in other directions,
he was trying his wings. If they did not sustain
him in long flights, he was distinctly successful in
short ones, and there are several songs [1] that are

[1] Here are two selections : —

THE REAPER.

I walked among the golden grain
That bent and whispered to the plain,
" How gaily the sweet summer passes,
So gently treading o'er us grasses."

exquisite in form, and tender and touching in feeling. Had he devoted to this art the time and labor necessary to the full unfolding of his powers, he might easily have ranked high. I cannot regret that he did not. He would at best have been one of no small number, and he could hardly have achieved the work he afterward performed.

> A sad-eyed Reaper came that way,
> But silent in the singing day, —
> Laying the graceful grain along
> That met the sickle with a song.
>
> The sad-eyed Reaper said to me,
> "Fair are the summer fields you see;
> Golden to-day — to-morrow gray;
> So dies young love from life away."
>
> "'T is reaped, but it is garnered well,"
> I ventured the sad man to tell;
> "Though Love declines yet Heaven is kind,
> God knows his sheaves of life to bind."
>
> More sadly then he bowed his head,
> And sadder were the words he said, —
> "Tho' every summer green the plain,
> *This* harvest cannot bloom again."

EGYPTIAN SERENADE.

> Sing again the song you sung
> When we were together young —
> When there were but you and I
> Underneath the summer sky.
>
> Sing the song, and o'er and o'er,
> Though I know that nevermore
> Will it seem the song you sung
> When we were together young.

Before he returned from Europe, he had formed the project of a life of Mehemet Ali, to whom one of the last chapters of the " Howadji in Syria " is given. He pursued it with much seriousness for several years, but finally gave it up. " Frankly," he said, " the motive that held me loyal to it is not the best : it was the desire to do something which, by the orthodox and received standard, should be con‑ceded to be a graver work than anything I have done. But the reason is puerile, although the senti‑ment is good." One thing which led him to drop the task undoubtedly was the conviction, as he wrote, that Mehemet Ali " was only a soldier of fortune, a condottiere upon the splendid scale, whose success was purely personal and therefore transitory." Such a subject could not keep Mr. Curtis up to his work. He was not a story-teller, not an artist in historical painting. The littérateur was already in bonds to the moralist.

His connection with " Putnam's Magazine " was in some ways extremely fortunate. It gave him work of a kind that he enjoyed and did well. It extended his acquaintance [1] with the men of letters

---

[1] The following is a note from Mr. Godwin's address upon Mr. Curtis delivered to the Century Club : —

" It may interest those who are curious as to our literary history to add, that among our promised contributors — the most of whom complied with their promises — were Irving, Bryant, Emerson, Longfellow, Lowell, Hawthorne, Thoreau, George Ripley, Miss Sedgwick, Mrs. Kirkland, author of *A New Home: Who 'll fol‑low?* J. P. Kennedy, author of *Swallow Barn;* Fred S. Coz‑zens, of the *Sparrowgrass Papers;* Richard Grant White, ' Shake‑speare's scholar;' Edmund Quincy, author of *Twice Married;*

of the day.   His intimate association with Charles
F. Briggs, the chief in the office, and with Parke
Godwin, his associate, was a healthful and fruitful
one, for both were men of fine fibre and strong purpose.   Especially the connection gave him a fairly
defined objective for his activity, and one requiring
sustained and concentrated attention.

Parke Godwin, in his "Commemorative Address"
before the Century Association, gives some reminiscences of the Putnams' days.   Referring to
"The Potiphar Papers" and to "Prue and I," he
says : —

"It was evidence of the fecundity and versatility
of Mr. Curtis's gifts that while he was thus carrying forward two distinct lines of invention — the one
full of broad comic effects, and the other of exquisite ideals — he was contributing to the entertain-

William Swinton, since the accomplished historian of The Army
of the Potomac; Richard Kimball, Herman Melville, of 'Ty-
pee' and 'Omoo' fame, Richard Henry Stoddard, E. C. Sted-
man, Ellsworth, Thomas Buchanan Read, Maria Lowell, Jer-
vis McEntee, and others.   We had a strong backing from the
clergy, — the Rev. Drs. Hawks, Vinton, Hanson, Bethune, Baird;
also the occasional assistance of Arthur Hugh Clough, the friend
of Tom Hughes, Matthew Arnold, and other pupils of Dr. Arnold,
who was then in the country; William Henry Herbert, reputed
grandson of the Earl of Pembroke, sportsman and naturalist,
known as Frank Forrester; William North, a frank and brilliant
young Englishman; Fitz James O'Brien, who died in our War for
the Union; and Thomas Francis Meagher, a gallant soldier in the
same war, and afterwards governor of Montana.   Miss Delia Bacon,
whose unhappy history is told by Hawthorne in *Our Old Home*,
began her eccentric Shakespeare-Bacon controversy by a learned
and brilliant article in the Monthly."

ment of our public in a half dozen other different modes,—monthly criticisms of music and the drama that broadened the scope and raised the tone of that form of writing ; rippling Venetian songs that had the swing of the gondola in them ; crispy short stories of humor or pathos ; reminiscences of the Alps taken from his Swiss diaries ; elaborate reviews of books, like Dickens's ' Bleak House,' the Brontë novels, Dr. Veron's ' Mémoires,' ' Hiawatha,' and recent English poetry, including that of Kingsley, Matthew Arnold, Thackeray, the Brownings and Tennyson, which, written forty years ago, have not been surpassed since by more appreciative, discriminating, and sympathetic criticism, even in that masterly and more elaborate book of our fellow-member, ' The Victorian Poets.' In addition to these he gave us, from time to time, solid and thoughtful discussions of ' Men of Character,' of ' Manners,' of ' Fashion,' of the ' Minuet and the Polka ' as social tide-marks, and of ' Rachel,' which may still be read with instruction and pleasure for their keen observation, their nice critical discernment, their cheerful philosophy, and their entrancing charms of style.

" Then, ever and anon, Mr. Curtis would be off for a week or two, delivering lectures on ' Sir Philip Sidney,' on ' The Genius of Dickens,' on ' The Position of Women,' and in one case a course of lectures in Boston and in New York on ' Contemporary Fiction.' In a galaxy of lecturers which included Emerson, Phillips, Beecher,

Chapin, Henry Giles, and others, he was a bright particular star, and everywhere a favorite. A harder-working literary man I never knew: he was incessantly busy, a constant, careful, and wide reader, yet never missing a great meeting or a great address, or a grand night at the theatre. From our little conclaves at No. 10 Park Place, where, I fear, we remorselessly slaughtered the hopes of many a bright spirit (chiefly female) he was seldom absent, and when he came he took his full share of the routine, unless Irving, Bryant, Lowell, Thackeray, or Longfellow sauntered in, and ‘that day we worked no more.’ ”

A few letters of this time from Curtis to Briggs give glimpses of the various life to which Mr. Godwin refers. He writes, December of 1853, from Milwaukee : —

My dear deluded Eastern, — Why do you stay in that dried-up, old-fogyish East? A man is nothing if not a squatter upon the prairies ; for, my dearest B———, I have seen a prairie, I have darted all day across a prairie, I have been near the Mississippi, I have been invited to Iowa, which lies somewhere over the western horizon. I feel as all the people feel in novels, — I confess the West ! Great it is and greatly to be praised.

Yesterday the almanac said December, but the sun said May, as we rolled out of Chicago towards the Mississippi. There was a boundless sky and a boundless earth. It was the old feeling of the desert minus the romance of association, minus history and the Arabian Nights. But if you could fancy the sun relenting, and blessing instead of blasting the wide level of the earth, then, having seen the desert, you would know the prairie.

I feel that I am on my travels once more. Detroit (where I delivered two lectures, had an ovation, was requested to stay and deliver more, and was magnificently lionized, and roared in my most dulcet tones) has drifted into the East.

In the East the note is equally gay : —

BOSTON, January 20, '54.

A being who whirls in a round of routs, dinners, and visits, who, as his friend Tom Appleton says, " nightly vomits fire and ribbons for the satisfaction of gaping multitudes, who is taken to balls, and rushes into small fishing towns to fascinate the alewives — who betakes himself with his rushlight to illuminate small villages whereunto gas has never been previously brought," — has little time for sublunary pursuits. Don't dream of a line from me until I fly these syren east winds and heavy rains, these beautiful women and hospitable men. To-morrow I go to the Longfellows, and I will write you a line soon again, that you may know that the rose-leaf has not been utterly fatal.

My lecture ? Oh, yes, it was fine. The hall was crammed ; see the " Transcript " of last night. I was immediately asked to deliver another, in the Monday evening course, but was too wise to accept.

From Cambridge, whither he had gone to prepare one of his articles for the " Homes of American Authors," he writes : —

Craigie House, June 8, '54.

I am staying now with the poet and his wife.
What though it rains, or shines? It is quite the
same to me. I sit and look over the melancholy
meadows at the winding Charles, and quote my host,
or, which is better, I contemplate my hostess, and
thank God for the gracious and beautiful woman
for whom, clearly, the woods, flowers, the stars,
suns, and men were created.

Lowell, the neighboring poet (the P's prevail
in Cambridge, — Poets, Philosophers, and Professors of religion and other things), is busy with a
sketch of Keats, which must be done to-morrow.
It is for Professor ——, of Boston, editor of the
" English Poets." Professor —— is one of the
cleverest and best of the Cambridge men. He has
just been to Holyoke, and brought home a worm
more brilliant than Herrick's glow-worm or the
Cuban curculio.

I write you in Washington's chamber. The tiles
adorn my fireplace. But I am lazy and thick-
headed.

He spent three months of 1854 at Newport, which
he calls " my country, where my airiest castles are
built and my fairest estates lie." I give, as they
run, a half dozen of letters to Mr. Briggs from
there : —

NEWPORT, June 29, '54.

I have left the poets behind, and awake amidst great historians and by the Poluphloisboio Thalasses. Lowell sends as much love as one man can send to another. Longfellow and his wife accompanied me even to the cars, and I came slipping along in the most gorgeous of summer sunsets, and found myself in the most perfect of climates, with a lofty compassion for those who celebrate the savage shores of Staten Island. Lowell is coming here in July to visit the Nortons, who arrive to-day. Your particular friends Evert and George D. were going out of the historian's house as I came in. I see their figures fluttering upon the edge of the cliff over the sea. They will be restored to your longing heart to-morrow, for they leave to-night.

NEWPORT, July 7, '54.

My young friend Curtis is here, immensely tickled to see his sentimental phiz in Putnam, and struggling with a poem! All the fools are not dead yet, it seems. But I, who have lived a lie for thirty years, — I, whose life was a riper romance than the most imaginative of these idiots can invent, — must laugh at that simple ass, Curtis, who is actually screwing out a poem in the regular old heroic style. It is a great pity that young men should waste themselves on literature and what not, instead of building steamers and laying up riches, like my best of friends, or speculating on the great scale, like my worst enemy. Curtis tells me he has written to Kensett to come here and stop, and give up that silly Saguenay business for the present.

If he does I will let you know, for your friend and chaplain, Dr. Choules, tells me that you are the friend of all loafers and give them passages, and I know not what else.

AQUIDNECK, July 12, '54.

For newspapers and editorial discrimination I have acquired the profoundest reverence, from having been half a year " upon " the " Tribune " and by having dined semi-occasionally with the Press Club. That editors are wise as well as witty, sagacious as well as sonorous, and as full of feeling as of fancy, are three alliterative facts of which I consider myself amply assured. And yet, spite of their witty wisdom, I love the loafers, the scapegraces, the sinners. I, too, am a Bohemian.

NEWPORT, July 23, '54.

That a man who did n't like Lawrence's head of Lowell and of Longfellow should admire the print of a beatified barber and irreproachable steamboat captain, which Hueston meant to publish as my likeness, was perfectly natural, only in future I am sure you will permit me to laugh out loud at your artistic admirations and censures. It is also entirely rational and to be naturally expected that you should be supported in your commendation of a melancholy libel by such eminent connoisseurs as were quoted to me by name in connection with your own. I am sorry that you will be deprived of the pleasure of having me in my favorite character of reformed George Barnwell, set in gold, with a circlet of Clark's hair worn in your cherishing bosom; for I have written Mr. Knickerbocker Hueston that, rather than make my bow to the world in such an unexceptionable coiffure, etc., I would snatch up my story and decamp from the " gallery."

You *are* a high old humbug.

Aquidneck (Isle of Peace and Plenty),
August 10, '54.

My dear friend Zaccheus, — Please climb a tree and consider the denizens of Newport, how they loaf; they write not, neither do they read; and yet I say unto you that Solomon with all his concubines had not a better time. Time goes I know not where, I care not how. Upon cool morning piazzas I sit talking with the Muses, in warm evening parlors I rush dancing with the Graces. Two hundred carriages with the dust of eight hundred wheels throng to Bateman's in the afternoon, or, dustless and delicious, prance along the hard bottom of the sea, or far out upon the island, driving the genial Kensett. We look back across woods, and meadows white to the harvest, and see the picture of peace and plenty framed in the soft sapphire of the sea. There are no end of pretty women. At the Bellevue dance on Monday I saw more really lovely girls than often fall to the lot of anybody's less than a sultan's eyes. Baltimore is especially brilliant. There are Southern women also, all wrong upon the great Question !!! — wronger and more unreasonable, but more courteous, than the men. Bob J—— is here dancing with all the girls, and sometimes so drunk that he cannot move across the floor. *I* dance and people say, "I thought you hated it." "I love it, madam!" "Yes, like other men, you say one thing and do another." "Pardon, most lovely of women, I write and say what I think. I have never been treacherous to my love of the dance."

Aquidneck (Isle of Peace), October 9, '54.

Where are you this bland Sunday morning? These great, gorgeous days chase each other through these spacious skies and die in unspeakable splendor along the sea. I am going to church, because I shall hear a man of earnest and solemn feeling chant a kind of religious reverie which his congregation love, but I am sure do not understand. The people, also, look calm and pious. There is not too strong a sense of millinery. Now that the flood-tide has fallen away from these shores of fashion, the pearls glisten in the sunshine.

I shall come home about the 23d of October, write a lecture, be away at the West in December, home in January, away at the East in February, and home in March. I mean to lecture during two months and make two thousand dollars. I have put my price up to fifty dollars.

CHAPTER VII.

FROM Mr. Curtis's work for "Putnam's Magazine" came two volumes by which he is, perhaps, even better known in American letters than by the Howadji books, "The Potiphar Papers" and "Prue and I." "It was while providing entertainment for our readers in a second number," says Mr. Parke Godwin, "that the vivacious Harry Franco (Charles F. Briggs, the editor-in-chief) exclaimed, 'I have it! Let us each write an article on the state of parties. You, Howadji, who hang a little candle in the naughty world of fashion, will show it up in that light.' Mr. Curtis . . . at once wrote a paper on the state of parties, which he called 'Our Best Society.' It was a severe criticism of the follies, foibles, and affectations of those circles which got their guests, as they did their edibles and carriages, from Brown, Sexton and Caterer, and which thought unlimited supplies of terrapin and champagne the test and summit of hospitality. Trenchant as it was, it was yet received with applause. Some thought the name of the leading lady more suggestive than facts warranted, and that in such phrases as 'rampant vulgarity in Brussels lace,' 'the orgies of rotten Corinth,' and 'the frenzied festival of Rome in her decadence,' the brush was overloaded. None the less, the satire delighted the public, and was soon followed by other papers in the same vein, since collected as 'The Potiphar Papers.' The older folks acknowledged them to be the best things of the kind since Irving and his friends had taken the town with the whim-whams and conceits of Evergreen Wizard and the Cockloft family. They were to some extent exaggerations, in which occasional incidents were given as permanent features; but their high and earnest purpose, their genuine humor, their amusing details, their hits at characters, and their sarcasms deodorized of offensive personality by constant drippings from the springs of fancy, won them great favor. If we behind the screen sometimes felt that we shook hands with Kurz Pacha and the Reverend Cream Cheese, they were, like sweet bully Bottom, ' marvelously translated.' "

I suppose that this summary of the impressions of a contemporary and a companion gives a fair view of the way in which " The Potiphar Papers," at the time of their appearance, affected intelligent minds familiar with the society of the day. There is plenty of evidence of the interest they excited. They had great vogue, and greatly helped the young magazine, while they brought to their writer much notoriety and some fame. As was natural, they made " hard feelings " among those who were, or thought they were, satirized in these pages; but on the whole they were greatly enjoyed, and their healthy purpose was recognized. Taken up now after forty years, a reader must be well through middle age to recognize their substantial basis of fact, and, so far as they survive, it is as satire on the one hand and a picture of the author's mind on the other, rather than as a description of society. Yet a description of society they really were, with a sadly substantial basis of fact. Mr. Curtis's own letters and those of his contemporaries, and the recollections of men who moved in the same circles, are not lacking in evidence that the brush was not very heavily overloaded. It was a period of swift money-making, when a great and increasing crowd of men and women were rapidly gaining the means for a life without work, and for the luxuries and indulgences that had previously been within the reach only of inherited wealth. To get money was relatively easy. It was a matter of energy and shrewdness amid abounding opportunities. To spend money rationally or with refinement was something far different, for which neither nature nor training had fitted the possessors, and for which the conditions of success in getting it had particularly unfitted them. The spending, like the getting, became an affair of competition, and in both it was quantity that told. But the latter competition was largely intrusted to the women, and they were, far less than their husbands, subjected to strong conventions, and wrought their wayward purpose with irresponsible, unenlightened, feverish energy. In such conditions Mesdames Potiphar and Crœsus and Gnu, Mr. Gauche Boosey and Miss Caroline Petitoes became not only possible or probable, but actual, so far as their conception of life goes, or their mode of acting. While, therefore, "The Potiphar Papers" are not pleasant reading for the children and grandchildren of the class represented in their pages, I should advise no one to put the book aside with the notion that it is a greatly exaggerated or even a particularly strongly colored account of what went on under the eyes of the writer.

If the book is to be considered independently of its accuracy, it must appear very uneven. The best parts of it by far are the serious parts, — the comment of the artist rather than the figures he draws. The spirit of the author is of one intense indignation, of anger and revolt and sorrow, at the unworthiness of what he depicts. Nurtured himself in the pure idealism of intellectual and moral New England, yet with a keen and warm delight in the joys — the sensuous as well as the spiritual and emotional joys — of life, bringing from wide travel and varied society an eager zest for the happiest and the best, a patriot moreover in every fibre of his being, with a sensitive pride in his native land and high hopes of what it might be, a high standard of what it should be, all doors flung wide open to his budding fame and his charming personality, Curtis was deeply moved by what he saw of greed and vulgarity and coarse display, and the unseemly strife in money-spending. The opening chapter, "Our Best

Society," expresses this feeling, and on some accounts it might have been better had he stopped with that. On some accounts, but not on the whole; for there is so much of good sense, so much fairness, humor, wit, philosophy in the other papers that it would have been a pity to lose them. As satire, however, they cannot be called highly successful. They fall distinctly below that of Thackeray, on which they are more or less consciously fashioned. Their bitterness is not caustic enough; the undertone of gravity is not deep enough; the fancy, though subtle and delicate, is not sustained or consistent, and the light dramatic machinery adopted does not work smoothly. Particularly the characters are not alive with any sense of reality. The reader is now and then puzzled and even annoyed by their variation from the types for which they are intended to stand. They frequently excite pity, but not sympathy. All of which means only that Curtis was not a creative writer, and, considering how small a part of his writing was in this direction, that is not a very important criticism. It would be, indeed, hardly worth making, were it not that in this instance the choice of a form not giving free scope to his strongest qualities, but cramping and slightly distorting their effect, obscures somewhat the real value of the work, which is substantial. That value comes from the force and elevation of the writer's purpose. It was no small thing in those days that a man of his knowledge and insight, wielding a pen of such singular charm, reaching so wide a class of intelligent readers, should have worked out that purpose in the way in which he worked it out, should have set in the pillory by the wayside the vices of a society unquestionably fascinating to many, and, with every word of scorn or ridicule or irony that he cast at them, should have made plainer and more respected the high ideals which they violated. As the satirist is not always the moralist, but is sometimes the hopeless cynic, wearying and discouraging and depressing the manhood and womanhood of his readers, I do not take it to be a serious qualification of Mr. Curtis's position in literature that he was not eminently a satirist. And as the sound moralist, however he may elect or be impelled to do his work, does work that lasts and blesses while it lasts, I find in this volume a service for which we may well be thankful, for which I feel deeply thankful, knowing that its influence was not only wholesome but strong and wide. Many a young man, reading the papers from month to month, found erected between him and the temptation of a frivolous and essentially low life the light but not easily disregarded barrier of the scorn of a guide who was at once a moralist, a philosopher, and an accomplished gentleman.

The second of the books issuing from the pages of Putnam's was "Prue and I." I am glad again to cite the words of Mr. Godwin, who says that "Mr. Franco and his colleague of the triumvirate used to look forward to these delightful papers as one does to a romance to be continued ; and when we received one of them, we chirruped over it, as if by some strange merit of our own we had entrapped a sunbeam." Sunbeams unfading they are, and I believe will be for long years yet to come, — tender, gay, rich, sweet, life-giving, touching the clouds that gather at evening with hues as lovely as those that ushered in the dawn. It is well-nigh forty years since " Prue and I " came to me, one of the innumerous books of my boyhood, and was my frequent companion in long strolls over the autumn hills or among the woods of spring. No year of the two-score has passed, I think, that the book has not been read again, and every year its subtle charm has grown more charming and more subtle. Had Curtis written only this, — had this alone represented to the world the character and gifts, the aspirations and the attainments, of the man, — his fame in one sense would rather have gained than suffered, because he would always have been associated with this singularly perfect production. I can imagine how we might then have mourned the fate that deprived us of further fruit of so rare a sort, and might have set ourselves to fancy how he would have developed, what sound wisdom, what serene dignity, what beautiful loyalty to the best and purest, what fine and delicate range of a warm and chaste imagination would have unfolded in the riper and wider work of the author of "Prue and I." It is one of the curious effects of the limits nature sets to even our mental appetites, that when what would have been but the imagined achievements of this author have become realities, and have multiplied through a long and fertile life, the fame that these have won for him is less distinct than the one book would have given him. Not less firm, certainly, nor less admirable, but less distinct; so that I find the book, with very many, an incidental association with Curtis's memory, and not, as it has grown to be with me, largely the embodiment, the type of all associations. I like to think that it was with this book in his mind that Lowell wrote: "Had letters kept you, every wreath were yours." For it seems to me that in this book there is more of the man, of the thinker, dreamer, artist, and moralist, than anywhere else in the great mass of his writings. And indeed, it could not but be very genuine. Here is no elaboration of years, no polished and repolished gem, slowly and carefully wrought with critical reflection and matured art. Here are a scant half dozen magazine articles, filling a couple of hundred of small pages, written with rushing pen, amid varied and pressing occupations, at times in the stolen moments of hurried journeys, and never in the calm of deliberate industry. What was put on paper was what sprang from the unforced mind. From the conditions of their writing the papers were a species of improvisation, and I think that in great part to that is due their unity and strength amid such rich variety, such bold and unreined fancy. What we get is the man, everywhere and always, nothing less or other.

In "Prue and I" the dramatic machinery, unlike that of "The Potiphar Papers," runs with entire ease. It is very slight and the persons are few — the old book-keeper and his immortal wife, Titbottom, and Bourne the millionaire. The motive is by no means very novel. The reflections of a philosopher of moderate or scant means upon the fortunes, successes, failures, realities, and shams of his fellow-beings have been written for ages in many tongues. The compensations for the deficiencies of life to be got from a lively imagination, the advantages of fancied adventure over the uncertain and trying reality, the riches of the world of books to him whose only possession — save a contented mind — they are, have been sung and painted ever since the favors of fortune began to vary the conditions of men. So far from being novel, the general theme of the book may be called dangerously hackneyed, and has spread pitfalls of commonplace in the way of numberless writers old and young. The world of readers yawns at the memory of the weary platitudes with which it has strewn the pages of books since before the invention of printing. But if the theme be not novel it is because the contrasts of life are as old as the race, and men who think at all are forced in one vein or another to think of them. It is the distinction of Curtis that his thought of them is so sweet, so sound, so subtle in its insight, broadly wise, gracious and luminous in its expression, essentially noble in spirit. It is not merely or chiefly the delight of the artist in the harmony brought out of variety that the author feels as he works in with rich fancy the different characters and scenes. It is deep and tranquil joy in the substance of purity, kindness, justice, and love which these variations illustrate. The modest and faithful and unimaginative **Prue** is the real inspiration of the piece. One feels that her love of poetry, her pleasure in the fine things of the finest books which her husband reads to her with glowing or tear-dimmed eyes, her enjoyment of the sunsets so magical, so infinitely suggestive to him, are almost purely sympathetic, are born of her love for him, and in the quaint humor, with which her husband admits this to himself and to his readers, one feels also that the love of this pure and gentle woman is the real thing before whose gracious radiance the splendors of nature and literature and imagination pale their ineffectual fire.

If the writer peoples the world of wealth and fashion, which he assumes to watch from afar off, with beautiful women whose " beauty is heaven's stamp upon virtue;" if he makes of his own fancy the ideal cavalier whose perfect reverence and grace and manly purity match the qualities of the woman, he never permits the suspicion that the reality is not possible : he only insists that, unless the reality is there, luxury is no better than poverty, and that true manliness and womanliness are common to all conditions. There is no suggestion of a sneer in the smile with which he greets the carriage of Au-

relia, and describes his own misadventure with the
" wrinkled Eve" whose apple-stand tempted him to
his fall. The smile suggests, indeed, the ephemeral
nature of Aurelia's social advantages, and even of
her youthful beauty, and implies that the accidents
of poverty are not of any more permanent seriousness than those of riches; but that is not because
the old book-keeper holds with the preacher that al!
is vanity, but because he holds that the only really
important thing is virtue, and that virtue bears
imperial sway wherever its throne may be set up.
This it is that gives to the book its perennial charm.
Its charm as literature I think very great, — it
grows with every reading. There is a wide range
of delightful literary suggestion in the little volume.
It teems with rich and varied allusion. One feels
in reading it that he is in intimate intercourse with
the best minds, and every literary association it
awakens is touched with a new light. The fantas-
tic characters that swarm unresting on the deck
of the Flying Dutchman, beneath the spectral
shrouds, and in the mystery of smoke and haze,
have been called from pages known to all the world :
but whenever the reader again sees them they will
be different, and more than they had been, for the
illumination bestowed by the pen of Curtis. Nor
has Curtis anywhere else, I think, sounded such
solemn depths. There are suggestions of them in
the Howadji books, but hardly more. The undertone of " Titbottom's Spectacles " is of pure tragedy,
and that of " A Cruise in the Flying Dutchman "

is only less so. But nowhere is it more than an undertone, and the last page leaves us again under the glance of Prue's pure eyes, safe from the questions that vex us with thoughts beyond the reaches of our souls.

In " Prue and I " Curtis's style, though not yet fully developed, was determined, and nearly every quality to be found in " The Easy Chair," in the great orations, and even in the editorial writings of after years, is here. The style of the Howadji is far in the past. There is no more opera, no more array of conventions splendid but artificial, no longer the gay and haughty demand on the assent of the reader. There is instead the most engaging candor, and, amid a wealth of fancy and imagery and glowing sentiment, there is the essential simplicity of sincerity. The book from first to last breathes integrity. It amuses, it delights, it stirs the imagination, it thrills delicately the most sensitive chords, but above all it inspires affection and respect. The writer, though he should be forever unknown, is henceforth forever a friend, to be loved and always to be trusted.

In December, 1855, at the close of the year in which " Prue and I " was begun, Mr. Curtis became engaged to Miss Anna Shaw, daughter of Francis G. Shaw, of Staten Island. On Thanksgiving Day, 1856, they were married. It was in every way a most happy union, and the marriage marked, if not a turning point, a distinct and important stage in the career of Mr. Curtis. Among the guests at the quiet wedding was Major John C. Frémont. I shall have occasion later to refer to the part Mr. Curtis took in the great campaign in which the "Pathfinder" led the first gallant and splendid charge of the Republican party against slavery, and to the influence of Mr. Curtis's connection with the Shaw family in stimulating and sustaining, if not in arousing, his zeal in the cause of freedom. That influence — pure, strong, inspiring, and in the highest sense moral — was to continue through life. I am sure that I violate no essential reserve in stating that, in the long and arduous years of Mr. Curtis's varied work, his home was always a haven where he constantly sought refuge and repose, and from which, refitted, reinforced, inspired with renewed confidence and courage, he set out to the "good wars" that invited him, and that to the gracious and noble lady who made that home is due no small share in his many and rich achievements.

CHAPTER VIII.

THE seven years following Mr. Curtis's return from Europe in 1850 were very busy, and generally very laborious, particularly after the establishment of " Putnam's Magazine."   While still engaged on that, he had begun the series of weekly contributions to " Harper's Weekly " by " The Lounger," to which I have already referred ; had written a number of social essays for " Harper's Monthly ; " and finally, in 1854, had undertaken the sole charge of the " Easy-Chair."   Meanwhile he kept up his lecturing, with what energy the extracts from his letters already given show.   For the most part he took his task lightly enough, and found " no end " of amusement, as well as much satisfaction, in his treatment by the local press of the cities he visited. He wrote January 15, 1853, to his father : —

" A Utica paper makes a rather amusing notice of the lecture.   It is to the effect that whoever has read Mr. C.'s books must have known what kind of a lecture to expect, — that it was full of gorgeous imagery, and that, although it had humor, beauty was its characteristic, but was full of sudden and quaint contrasts that presented an endless series of grave and gay imagery. Yet an almost feminine perception of beauty, an unlimited command of language, an imagination chastened but rich, and evidently moulded by the most soothing influences of the Orient, resulted in a work which the hearer could not forget, — a series of pictures that would linger long in the memory of every one present. That is about the pith of it, which has the invaluable merit of praising the lecture for just what it was not ! So, what with commendation for what it is and for what it is not, it will go hard with it if it does not secure all suffrages."

The few letters to his father that have come into my hands are extremely interesting, and some of them very touching. There was a very sound and wholesome relation between father and son. The early essential independence of mind shown by the latter, always accompanied by and indeed resting on a strong affection and sincere respect, together with the gayety of many of the letters, show the intimacy that existed. Mr. Curtis was not yet thirty-two when his father died. Shortly after that loss he wrote to his mother (January 21, 1856) : —

" You may imagine how sad and strange it is not to feel father's interest and anxiety in my success. I used to read everything that was said about me with his eyes, and so gladly sent him all the praise. But I do not feel at all removed from his real sympathy and interest even now. He is lost to the eye, but not at all, even as a father, to the heart. I shall always live as if in his eye. In every act 1 shall always feel his judgment. . . . To children, parents are matters of course, like trees and stones. But when we become men and women, we reverence their individual excellence, and when we lose them we know that we have lost friends. How just and calm and generous a friend my father was to me! He was so candid and simple in his love that I never ceased to feel myself a boy when I was with him."

He was soon to gather some of that harvest of experience which tells us beyond all question that the springtime of life has passed forever. In the spring of 1856 he had put some money into the publishing firm of Dix, Edwards & Co., to whom had passed the ownership of "Putnam's Monthly." They failed the next year in April, and in August Curtis, in a letter to Mr. Charles Eliot Norton, describes his experience in business: "I was responsible as a general partner. To save the creditors (for I would willingly have called quits myself), I threw in more money, which was already forfeited, and undertook the business with Mr. Miller, the printer, who wanted to save himself. Presently Mr. Shaw put in some money as special partner. But what was confessed to be difficult, when we relied upon the statements given us, became impossible when those statements turned against us, and last week we suspended. In the very moment of arrangement, it appeared that by an informality Mr. Shaw was held as a general partner: the creditors swarmed in to avail themselves of the slip, and we are now wallowing in the law. Of course I lose everything and expected to, but there is now, in addition, this ugly chance of Mr. S.'s losing sixty or seventy thousand dollars, and all by an accident which the creditors fully comprehend."

Without going into the details of the arrangement by which this trouble was finally settled, it is sufficient to say that Mr. Curtis assumed a large indebtedness for which he was not legally bound, and for nearly a score of years labored incessantly to pay it, devoting to that purpose the money earned by lecturing. It was an arduous task, involving not merely the work of preparation and the time spent in traveling, but much hardship and exposure, much sacrifice of the joys of a home peculiarly dear, and the almost complete abandonment of sustained scholarly pursuits to which he had looked with longing. It was not, however, without compensations, and some of high value. Of these, necessarily, the greatest was the one he rarely if ever mentioned, — the satisfaction of his conscience. Besides this, however, there was the close acquaintance he formed in every part of the Union with the many of those who were to march with him in the field of the better politics. When he took up the work of an editor a few years later, this acquaintance was continued and extended, and was of inestimable value to him and to the country. It gave him the sureness of aim which made his writing more effective, perhaps, than that of any other man in his generation; and it helped to give him also the sense of confidence in the final triumph of the causes in which he successively engaged, which was at once a source of strength to himself and an inspiration to others. This experience, moreover, was a constant training in the art of public speaking, of which he became easily, I think, the greatest master of his country in his time. But of these compensations there was, of course, no thought when Mr. Curtis calmly took up the heavy burden which he knew would not be discharged for many years, if ever. That was done in the quiet and unquestioning obedience to the law of simple, manly fidelity that was a law of his nature, and as integral a part of it as his kindness of heart and gentleness of manners. So modestly was it done that I have almost a sense of offending his proud and delicate self-respect in thus speaking of it, as if it were a thing he could have helped doing. But we all know that it was a thing of a sort rarely done: any account of Mr. Curtis's life would be deficient were it omitted.

CHAPTER IX.

THE CAMPAIGN OF 1856.

In 1846, ten years before the first candidate of
the Republican party had been named, James Russell Lowell had written, apropos of the movement
for the annexation of Texas : —

> "Slavery, the Earth-born Cyclops,
>   Fellest of the giant brood,
> Sons of brutish Force and Darkness
>   That have drenched the Earth with blood,
> Famished in his self-made desert,
>   Blinded by our purer day,
> Seeks in yet unblasted regions
>   For his miserable prey.
> Shall we guide his gory fingers
>   Where our helpless children play ? "

For ten years devoted men and women, with
the utmost energy and courage and persistence, if
not always with discretion, had been pressing this
question upon the American people. The people
would hardly listen when only the almost unknown
territory involved in the annexation of Texas and
in the Mexican War was concerned, but when the
slave power forced the same question upon their
reluctant ears with reference to Kansas and Nebraska, the land toward which the restless children

of the free States had begun to push forward, there was no stilling it. And then it was that Mr. Curtis seems first earnestly to have considered it. He could not long have resisted it, we may be sure, but it is to be remarked that the connection he had formed with the Shaw family undoubtedly quickened his sympathies, and aroused him to a sense of what it was possible, and therefore imperative, for him to do. The father and mother of the woman who was to be his wife were of the early school of intensely earnest, unflinching, uncompromising, unwearying foes of slavery. It was a part of their religion to fight the evil at all times and in all ways that offered or could be found, and it is certain that, if the flame of his zeal was not kindled, it was nursed and fanned by theirs.

As the extracts given from his letters to his father from Brook Farm and from Concord, and later after his return from Europe, clearly show, Mr. Curtis's mind was never closed to the essential nature of slavery, never misled as to the specious claims made for it founded on the Constitution, and especially never dull to the moral question involved. It was the latter that most deeply moved him, and aroused him to a series of appeals to young men of the Union which had a deep and lasting effect. In the spring of 1856 had occurred the assault upon Charles Sumner in the Senate Chamber by Preston Brooks, of South Carolina. In that year also culminated the struggle in Kansas between the free-state immigrants and settlers, largely from New England, and the pro-slavery men from the South, chiefly from Missouri, the latter aided by the force and authority of the Federal government under President Pierce. This is not the place to trace even in outline the features of the tremendous conflict of which these were incidents. It was in these that the tendencies of the slave power, which gave to the presidential canvass of that year its distinctive character, were most strikingly exposed.

The first speech of importance by Mr. Curtis was delivered August 5, 1856, before the Literary Societies of Wesleyan University, at Middletown, Conn. Its title was, "The Duty of the American Scholar to Politics and the Times." He was thirty-two years old. "Too young," he told the college boys, " to be your guide and philosopher, I am yet old enough to be your friend. Too little in advance of you in the great battle of life to teach you from experience, I am yet old enough to share with you the experience of other men and of history. I would gladly speak to you," he went on, " of the charms of pure scholarship; of the dignity and worth of the scholar; of the abstract relation of the scholar to the state. The sweet air we breathe and the repose of midsummer invite a calm ethical or intellectual discourse. But would you have counted him a friend of Greece, who quietly discussed the abstract nature of patriotism on that Greek summer day through whose hopeless and immortal hours Leonidas and his three hundred stood at Thermopylæ for liberty? And to-day, as the scholar meditates that deed, the air that steals in at his window darkens his study and suffocates him as he reads. Drifting across a continent, and blighting the harvests that gild it with plenty from the Atlantic to the Mississippi, a black cloud obscures the page that records an old crime, and compels him to know that freedom always has its Thermopylæ, and that his Thermopylæ is called Kansas."

Of Sumner he said: " In a republic of freemen this scholar speaks for freedom, and his blood stains the Senate floor. There it will blush through all our history. That damned spot will never out from memory, from tradition, or from noble hearts."

Of the function of the scholar class: —

" The very material success for which nations, like individuals, strive, is full of the gravest danger to the best life of the state as of the individual. But as in human nature itself are found the qualities which best resist the proclivities of an individual to meanness and moral cowardice, — as each man has a conscience, a moral mentor which assures him what is truly best for him to do, — so has every state a class which by its very character is dedicated to eternal and not to temporary interests; whose members are priests of the mind, not of the body; and who are necessarily the conservative body of intellectual and moral freedom. This is the class of scholars. The elevation and correction of public sentiment is the scholar's office in the state.

"If, then, such be the scholar and the scholar's office, — if he be truly the conscience of the state, — the fundamental law of his life is liberty. At every cost, the true scholar asserts, defends, liberty of thought and liberty of speech. Of what use to a man is a thought that will help the world, if he cannot tell it to the world? Such a thought comes to him as Jupiter came to Semele. He is consumed by the splendor that secretly possesses him. The Inquisition condemns Galileo's creed: '*Pur muove*' — still it moves — replies Galileo in his dungeon. Tyranny poisons the cup of Socrates: he smilingly drains it to the health of the world. The church, towering vast in the midst of universal superstition, lays its withering finger upon the freedom of the human mind, and its own child, leaping from its bosom, denounces to the world his mother's madness."

After tracing the character of Milton as most nearly fulfilling the conditions of the ideal scholar, Mr. Curtis made a concise but careful and strong statement of the advance of the slave power, from the framing of the Constitution to the passage of the Kansas-Nebraska Bill. He drew a pathetic and impressive picture of the men of Connecticut who answered the call to Lexington and Boston.

"Through these very streets they marched who never returned. They fell and were buried, but they can never die. Not sweeter are the flowers that make your valley fair, not greener are the pines that give your valley its name, than the memory of the brave men who died for freedom. And yet no victim of those days, sleeping under the green sod of Connecticut, is more truly a martyr of Liberty than every murdered man whose bones lie bleaching in this summer sun upon the silent plains of Kansas. And so long as Liberty has one martyr, so long as one drop of blood is poured out for her, so long from that single drop of bloody sweat of the agony of humanity shall spring hosts as countless as the forest leaves and mighty as the sea.

"Brothers! the call has come to us," he concluded; "I bring it to you in these calm retreats. I summon you to the great fight of Freedom. I call upon you to say with your voices whenever the occasion offers, and with your votes when the day comes, that upon the fertile fields of Kansas, in the very heart of the continent, the Upas-tree of slavery, dripping death-dews upon national prosperity and upon free labor, shall never be planted. I call upon you to plant there the palm of peace, the vine and olive of a Christian civilization. I call upon you to determine whether this great experiment of human freedom, which has been the scorn of despotism, shall by its failure be also our sin and shame. I call upon you to defend the hope of the world. The voice of our brothers who are bleeding, no less than of our fathers who bled, summons us to this battle. Shall the children of

unborn generations clustering over that vast Western Empire rise up and call us blessed or cursed?
Here are our Marathon and Lexington. Here are
our heroic fields. The hearts of good men beat
with us. The fight is fierce ; the issue is with
God, but God is good."

In this, the first serious address on public affairs
that Curtis made, there are indications of some of
the most distinctive and the finest traits of his oratory at its best. The happy expression of the influence of the season and the place with which he
frequently began, the vivid and inspiring use of
historic associations fitted with aptness to the purpose of the discourse, very jewels upon its thread,
but beaming a steady light upon its object ; the
stately march of broad recital ; the solemn and
simple, tender and stirring appeal ; and through
all the sense of the high level of principle and conviction from which the speaker surveyed the field
of fact and argument, — all these are here. There
are points in the discourse where the fine restraint
of the rhetoric which was the characteristic of his
riper years was not attained, and there are signs
that his subject had not been so severely studied,
its details not so closely subordinated and marshaled, as was his later habit. The logic does not
fail, but it is not so sustained, and the view of the
hostile critic had not been so clearly imagined as
became his wont. Experience and observation had
not done their whole work at thirty - two, but
they had begun it, and were well advanced. With

this speech the party of resistance to the extension of slavery, the party of freedom, knew that a champion had taken up its cause, who brought to it not only the dashing courage of the cavalier, but the unyielding firmness of the Puritan; a bright and tempered sword flashed upon the combat in the hand of one who could not turn back if he would, so high he felt to be the behest that summoned him. "The fight is fierce," he cried; "the issue is with God, but God is good."

In the autumn Curtis was fairly enlisted in the "campaign." He made an extended tour of Pennsylvania for the state election, which was then held in October, and which made the State one of the most hotly contested in every presidential year. Returning, he spoke frequently in Connecticut and New York. Mr. Rhodes, in his recently published history, says: " N. P. Willis, one of the best known littérateurs of his day, relates how he drove five miles one night to hear Curtis deliver a stump speech. He at first thought the author of the Howadji 'too handsome and well dressed' for a political orator, but as he listened his mistake was apparent. He heard a logical and rational address, and now and then the speaker burst into the full tide of eloquence unrestrained. Willis declared that, though fifty-four years old, he should this year cast his 'virgin vote,' and it would be for Frémont."

Writing October 31, on the eve of the election, Curtis said to a near friend: "I shall not tell you of the great struggle which is advancing. The election is but an event. God is still God, however the election goes and whoever is elected. The movement which is now fairly begun will not relapse into apathy or death."

CHAPTER X.

A NOVEL AND A LECTURE.

MR. CURTIS, as I have said, was married in November, 1856, and went to live on Staten Island, where his wife's father had a spacious home with large grounds. His first child, a son, was born there in December, 1857. His home life, though constantly broken in upon by his lecturing tours and by his journeyings for the delivery of political speeches, was always happy, peaceful, the source of incalculable comfort and delight. The following extracts from letters to his intimate friend, Charles Eliot Norton, of Cambridge, will give the reader a glance at his life during the few years preceding the great campaign of 1860 and the Civil War: —

NEW YORK, June 17, '58.

Your kind note floats into my hand just as I am " stepping westward," for a fortnight. I go to the University of Michigan and Antioch College with an oration upon " The Democratic Principle, and its Prospects in our Country," with every word of which I think you would agree, and not find a single thing which you would be sorry to have a friend of yours say. When I come to you I will bring it, and take the taste of some other things of mine out of your mouth.

NORTH SHORE, September 25, '58.

I have promised to deliver my " Democracy and Education " before a teachers' institute in Newport on the 8th October, and I shall put off coming to you till then.

> " For tho' on pleasure he was bent,
> He had a frugal mind."

What else could you expect of a seditious Sepoy, — a Chairman of the Republican County Committee, an agricultural orator, and your most affectionate

G. W. C.

On his return from this trip he describes his home-coming : —

10th October, '58.

I saw the receding tower of Trinity, and presently beheld the camp of the army of occupation upon the wharf — who but she? — and along the Kills we drove, while I talked of Newport friends and fields, and watched the autumn waiting for me in the woods and on the flowery hills. All were well. The boy of boys — the man-child — shouted and jumped into my arms, and in an hour he was riding behind his goat with his mamma and papa in waiting."

8th November, '58.

We have finished our fight and elected our governor. He is a merchant, an average merchant, but our congressional majority, which shows by districts the complexion of the State, is nearly seventy thousand.   That shows a change of heart.

And yet, while we have won, the *one* thing clear seems to be that Douglas is the next President, unless the Slave party offers us some new issue. We cannot beat them upon that of Popular Sovereignty, upon which D. will make his stand and his battle.

Next week I begin my lecturing, and have already engaged sixty evenings.

January 30, '59.

At the Burns festival in Troy I led off Auld Lang Syne at four in the morning and hoarsened my voice.

March 2, '59.

I am glad you succeeded in amusing your little sister.   I have often wished she were here to join Master Frank's class in Little Bo-Peep.   Don't stimulate her mind with too much House-that-Jack-Built at once, but lead her gradually on from Cock Robin to Mother Hubbard.

In September, 1859, he writes : —

" The ' Weekly ' now circulates 93,000, and is very thoroughly read. I make my Lounger a sort of lay pulpit, and the readers have a chance of hearing things suggested that otherwise there would be no hint of in the paper. And, after all, an author has something besides his own fame to look after."

It was in this year that Mr. Curtis, tempted, I

imagine, by what the publishers could offer not only in money, but in the security of a very wide circle of readers, began the novel of " Trumps " as a serial in " Harper's Weekly." It was not an unnatural venture. He was a lover of good fiction, and an intelligent critic of it. He was in the very prime of his manhood. He had won notable success in varied directions. He had seen much of the world, not only of society, but of affairs and of politics. He had traveled widely abroad and in his own land. He was a welcome intimate in the houses of gifted men and women. He was conscious of the possession of the literary faculty. Expression fitting the thought was not difficult to him. He had quick and sensitive sympathies, a sound and trustworthy judgment, and his fellow-beings, of all sorts and on all levels, interested him much. He could not but know that when he talked of them, of their character, their doings, their oddities, adventures, aims, humors, his talk charmed his hearers. Why should he not write a novel? Why should he not group in a well-connected story the acts and words that should reveal men and women as he saw and knew them, not forgetting the lesson of the supreme value of goodness which every life, good or evil, disclosed to him, and of which his own was a half-unconscious reading? Why cannot the eagle swim?

I think it is not to be denied that " Trumps " is depressing reading, despite its many excellences. It is the fruit of an author's mistake as to his powers. It is Thackeray's pictures, George Eliot's poetry, Dickens's portrayal of aristocracy. It shows how many and how great gifts the author had, and how little he had of the rare art of sustained story-telling. Five years before, Lowell had written to Briggs (he had just said of the "Chateaux in Spain," "I think it one of the best essays I ever read, I don't care by what author"): "The fault of 'The Potiphar Papers' seems to me that in them there are dialogizing and monologizing thoughts, but not flesh and blood enough." And it is with "dialogizing and monologizing thoughts" that the pages of "Trumps" fairly swarm. The title, the intention of which is emphasized in the last sentence, shows that the real purpose of the writer was not to write a novel, but to point a moral. "Patient and gentle reader," he says, as he closes his work, "it is for you to say who, among all the players we have been watching, held Trumps," and the reader is expected to answer that Trumps were held by the benevolent and beneficent Lawrence Newt, and by that heaven-born vision of earthly beauty and unspotted soul, Hope Wayne, and, as the proportions of the pack allow, by the lesser embodiments of kindness and purity and rectitude, and that all the low cards fell to those who were playing for self. It is a gracious view of life, and one that cheers the good in adverse conditions, even if it escapes the attention and leaves uncorrected the wayward will of the mean and wicked. But this naïve indiscretion as to the title of the

book seems to me to show the peculiar failure of
the writer to grasp the cardinal principle of his
art, that the moral, if moral there must be, should
point itself. And, worse than this, the title does
not fit the avowed purpose. Trumps are the gift
of the gods. It is the duty of a skillful player not
to waste them on his partner's trick, and to make
and take all the chances of the game in order to get
the most good of them, and it is the duty of an
honest player not to supply them when wanting
from up his sleeve. But to find them in his hand
when the deal is made is no merit of his, and to
miss them is not his fault. Now the lesson of
Curtis's novel is clearly that the reward of virtue
is in great part earned, and not a matter of chance.
The joy of honorable self-denial, the peace that
comes from generous sympathy with the good fortune of others, through one's own loss, — these are
urged, and with winning earnestness. They are
not the fruit of chance. Indeed, the life that Curtis tries to depict and does very clearly suggest,
and of which he gives us most engaging chapters,
is not in reality a game at all, neither a game of
hazard nor of sport. Nor, on the other hand, —
that is the shortcoming of the writer, — is it a
drama. It is a modern version of the mediæval
" morality,"— a long and elaborate lesson, without,
indeed, the tediousness of its ancient prototype,
and also without the picturesqueness gained by
that from the very concrete notions of the Devil and
his conqueror then prevailing. I may say, I hope

without offense, that it is in its general effect a
Sunday - school story, written by a man of rare
gifts, some of which betray the elusive charm of
genius, but still essentially of that class, producing,
and apparently intended to produce, the impression
that in the end virtue triumphs and vice comes to a
miserable end.

Yet there are the materials, the raw materials, of
a strong story in "Trumps," and the writer's conception of their significance is vigorous. The brilliant viciousness of Abel Newt, started at school
and developed in society, in dissipation, in politics,
in the corruption of the capital, in the desperation
of the culminating crime ; the wasted and misdi-
rected loves of the two sisters whose lives are shad-
owed and nearly wrecked by one man ; the un-
disclosed experiences by which the character of
Lawrence Newt is moulded ; contrasted with these,
the simple and sunny life of Amy Waring, the more
delicate and remote nature of Hope Wayne, the
hopeless final kindling of real affection in the heart
of Abel's mistress, — here is the stuff of which romance and tragedy are woven, and with it are plentiful minor threads of comedy and sentiment. Nor
can I resist the impression that, had Curtis taken
up the study and practice of the story-telling art
earlier, or with a firmer purpose, the product would
have been, if not perfect, not only far more satisfactory than this single fruit, but of a marked distinction and value. There are few more real figures than "Prue" and her husband, and Titbottom

is only slightly less real. But I cannot regret that
his energies, great and efficient as they were (" his
mind works so easily," wrote Lowell), were not
turned in this direction. He might possibly have
won a more lasting fame; and perhaps a wider one.
I cannot think he would have done wider or more
lasting service. He could not seriously have
changed his aim. He might have attained the art
that makes the moral point itself; he could never
have really forgotten or wished to forget the moral.
The highest achievement, I take it, in fiction, certainly in the more modern fiction, is the impressive
unfolding of the complexity, the contradiction, the
pathetic or amusing or baffling conflict, in human
nature. Perhaps Curtis saw these. I doubt if he
felt them with the intensity and depth that are requisite to embody them. Life does not seem to me
to have been to him a supremely complex problem,
but rather, simple with the simplicity of his own
rare and beautiful nature. It is delicate ground to
traverse, but I think that, as his own conscience
was in no wise a Delphic oracle, but spoke to him
with the directness of Sinai, — " thou shalt " or
" thou shalt not " — he may easily not have understood the infinite difficulties that men less morally
gifted meet and so seldom conquer, not always because they will not do what is right, but because
they cannot decide. And again, as conscience having once answered his questioning, his obedience,
if not easy, was singularly certain and prompt and
steadfast, he may not quite have been able to see

or to portray those impulses of evil before which a
fine nature becomes the helpless victim of passion,
the clearest aspiration toward the best vanishes,
and the soul lies weak, weary, defeated in the tan-
gled meshes of a life it loathes. He might have
trained himself to imagine, but I believe it would
not have been easy for him, the multiform effects
of circumstance, of heredity, of all that sways the
will, which are so important and so fascinating a
part of the creations of such writers as George
Eliot, and, with less betrayal of conscious philosophy, of such a writer as Thackeray. And since, if
he had worked through fiction, his aim must still
have been what it practically was in everything he
wrote after the Howadji books, it is surely best
that he pursued it in his own way. This, I believe, he felt strongly himself. He did not regard
" Trumps " with any great satisfaction, and he
never renewed an attempt which, relatively at least
to others of his own, was a failure.

Mr. Curtis's lectures were generally received with
great admiration, and his welcome was almost always
cordial, even though he went, as he did frequently
after 1856, with an incendiary address in his bag.
But there were experiences of a different sort.

In the summer of 1859 Mr. Curtis accepted a
proposition to deliver a lecture in Philadelphia on
the 15th of December. It came from two young
men who had planned the course purely as a business enterprise ; and though Mr. Curtis chose as his
subject " The Present Aspect of the Slavery Ques-

tion," it was a mere coincidence that the Anti-Slavery Society of Pennsylvania was to hold a fair at the same time. In October came the raid of John Brown upon Harper's Ferry, and on the 2d of December Brown was hanged. The excitement roused by these events over all the country ran very high in Philadelphia, much of the richest trade of that city being with the South. On the day before the lecture was to be given, handbills summoned a mass meeting at National Hall, where Curtis was to speak, with the avowed purpose of preventing him from speaking. This hall was in the upper part of a building the lower part of which was used as a warehouse, into which railroad cars were run to be unloaded. Mayor Henry, though not in favor of the views Mr. Curtis was known to hold, did not oppose the delivery of the lecture; and Mr. Ruggles, the chief of police, though a firm Democrat in politics, declared that free speech must be defended at any cost. Mr. Curtis went to the hall accompanied by Dr. Furness and Mrs. Furness, by Lucretia Mott, and the Hon. William D. Kelley, who introduced him. Approach to the stage was had from the floor by a narrow, winding stairway on either side, which also descended to the warehouse below. These were blocked, so soon as Mr. Curtis and his party reached the stage, by benches thrown one on another, and by a couple of members of the junior Anti-Slavery Society armed with heavy sticks. In the hall a policeman was stationed at the end of each seat, and several hundred below guarded the entrances and the warehouse. Mr. Kelley was allowed to introduce the lecturer, but the latter had hardly risen when rioting began. Repeated attempts were made to storm the stage, but were repulsed. Stones were thrown through the windows, and bottles of vitriol, and one of the auditors was terribly burned. Meanwhile there was in the warehouse below a series of determined and furious attempts by the mob to get to the hall from that point. The police repelled them, making many arrests. At first Chief Ruggles sent the prisoners to the police station ; but soon seeing that this weakened his force too much, he had offenders locked in empty cars standing on the tracks in the warehouse. Two attempts were made to set fire to the building. Then Chief Ruggles mounted a car and announced that if this were again tried every effort would be made to save the persons in the hall, but that the prison-cars and their human freight would be left to the flames. The attempt was not renewed.

Mr. Henry C. Davis, of New York, then a resident of Philadelphia, a grandson of Lucretia Mott and one of the young guards on the stage, from whom the above recounted facts are obtained, says that "there were only brief intervals in which Mr. Curtis could be heard, but that he delivered his address in full." "When I could hear him," says Mr. Davis, "his voice was firm and clear and resonant, and his delivery sustained and self-possessed." "It was," says Mr. Isaac H. Clothier, who was Mr.

Davis's companion, " an eventful and dangerous evening, but the meeting did not break up until the lecture was fully delivered, and until free speech had been triumphantly vindicated in Philadelphia. Mr. Curtis, with all his well-known gentleness and sweetness of spirit, proved himself on that occasion to be a man of mettle and undaunted courage."

CHAPTER XI.

ONCE entered on politics, Mr. Curtis gave to it most careful study as well as much hard and detailed work. He was very active in the Republican party organization in the county of Richmond, N. Y., formed by Staten Island, and was early chosen chairman of the County Republican Committee, a post he held, with the greatest assiduity in its duties, almost uninterruptedly for many years. Evidence of the clear fashion in which he reasoned on the practical as well as the theoretic side of politics is found in a letter to Mr. John J. Pinkerton, of West Chester, Pennsylvania, then a young man, who had made Mr. Curtis's acquaintance at Union College, on the delivery of the address on " Patriotism " in 1857. This acquaintance ripened into a warm friendship which lasted unshaken to the time of Mr. Curtis's death. The letter followed an answer to Mr. Curtis's inquiry as to the state of opinion in Pennsylvania with reference to the approaching presidential contest.

NORTH SHORE, 13th April, 1860.

MY DEAR PINKERTON, — Thanks for your kind response. I have had the same suspicion of Pennsylvania, but my general feeling is this: that the nomination of Mr. Bates would so chill and paralyze the youth and ardor which are the strength of the Republican party; would so cheer the Democrats as a merely available move, showing distrust of our own position and power; would so alienate the German Northwest, and so endanger a bolt from the straight Republicans of New England,— that the possible gain of Pennsylvania and New Jersey, and even Indiana, might be balanced. Add to this that defeat with Bates is the utter destruction of our party organization, and that success with him is very doubtful victory, and I cannot but feel that upon the whole his nomination is an act of very uncertain wisdom.

It is very true that there is no old Republican, because the party is young, and it will not do to ask too sharply *when* a man became a Republican. Moreover, a man like Mr. Bates may very properly have been a Fillmore man in '56, because he might not have believed that the Slavery party was as resolved and desperate as it immediately showed itself in the Dred Scott business; this is all true, but human nature cries out against the friends of Frémont in '56 working for a Fillmore man in '60, and there is a good deal of human nature in the public. The nomination of Mr. Bates will plunge the really Republican States into a syncope. If they are strong enough to remain Republican while they are apathetic, then in the border States you may decide the battle.

I think New York is very sure for the Chicago man, whoever he is; but if Bates is the man, we shall have to travel upon our muscle!!

Individually believing, as I do, in the necessary triumph of our cause by causes superior to the merely political, I should prefer a fair fight upon the merits of the case between Douglas and Seward, or Hunter or Guthrie and Seward. I think Douglas will be the Charleston man.

Thank you once more.

Yours faithfully,

George William Curtis.

Mr. Curtis went as a delegate to the Republican National Convention at Chicago in May, 1860. It was his first experience in those vast representative assemblies so peculiar to American political life, and yet so firmly established in it that it is not easy for an American to realize that they are without a counterpart in any other nation. It was a field calculated to bring out the political capacity of any man of ability entering it with a definite purpose and willing to face its difficulties. In theory the convention is absolutely free. It is a gathering of delegates chosen in congressional districts to discuss and announce the policy and name the candidates of their party. In practice very important limitations have grown up. Some of these are almost purely physical, and spring from the nature of the organization necessary to the performance of complex functions by a body of numerous members. Others, however, have their source in the inevitable desire of men intrusted with representative power to use it to advance their own views or their own interests. Though the Republican party was then young and its spirit was more free, unselfish, and more nearly purely moral than that of any other great party that had preceded it in our history, it was not without leaders actuated by ambition, by appetite, and by jealousy. Mr. Seward, then United States Senator from New York, was the " logical candidate " of the party for the Presidency. His eminent ability, his long and honorable service in the Senate, his breadth of view, his courageous and enlightened advocacy of the essential principles of his party, his political sagacity, were claims that could not be ignored. Mr. William M. Evarts was the chairman of the New York delegation, and presented Mr. Seward's name to the convention in a speech of great force and noble enthusiasm. Mr. Curtis, as the letter just cited shows, believed the nomination of Mr. Seward to be both just and wise. But he was to distinguish himself in the convention by a most brilliant and unexpected assault on the lines of Mr. Seward's supporters. These were led by Mr. Thurlow Weed, of New York, a politician whose rare qualities as a manager rested largely on his instinctive and acquired knowledge of the weaknesses of his fellow-men, of their prejudices and personal desires, and who was not fond of leaving much to the unguided impulses of a convention.

It had been determined that the declaration of principles — the platform — of the convention should be so shaped that the more timid and less convinced of the opponents of the rival party should not be scared from its acceptance by too radical utterances. Among the more advanced of the Republican leaders at Chicago was Mr. Joshua R. Giddings, of Ohio, who hoped to make of the party an instrument not only for checking the extension of slavery, but for its ultimate extinction. To serve this purpose, he proposed to add to the platform the words of the preamble of the Declaration of Independence: " That the maintenance of the principle promulgated in the Declaration of Independence and embodied in the Federal Constitution, 'that all men are created equal; that they are endowed by their Creator with certain inalienable rights; that among these are life, liberty, and the pursuit of happiness; that, to secure these rights, governments are instituted among men, deriving their just powers from the consent of the governed,' is essential to the preservation of our republican institutions." The amendment was rejected, and Mr. Giddings in despair turned to leave the hall. " It seemed to me," Mr. Curtis afterwards said, " that the spirits of all the martyrs to freedom were marching out of the convention behind the venerable form of that indignant and outraged old man." He rose to renew the motion of Mr. Giddings. A writer in the " Boston Herald" of January 10, 1880, gives the best ac count of the scene that followed that I have been able to find. Mr. Curtis's voice was at first drowned in the clamor of the followers of the managers: —

"Folding his arms, he calmly faced the uproarious mass and waited. The spectacle of a man who would n't be put down at length so far amused the delegates that they stopped to look at him. 'Gentlemen,' rang out that musical voice in tones of calm intensity, 'this is the convention of free speech, and I have been given the floor. I have only a few words to say to you, but I shall say them if I stand here until to-morrow morning.' Again the tumult threatened the roof of the Wigwam, and again the speaker waited. His pluck and the chairman's gavel soon gave him another chance. Skillfully changing the amendment to the second resolution, to make it in order, he spoke as with a tongue of fire in its support, daring the representatives of the party of freedom, meeting on the borders of the free prairies in a hall dedicated to the advancement of liberty, to reject the doctrine of the Declaration of Independence affirming the equality and defining the rights of man. The speech fell like a spark upon tinder, and the amendment was adopted with a shout of enthusiasm more unanimous and deafening than the yell with which it had been previously rejected."

The following extracts from letters to his friend, Mr. Norton, indicate Curtis's occupation and the tenor of his thoughts during the remainder of the year 1860, marked by the triumph of the contest

against slavery in the political field. In response
to a request to address a meeting in behalf of the
Italian cause he wrote : —

June 12, 1860.

Your note reached me at sunset this evening as
I stood upon the lawn, in the midst of green trees,
blooming flowers, and the fairest fair. It was the
moment to be asked to speak for Italy, but — I
must stay at home. I have made several engage-
ments, near at hand, to say something for Abra-
ham. I have also promised to deliver a Fourth of
July oration upon the Island. I am putting my
hand of "Trumps" into order for the printer. I
have my little jobs at Franklin Square, and I have
been away so much, and my home, my wife, and my
boy are so dear and lovely! You will not think
that I love Italy and you less if I cannot say yes
to you just now. How grandly Garibaldi stalks
through that magnificent, moribund Italy, each
step giving her life and hope! When I speak of
liberty on the Fourth, I shall not forget the soap-
boiler of Staten Island !

Under the elms and the sassafras, and among the
thick flowering shrubs, I think of you girdled with
your sapphire sea ! Then Nanny and I jump on
the horses, and gallop through the woods until we
can see it, too. I wish you could come and see us
here. If you want to run off and be entirely alone,
won't you let me know ? Have you seen how uni
versally your book is commended? I have.

3d August, 1860.

Have you read Olmsted's new book? It is the third of the series, and completes his view of the slave States. It is a curious confirmation of Sumner's "Barbarism," and seems to me about the heaviest blow (being true and moderate) that has yet been dealt at the system. It shows conclusively what a blight it is, but at the same time how difficult and distant the remedy seems to be. It is the most timely of books, for no man who believes that the picture is faithful would be in any manner accessory to planting such a curse in the territories.

How bravely the battle goes on! I am speaking a good deal here upon the Island and in our [first] district, and, although I shall never again have the sanguine hope of my first campaign, yet I can see how every sign promises.

I find myself looking over the sea sometimes and thinking of Italy, but I know that it is not Italy I look at, but the old days in Italy.

NORTH SHORE, 14th October, 1860.

MY DEAR CHARLES, — I have been scribbling and scrabbling at such a rate that I have recently cut all my friends for my country. We are having a glorious fight. This State, I think, will astonish itself and the country by its majority. The significance of the result in Pennsylvania is, that the conscience and common sense of the country are fully aroused. The apostle of disunion spoke here last week, and, if there had been any doubt of New York before, there could have been none after he spake. Even Fletcher Harper, after hearing it, said to me, "I shall have hard work not to vote for Lincoln."

I have been at work in my own county and district, and the other day I went to the convention to make sure that I was not nominated for Congress!

I have been writing a new lecture, " The Policy of Honesty," and am going as far as Milwaukee in November. Here's a lot about myself, but we country philosophers grow dreadfully egotistical. I did cherish a sweet hope (it was like trying to raise figs in our open January!) that I should slip over and see you, and displace my photograph for a day or two, but I can only send the same old love as new as ever. The ball for little Renfrew [1] was a failure, though I was one of the 400, — and his reception was the most imposing pageant, from the mass of human beings, that I *ever* saw.

19th December, '60.

No, I did not speak in Philadelphia, because the mayor thought he could not keep [the peace], and feared a desperate personal attack upon me. The invitation has been renewed, but I have declined it, and have recalled another acceptance to speak there. It would be foolhardy just now. I am very sorry for the Mayor.

There must be necessarily trouble of some kind

The Prince of Wales.

from this Southern movement. But I think the North will stand firmly and kindly to its position. If the point shall be persistently made by the South, as it has been made so far, the nationalization of slavery or disunion, the North will say, and I think calmly, Disunion, and God for the right. The Southerners are lunatics, but what can we do? We cannot let them do as they will, for then we should all perish together.

The political fight was over. The party of slavery limitation — it would not be exact to call it even the anti-slavery party — had elected its President, and held a safe majority in the House of Representatives. The men who had brought the fight thus far were called to face a wholly new situation, one that they had not clearly foreseen, and had not consciously produced, and yet one which was inevitable. It is true that both Mr. Lincoln and his chief rival for the Republican nomination, Mr. Seward, had declared in general terms the irrepressible, irreconcilable conflict between slavery and freedom; but there is little probability and less evidence that they had formed a distinct idea of what the direction or force of such a conflict would be, or how they should meet it if the people gave them the power and imposed the duty of meeting it. Moreover, the victory they had won was not so complete as to force the problem upon them, or even to enable them to take up its solution in the ordinary progress of public affairs.

The Democratic party still held the Senate and the Supreme Court. No affirmative legislation was possible. The Republicans had elected their President through the division of their opponents, and had cast less than two fifths of the popular vote. Their leaders, therefore, were not to be blamed that they had no plan, nor any very clear principle on which to frame one, for the complete conduct of the government. The threats of secession, which had multiplied and become constantly fiercer during the presidential canvass, were not taken to be so serious as they proved to be, and were perhaps not intended to be carried so far as afterwards they were carried. The few words last quoted from Mr. Curtis expressed a feeling very general at the time they were uttered and for some months later. When South Carolina passed its ordinance of secession, and one after another of the Southern States followed her example, the Federal government was still under the guidance of Mr. Buchanan, who, whatever his motives, — and they are not now judged with such severity or such certainty as they once were, — took no decisive step. The public mind was startled, puzzled, and could not know its own real purpose. The first impulse — and it was a sound one — was toward the avoidance of civil war. Rather than *that*, " Disunion, and God for the right."

Early in January came Mr. Seward's famous speech in the Senate, — a speech intended to bring the minds of men together, but which appealed

only to the calm judgment when calm judgment
had already become almost impossible. Mr. Curtis received it with eagerness. " I hope," he wrote
to Mr. Norton on the 16th of January from Roxbury, Mass., — " I hope you like Seward's speech
as I do. I see by the New York papers that
people are beginning to see how great a speech
it is. Webster had his 7th of March and went
wrong ; Seward his, and went right. If you don't
agree, load your guns, for mine are charged to the
muzzle." Nearly a month later he wrote to his
friend Mr. Pinkerton more fully :—

North Shore, 11th February, 1861.

My dear Pinkerton, — Your letter of the
18th of January reached me in Boston while I was
upon the wing, where I have been ever since. I
wanted to reply at once, but I was to come to
Philadelphia this evening, and I hoped to see you
and say what was too long to write. But it seems
that I am so dangerous a fellow that no hall-owner
in Philadelphia will risk the result of my explosive
words, and not a place can be had for my fanat-
ical and incendiary criticism of Thackeray ; so I
shall not see you. Four words in Seward's speech
explain it, and especially " justify " it, as you use
the word, — " Concession short of principle." Do
you ask what and why we should concede ? Mr.
Adams answers ; he has learned from history and
common sense that no government does wisely
which, however lawful, moderate, honest, and con-

stitutional, treats any popular complaint, however foolish, unnecessary, and unjustifiable, with haughty disdain.

Those sentences of Seward and Adams furnish the key to our position, and the wise triumphant policy of the new administration. You have no fear of Lincoln, of course. Well, do you suppose that his secretary of state makes such a speech at such a time without the fullest understanding with his chief? Does any man think that the plan of the new government could wisely be exposed in advance while the traitors had yet nearly two months of legal power? Seward's speech indicates the spirit of the new government, a kindly spirit. Special measures he does not mention, saying only no measure will compromise the principle of the late victory. In his career of thirty-seven years you will find that under every party name he has had but one central principle, — that all our difficulties, including the greatest, are solvable under our Constitution and within the Union. And the Union is not what slavery chooses to decree. It is a word which has hitherto been the cry of a party which sought to rule or ruin the government, without the slightest regard to its fundamental idea. Now the people have pronounced for that idea, and now therefore, when a Republican says Union, he means just what the fathers meant, — not union for union, but union for the purpose of the union. But you say he subordinates his party to the union. Yes, again, but why? Because (as he said two years ago, when, thanks to Hickman and the rest, the Lecompton crime was prevented), because "the victory is won," the peculiar purpose of the party has been achieved, the territories are free. Even South Carolina concedes that. The South allows that we have beaten them in the territories, and they secede because they think we must go on and emancipate in the District and navy yards, and then, from the same necessity of progress to retain power, emancipate in the States. Remember that by the bargain of 1850 New Mexico has a right to come in slave or free. Mr. Adams proposes that she shall come now, if she wants to ; that is all. And he and Seward, and I suppose you and I, know perfectly well that she will come free. Yet even Seward says that, while he would have no objection to voting for such an enabling act, he is not quite sure that it could be constitutionally done.

I shall not tire your soul out by going on, but if we could sit for an evening in MacVeagh's office and smoke the calumet of explanation and consideration, I am perfectly sure that I could make you feel that Seward is greater at this moment than ever before. At least *wait*, wait until something is done, before you believe that a man who is a Democrat in the only decent sense, — who believes fully and faithfully in a popular government, who for nearly forty years, under the stinging stress of obloquy and slander and the doubt of timid friends, has stood cheerfully loyal to the great idea of liberty, and has seen his country gradually light up

and break into the day of the same conviction, with
the tragedies of Clay and Webster before him perfectly comprehended by him, with a calmness and
clearness of insight and a radical political faith
which they never had, — wait, I say, and do not
think that such a man has forsworn himself, his
career, and his eternal fame in history, until you
have some other reason for believing it than that,
when his country is threatened with civil war, he
says he will do all that he can to avoid it *except*
betray his principles.

All things are possible.   Great men have often
fallen in the very hour of triumph.   But my faith
in great men survives every wreck, and I will not
believe that our great man is going until I see that
he is gone.   Indeed, as I feel now, I should as soon
distrust my own loyalty as Seward's, and what can
any individual say more ?

Believe me, full of faith, your friend,

GEORGE WILLIAM CURTIS.

In one of the crowded days of that eventful
April, Curtis wrote to Mr. Norton : —

HOME, 17th April, 1861.

MY DEAR CHARLEY, — Night before last, at
eleven o'clock, the loveliest of *girls*.   By midnight
I was wondering to think how glad and thankful a
man may be even in the midst of civil war.   Frank
is perfectly fascinated, and laughs with shy delight
as he calls me to look at the baby's nose, and puts

his finger carefully upon the little soft red cheek. If it were not for the bitter days before us, I should feel that I was having more than my share of happiness.

Three days later to the same friend : —

20th April, 1861.

Anna and the baby are perfectly well. Her brother Bob and my brother Sam marched yesterday with their regiment, the 7th, both the Winthrops, Philip Schuyler, and the flower of the youth of the city.

This day in New York has been beyond description, and remember, if we lose Washington to-night or to-morrow, as we probably shall, we have *taken New York*. The grand hope of this rebellion has been the armed and moneyed support of New York, and New York is wild for the flag and the country, and our bitterest foes of yesterday are in good faith our nearest friends. The meeting to-day was a city in council. The statue of Washington held in its right hand the flagstaff and flag of Sumter. The only cry is, " Give us arms ! " and this before a drop of New York blood has been shed. What will it be after?

I think of the Massachusetts boys dead. " Send them home tenderly," says your governor. Yes, " tenderly, tenderly ; but for every hair of their bright young heads brought low, God, by our right arms, shall enter into judgment with traitors ! "

CHAPTER XII.

THE next two or three years of Curtis's life may,
I think, be told, so far as falls within the scope of
this work, in the extracts from his letters that follow. There was no marked change in his occupations, except such as the war and its interests and
duties brought. He continued "The Lounger" in
"Harper's Weekly" and the "Easy-Chair" in the
magazine, and his lecturing, with the object that
we know, and the further one which the times imposed.

TO CHARLES ELIOT NORTON.

July 30, '61.

What a summer it is and has been! That nothing shall be wanting, we have a comet, too; a
comet seen last when Charles Fifth was abdicating
and Calais was falling, and Elizabeth was coming
to the throne, and Ben Jonson and Spenser and
the Dutch William were alive, and Philip Sidney
was a gray-eyed boy of two. Can you see all that
in the bushy swash of the comet's tail?

Winthrop's death makes a great void in our
little neighborhood. We all knew him so well and
loved him so warmly, and he was so much and inti-

mately with us, that he seems to have fallen out of our arms dead.

Thank Jane for her most welcome letter. Give our dear loves to your dear mother, to Jane and Grace; and may God have us all and our country in his holy keeping.

TO JOHN J. PINKERTON.

North Shore, Richmond Co., N. Y.,
July 9, '61.

My dear Pinkerton, — I have been long meaning to say how d' ye do, and now your note is most welcome. No, I stayed at home, resisting several very tempting calls, nor shall I be lured to any college halls this year.

I have two brothers at the war, and my wife has one. My neighbor and friend, Theodore Winthrop, died, at Great Bethel, as he had lived. Many other warm friends are in arms, and I hold myself ready when the call comes. I envy no other age. I believe with all my heart in the cause, and in Abe Lincoln. His message is the most truly American message ever delivered. Think upon what a millennial year we have fallen when the President of the United States declares officially that this government is founded upon the rights of man! Wonderfully acute, simple, sagacious, and of antique honesty! I can forgive the jokes and the big hands, and the inability to make bows. Some of us who doubted were wrong. This people is not rotten. What the young men dream, the old men shall see.

Well, I will not discuss Seward just now. I do not believe him to be a coward or traitor. Chase said to a friend's friend of mine last week, " Mr. Seward stands by my strongest measures."

I should like greatly to sit with you and the P. M. and the D. A., and talk the night away, even if the newspaper did find us out and tattle! But I can only shake your hand and theirs, which I do with all my heart.

My wife sends her kind remembrance. We have a little girl, born on the day of the Proclamation.   Yours always,

GEORGE WILLIAM CURTIS.

TO CHARLES ELIOT NORTON.

July 29, 1861.

MY DEAR CHARLES, — I have your notes and the good news of Longfellow. A week ago Tom Appleton wrote me about himself and L——. It was a very manly, touching letter. How glad I am that L—— is not crushed by the heavy blow!

No, nor am I nor the country by *our* blow. It is very bitter, but we had made a false start, and we should have suffered more dreadfully in the end had we succeeded now.

The " Tribune," as you see, has changed. There was a terrible time there. Its course was quite exclusively controlled by my friend, Charles Dana. The stockholders and Greeley himself at last rebelled and Dana was overthrown. It may lead to

his leaving the " Tribune ; " but for his sake I hope
not.

As for blame and causes (for the defeat at Bull
Run), they are in our condition and character. We
have undertaken to make war without in the least
knowing how. It is as if I should be put to run
a locomotive. I am a decent citizen, and (let us
suppose) a respectable man, but if the train were
destroyed, who would be responsible? We have
made a false start and we have discovered it. It
remains only to start afresh.

The only difficulty now will be just that of
which Mr. Cox's resolutions are an evidence, the
disposition to ask, " Will it pay ? " And the duty is
to destroy that difficulty by showing that peace is
impossible without an emphatic conquest upon one
side or the other. If we could suppose peace made
as we stand now, we could not reduce our army by
a single soldier. The sword *must* decide this radical quarrel. Why not within as well as without
the Union ? Then, if we win, we save all. If we
lose, we lose no more.

August 19, '61.

I say these things looking squarely at what is
possible, looking at what we shall be willing to do,
not what we ought to do. There is very little moral
mixture in the " anti-slavery " feeling of this country. A great deal is abstract philanthropy ; part
is hatred of slave-holders ; a great part is jealousy
for white labor ; very little is a consciousness of
wrong done, and the wish to right it. How we

hate those whom we have injured. I, too, "tremble when I reflect that God is just."

If the people think the government worth saving they will save it. If they do not, it is not worth saving. And when it is gone, he will be a foolish fellow who sees in its fall the end of the popular experiment. All that can truly be seen in it will be the fact that principles will wrestle for the absolute control of the system. That is my consolation in any fatal disaster. Meanwhile I hope that the spirit of liberty is strong enough in our system to conquer.

I am elected a delegate to our State Convention on the 11th September. There was a strong effort to defeat me, but it was vain. In the reorganization of the County Committee, the opposition triumphed, though I and my friends were unquestionably strongest. But none of us moved a finger, and the enemy had been busy for a fortnight. We were displaced in the Committee by a conspiracy based upon personal jealousy of me as the "one-man power" in the distribution of political patronage in the county. I am not sorry at the result, for the post of chairman was very irksome, but I *am* sorry for the method, for it is an illustration of the way in which we are governed.

Don't think I am lugubrious about the country, for I am really very cheerful. The "old cause" is safe, however in our day it may be checked and grieved. The heart of New England is true. So I believe, is the heart of its child, the West. We go out alone to fight Old England's battle, and she scoffs and sneers. "The Lord is very tedious," said the old nurse, "but he is very sure."

23d August, '61.

I am very firm in the faith that there can be but the government and anti-government parties, and then that the Republican party, though strictly loyal, does not by any means include all loyal men, and that recent political opponents have a right to demand, as a condition of concerted action, that some of the candidates shall be taken from among them. Is n't this *exactly* right?

7th October, '61.

Well, and how goes the day in your heart? Mrs. Shaw had a few lines from Mrs. Frémont the other day. It is fine to see her faith in her husband. Can there be any who do not wish him well and hope for his success?

I am putting down some of my thoughts about the war in a lecture upon "National Honor." It is really a speech upon the times. The Fraternity wanted me to open their course upon the 15th, but I cannot be ready before the 29th October. Then I shall come; and I shall see you, I hope, though I do not know that I can do more than front, fire, and fall back.

2d December, 1861.

At the Astor we saw General and Mrs. Frémont. She seems bitter, I think, but he is the same old simple, winning soul that he always was. He is perfectly calm and sweet. He evidently thinks the administration do not yet understand that there is a *war*.

HOME, 28th December, 1861.

The New London business was utterly dreary. The audience was fair, the best they had had, as they kindly say to every lecturer, but the course is a failure. I came away at twelve, midnight, and slept and waked, cold, back to New York. The wind had blown the water out of the Connecticut (high old Yankee river!) so that we lay for three hours upon the shore. I was not very sorry, for it prevented our arriving before dawn, and I came in upon mother and E. and N. at nine o'clock to breakfast.

I have just read the correspondence of Seward. It seems to me admirable and honorable. He puts it upon a true ground, — that we, in like circumstances, should demand reparation and apology. It is calmly and well argued, and the conclusion is ingenious and masterly. We have nothing to be ashamed of. Our pride may be wounded, but our honor is untouched. The third and last trump card of the rebellion has failed.

24th February, 1862.

MY DEAREST CHARLES, — The heart of thirty-eight, although of course frosted with extreme age, is yet sensible of the glow of friendly emotion. When Nannie gave me the book this morning, I felt, with Coleridge, "And dearer was the mother for the child," the wife for the friend. Or, as Emerson has it in his poem of Etienne : —

> "The traveler and the road seem one
> With the errand to be done."

So it seemed this morning. You are always thoughtful, always generous. How have I deserved such a friend?

March 6, '62.

I think I am a little more cheerful in the [Washington] matter than you, because I have rather more faith in the President's common sense and practical wisdom. His policy has been to hold the border States. He has held them; now he makes his next step and invites emancipation. I think he has the instinct of the statesman, — the knowledge of how much is practicable without recoil. From the first he has steadily advanced, and there has been no protest against anything he has said or done. It is easy to say he has done nothing until you compare March 6, '61 and '62.

As other signs of the current, I observe these things in the papers of to-day: 1st, Mr. Adams' speech distinctly saying that Slavery is the root of all evil; 2d, Cyrus Field, a stiff old Democrat, repeating it. 3d, Prosper Wetmore introducing into our Chamber of Commerce, he an old Commercial Democrat, a resolution of thanks to John Bright, the eloquent defender, etc., of *freedom*,— a word that your true-blue pro-slavery modern Democrat shies as a bat shies the sun.

All the omens are happy, it seems to me. For what is it but a question of our national common sense? and if that, as the year has proved, was strong enough to smother so furious a party spirit as ours in this country, why should we suppose it will fail us suddenly?

25th March.

Fletcher Harper has asked me to take into consideration the writing of a history, a chronicle of the war, to be illustrated by the war pictures of the " Weekly," a huge (in size) book for popular reading, and to be especially a Northern book, to show what the Rebellion came from, and what its end would probably be! That is not bad for Mr. Harper. I told him that if I wrote about the Rebellion I should want to write a proper history; that his work, though admirable in intention, could be but a ' job' for me; that the study would be useful to any subsequent work upon the subject, but that the public never could believe that the later was more than a hash of the earlier. He said that I could easily do it in three months, and he would pay me well, and begged me to think it over.[1]

TO MISS NORTON.

June 11, '62.

Everything is so soft and ample and rich in form and color during this month! Yet I regret the rain that makes the freshness, on account of Mac and his boys before Richmond. What a pity

---

[1] The book was not undertaken.

that we have not a hundred thousand more men, so that everything might be as sure as speedy! And what a tremendous contest! I go back to Persia and Greece and Carthage and Rome to find its parallels. The Rebels are as united and sullen and desperate as I always knew they must be. They hate us with ferocity. The task before us is greater than any people ever was called upon to accomplish. Great nations have conquered and subjugated others, but we have to conquer and assimilate half of ourselves.

TO CHARLES ELIOT NORTON.

18th June, '62.

What a resplendent summer! How densely rich and blooming! I am out all I can be. This moment A. darts in and out again, asking, "What's your hat on for?" I've just been pruning and quiddling, and feeling of the ground with the roots of the Virginia creeper (no allusion to McClellan), and of the air with the white blossom sprays of the deutzia. I am grand in my square foot principality! My patch to me a kingdom is, and that elm-tree! (do you remember it?) my prime minister.

Colonel Raasloff waits to see what Congress will do about his St. Croix proposition. I have written to him that it seems to me we want our Southern laborers where they are, but we want them free, and, until they are so, I should cry godspeed to any man who wanted to escape as a free man to another country. Consequently I shall work all the harder upon public opinion to hasten the day of their freedom. It is better they should be a " free rural population " in their native land, which wants their labor, than in another country, is n't it ?

Colonel Raasloff says, and this is *entre nous,* that he saw Sumner the day before; and when the colonel said that the war would be long, the Senator was evidently " delighted," which R. says he was sorry to observe. He says that Speaker Grow told him that Congress would not adjourn before the middle of July, or certainly until Richmond was taken, adding, " The army is encamped before Richmond, and we are encamped behind the army."

Fortunately for us all, Mr. Lincoln is wiser than Mr. Sumner. He is *very* wise.

26th June, '62.

What an extraordinary paper by Hawthorne in the " Atlantic "! It is pure intellect, without emotion, without sympathy, without principle. I was fascinated, laughed and wondered. It is as unhuman and passionless as a disembodied intelligence.

North Shore, Sunday, 3d August, '62.

It is not easy to say who is responsible for this extremity. I do not blame any one man ; the difficulty is ultimately in the nation, but a good deal must be shouldered by those who so attacked McClellan that he became the centre of party combinations. I think that he must soon retire from his command, for the faith of his own army is leaving

him.   Yet I think that history will record that he
was a faithful and devoted citizen and soldier, and
that, if he was unequal to his task and did not
know it, it was an ignorance he shared with the
most accomplished of our military men, and with
the mass of the people.

The country seems to me to be making up its
mind whether it will own itself beaten.   But I do
not lose heart, although in events there is little to
encourage.   I cannot believe that a people which
has shown itself so singularly ready to learn what
to do and how to think will fail in this crisis.   If
the government continues to move as fast as the nation, all is saved.   I don't know whether I think it
will or not.

NAUSHON ISLAND,[1] 11th August, 1862.

MY DEAR CHARLES, — Here we have been for a
week to-morrow, and in the salt sea air we all seem
to be perfectly well.   It is only about thirty miles
from the southern point of Rhode Island, so I
breathe my native Narragansett air and am electri-
fied.   The island is about eight miles long and one
or two broad.   It is beautifully broken, with superb
beechwoods rising and opening into bare uplands,
from which you see the ocean or Vineyard Sound,
and again opening into sunny, grassy nooks and
spaces with clusters of shrubs in which the deer lie
or feed.   Day before yesterday we started a pair
of magnificent bucks.   The paths and dells are endless.   From the house you have a sea horizon and

[1] The summer residence of Mr. John M. Forbes.

the entire sky, with woods almost to the horizon, and holding azure crescents of sea (as in " Maud ") in their tops.   The house is immense, the life simple, the hospitality unbounded.   To-day the governor and three of his suite are here, beside ourselves and three or four other visitors.   There are riding, driving, rowing, sailing, shooting, fishing, billiards, dancing, — what you will.   You join the doers, or you go apart and do nothing or mind your own business.   Mrs. Forbes is incessantly working on preserves and comforts for the soldiers, and we all pull lint at intervals.   I have been reading here Tocqueville's " Ancien Régime."   It is very calm and wise.

NORTH SHORE, 25th September, '62.

MY DEAR CHARLES, — I hoped to hear from you, for I knew you would say what I felt.

Coming at this moment, when we were in the gravest peril from Northern treachery, the proclamation clears the air like a northwest wind.   We know now exactly where we are.   There are now none but slavery and anti-slavery men in the country.   The fence is knocked over, and straddling is impossible.

Now, if my friends nominate me for Congress, I shall accept.   Success I should like, but I don't count upon it.   I should stump the district and sow the seed.

When I think of Wilder Dwight and the brave victims, my joy is very sober.   How the country will be filled with mourning as our victory goes on!

For victory it must be now. We heard of Bob[1] through Dr. Stone. They were both in the thick of the fight and escaped unhurt. You saw the account of our brave Joe. Think of the service these soldiers of less than two years have seen! I saw a banner of Sickles's brigade. It has been in *ten* battles!

North Shore, 6th October, 1862.

As for me and my chances, and the peace of the estimable Jane, — which is the only peace I care for just now, — they are in great peril! The "outs" in the county here have worked like beavers against me, who represent the "ins." The free and native citizens of the island (especially those born *trans mare*) are resolved that a foreigner shall no longer carry the county in his fob. They beat me in going to Syracuse, and they have elected an anti-Curtis delegation to the Congressional Convention. There will be an unofficial delegation from this county which will urge me upon the Convention, and will say that I have n't the delegation because I refused to work for it. They will also say that I shall accept if nominated, although I do not think that the nominee will be elected. If they say what I have said to them — that for the right kind of a man I shall do exactly as I should for myself, they will probably secure another nomination, — because the convention will say: "Let us, then, have a candidate who will unite Richmond." I should be very glad to be nominated, and gladder

[1] Robert Gould Shaw.

to be elected, but I have not taken the necessary steps.[1]

I am going up to town this evening to dine with Colonel Raasloff and Count Piper and two or three more.   The colonel goes to China immediately.   I shall have to espouse the proclamation and make them like it, which they do not yet.

Lowell, December 10, '62.

I had a very large audience this evening, and the lecture was admirably received.   One man said, in the Cambridge vein, " He is a very dangerous man, he puts it so plausibly ! "   An American says so of the doctrine of the Declaration ! You see there is work before us.

New York, December 15, '62.

I am at my mother's, — a house of mourning. On Saturday afternoon my brother Joe fell dead at the head of his regiment, ending at twenty-six years a stainless life in the holiest cause and in the most heroic manner.   God rest his noble soul, and grant us all the same fidelity !   My mother, who has felt the extreme probability of the event from the beginning, is as brave as she can be ; but it is a fearful blow.   She does not regret his going, and she knew the risk, but who can know the pang until it comes ?[2]

---

[1] He was not nominated.

[2] Joseph Bridgham Curtis was born in Providence, R. I., October 25, 1836.   Educated as a civil engineer at the Lawrence

December 28, '62.

This will be a crucial week. The counter proclamation, the edict of emancipation, the opposition of Seymour & Co., and the mad desperation
of the reaction, — all will not avail. The war must
proceed, and to its natural result. Even Joseph
Harper, the most Southern of the firm, said to
me yesterday, "The negroes must be armed, and if
Seymour does not support the war he will have no
support." Perhaps, if any possible way of settle-
ment could be devised, there might be a strong
party for it, but in deep water we must swim or
drown. All our reverses, our despondence, our
despairs, bring us to the inevitable issue: shall
not the blacks strike for their freedom?

February 6, 1863.

Why should Dr. Holmes trouble himself about
the base of McClellan's brain? McClellan has

Scientific School, Cambridge, **Mass.**, he entered the Union service at the outbreak of the war in 1861 as engineer on the staff
of the Ninth Regiment of the New York State National Guard.
On the organization of the Fourth Rhode Island Regiment, **he was**
appointed Adjutant. He served with Burnside at Roanoke and
in the Army of the Potomac. The regiment was cut to pieces
at Antietam, and fell back **in disorder.** Lieutenant Curtis seized
the colors, shouting, "I go **back no** further! What is left of
the Fourth Rhode Island, form here!" But there was not enough
left to form, and Curtis, for the rest of the day, fought **as** a pri-
vate in an adjoining command. He was made Lieutenant-Colonel
on the reorganization of the regiment, **and** was in command at
Fredericksburg. He was instantly killed at the head of his men
on the evening of the battle of December 13, 1862.

nothing to do with all this McClellanization of the public mind. The reaction requires a small Democrat with great military prestige for its presidential candidate. The new programme, you know, is a new conservative party of Republicans and Democrats, and all mankind except Abolitionists. It will work, I think, for as a party *we* have broken down. I blame nobody. It was inevitable. The "Tribune," through the well-meaning mistakes of Greeley, has been forced to take (in the public mind, which is the point) the position of W. Phillips, — the Union if possible, emancipation anyhow. As a practical political position that is not tenable. If, by any hocus-pocus, the war order of emancipation should be withdrawn, we should be lost forever, beyond McClellan's power, assisted by John Van Buren, the "Boston Courier" and "Post" and the "New York Herald," to save us. There's nothing for us but to go forward and save all we can.

February 14, '63.

General Burnside came to see mother a day or two since. He spoke with utmost respect and love of Joe. He said that he was one of the few officers that "rose" in the fight; that his coolness, valor, and sagacity kept pace; and that he would have been necessarily a distinguished officer. Dear boy! I see his calm, sweet, dead face, and I think of his lovely life, "wrapped sweet in his shroud, the hope of humanity not yet extinguished in him."

TO JOHN J. PINKERTON.

February 17, 1863.

The fate of the country is being settled in this lull. If it awakes divided, we have a long, sharp fight before us all. The instinct of union, if not stronger than that of liberty, in this people, as Mr. Seward once said, is yet too strong to be squelched like a tallow dip. There was never but one government that merely tumbled down and died, and that was Louis Philippe's! We are too young, and the government has been too long consciously a general benefit, to allow such a result here. Even Vallandigham, braying to Copperheads in New Jersey, is obliged to say that he is for union. John Van Crow has jumped to the dominant tune, and the wayward sisters are rebels to be put down. The " Herald " is afraid of the " Express " and " World " for rushing reaction into absurdity, and plants itself square upon war. Bennett told Mahoney, when he asked him to print his letter, that he was a damned fool.

When the question is fairly put, " Shall we whittle this great sovereign power down to a Venezuela or Guatemala ? " if the soul of the people does not snort scorn and defiance, then good-night to Marmion.

I feel steadily cheerful, and yet, as you know, I am a traveler, not a recluse.

Do you mean that you have evacuated West Chester finally ? What says MacVeagh ? My friendly regards to him if ever you write.

Faithfully yours, GEORGE WILLIAM CURTIS.

TO CHARLES ELIOT NORTON.

11th March, 1863.

Not only has the reaction consumed itself, but it is of the greatest significance that the result is not due to a victory, but is a purely intellectual and moral recuperation. I have been very sure that, when the Democratic party found that they could not operate on the base of peace, they would hurry over to war, as McClellan from the Pamunkey to the James. But the movement shows that the strongest and most sagacious men of the party are its old Southern leaders. Jeff and his friends have known from the beginning that it was a war of ideas, which had exhausted compromise and had to fight. The Northern Democrats refuse to acknowledge the truth, but they are forced to act upon it, which comes practically to the same thing.

The following letter refers to incidents following the draft riots in New York in July, 1863, by far the most exciting experience of any Northern community during the war. The disturbance was started by an attack upon a building in which the provost-marshal was conducting the draft. Most of the militia were absent in Pennsylvania; there was but a small number of Federal troops available; the police, taken by surprise, were for two days able to do but little in restraining, and nothing in repressing the mob, which, with the usual rage for plunder and destruction, showed especial fury against the negroes, on whom atrocious outrages were committed.

NEW YORK, July 19th, '63.

On Tuesday evening, upon an intimation from a man who had heard the plot arranged in the city to come down and visit me that night, and find Horace Greeley and Wendell Phillips, "who were concealed in my house," I took the babies out of bed and departed to an unsuspected neighbor's. On Wednesday a dozen persons informed me and Mr. Shaw that our houses were to be burned ; and as there was no police or military force upon the island, and my only defensive weapon was a large family umbrella, I carried Anna and the two babies to James Sturgis's in Roxbury. Frank was with Mrs. Shaw at Susie Minturn's up the river. To-day I am going with him to Roxbury, but shall return immediately, so that I cannot see you. We have now organized ourselves in the neighborhood for mutual defense, and I do not fear any serious trouble.

The good cause gains greatly by all this trouble. The government is strong enough to hold New York, if necessary, as it holds New Orleans, Baltimore, and St. Louis. There must be a great deal more excitement, and if Seymour can bring the State, under a form of law, against the national government, he will do it. It will be done by a state decision of the unconstitutionality of the conscription act. But as a riot it has been suppressed, as an insurrection it has failed. No Northern conspiracy for the rebellion can ever have so fair a chance again as it had in this city last week, without soldiers, with a governor friendly to the mob, and with only a splendid police which did its duty as well as Grant's army.

TO JOHN J. PINKERTON.

NORTH SHORE, STATEN ISLAND,
2d October, 1863.

MY DEAR PINKERTON, — I wish you joy with all my heart, and the voice of a married man of seven years ought to have some weight in felicitation. It has always seemed that my fancy was fleet enough to outrun the fact, and yet I have been always distanced. As a lover you think marriage is a very Paradise, but as a husband you will feel that it was the beginning of life. But I leave the sermon to the good clergyman who will breathe upon you the heavenly benediction for your voyage. I only stand on the shore and fling after you my well-worn marriage slipper, and believe all that you know of your companion, and whistle for the softest and most favorable gales. God bless you and yours always.

Your friend,
GEORGE WILLIAM CURTIS.

TO CHARLES ELIOT NORTON.

15th October, 1863.

Whatever is happening to Meade, let us rejoice over Pennsylvannia and Ohio. It is the great vindication of the President, and the popular verdict upon the policy of the war. It gives one greater joy than any event which has lately happened. Is it not the sign of the final disintegration of that rotten mass known as the Democratic party? In this State we have sloughed off the name Republican and are known as the Union party. How glad I am that we can gladly bear that name, and that the Union at last means what it was intended by the wisest and the best of our fathers to mean!

24th October, 1863.

What a splendid succession to the editorship of the ancient quarterly! The great literary question of this epoch in my mind has always been, who pays for the " North American "? (I do not mean the writers, dear Mr. Editor, but the running expenses of the institution). I am sincerely glad that you and Lowell have taken it in hand, but my own are so full that I cannot promise you anything, now at least. I am at another lecture, and rewriting my oration of September 1, and am speaking hereabouts in the canvass, and go to a Loyal League on Monday evening in Bridgeport and keep the mill going pretty steadily. I have a busy winter of lecturing before me."

CHAPTER XIII.

In 1863 — I have not been able to fix the exact date — Mr. Curtis became the political editor of "Harper's Weekly." His relations with Harper & Brothers had always been intimate and cordial. They had published his books; he had for nearly ten years been a regular writer for the Monthly, and later for the Weekly. Fletcher Harper, in whose charge were the periodicals, had long been a trusted and beloved friend and adviser. The Weekly was then, as it is still, the most important illustrated paper of the country, and had a very large number of readers. Before the outbreak of the war, its tone in politics had been conservative and mild, so that it was the habit of the "Tribune" in its more radical moods — the moods of that journal were by no means consistently radical — to speak of Harper's as a "Journal of Weakly Civilization," a *mot* which in those hot times had much vogue. When, however, slavery led to secession, and secession to rebellion, the Weekly gave to the government of Mr. Lincoln and to the Union Republican party hearty support. Mr. Curtis took control as editor with a perfectly clear understanding, equally honorable to him and to the publishers, that he was to have entire independence. He could not otherwise have taken it at all, nor could he have made of the journal the power that it became. At first and for some time he did only a part of the writing for the editorial page, but gradually did more and more until, for some years before his death, except in rare instances (chiefly when he was ill), the entire page was from his pen. He retained his home on Staten Island, and could never be persuaded, though often urged, to remove to the city. Doubtless it was the better plan. He lost something in absence from the daily intercourse with men, and the daily participation in affairs, but he gained more in the disposition of his time, which was always urgently occupied, leaving him but very little that could be called leisure. His semi-rural life also gave him two privileges of the greatest value to him, — a certain amount of seclusion with his family, safe from the incessant and consuming interruptions almost inevitable in the city, and a certain amount of unforced intercourse with nature, and these counted for much in that fine serenity of character, that calmness wedded to vigor in his spirit, which marked him as a man apart in the strenuous times in which his part was so large, so important, and so exacting.

In one sense, the taking of the editorship of the Weekly was a decisive step in the life of Mr. Curtis. He did not and could not cease to be a man of letters, a student, and in certain broad fields a scholar. His writing in the " Easy-Chair," which

of itself sufficed to fill a volume each year, continued and was purely literary. Some of his editorial
writing was almost equally so, and all of it was ex-
ecuted with sustained fidelity to his literary standard, so far as conditions permitted ; and his standard was high. He was still to produce that series of
orations, some of which — that on Bryant, that on
Lowell, that on the unveiling of the statue of Washington, that at Gettysburg — have a very high
value, and must always have, wholly apart from the
charm or impressiveness of their delivery. But
from this time on, his chief interest and occupation
were to be with the public affairs of the time, and,
indeed, of the day ; he was in the movement of his
country, shared it, was swayed by it, and in no small
degree contributed to its direction.

The readers he addressed were far more numerous than books could reach, but what he said to
them was necessarily briefly said, generally for a
specific purpose, often a temporary one, on matters
of supreme moment at the time, often also of enduring interest, but demanding instant action which
he sought to influence. The editor of even a weekly
journal is rather a talker than a writer. He keeps
up a continual one-sided conversation on whatever
he deems of greatest immediate concern, and his
subjects may be of infinite variety, but none of
them can at any one time be treated completely, or
with any detailed preparation.

Mr. Curtis, moreover, was active in the affairs
he discussed, and his action and his writing, with

a common object of the most absorbing nature, left him scant time for purely scholarly pursuits. From time to time, as after the death of Mr. Lincoln, there came to him pressing suggestions and solicitations for historical and biographical work that would have given scope for the more sustained exercise of his literary powers; but he put them aside, not without reluctance, and even something of the despairing pang that the strong man must feel in the presence of the relentless limitations of time, but with firmness. He had chosen his pathway with the conscientious care and deliberation that in him were both native and cultivated, and no considerations less strong or worthy than those that had determined his choice could swerve him from it.

Mr. Curtis entered on the editorship of the Weekly at the crisis of the War for the Union. Gettysburg had been fought and won, Vicksburg had fallen, Sherman in the West and Grant in the East were about to enter on that tremendous series of movements and battles between the slowly converging forces of which the rebellion was to be crushed. The proclamation of emancipation had determined the purpose of the final struggle on both sides, and what the issue must be if the government should succeed. Mr. Curtis, and those who with him had felt that the war was in reality resistance to the aggressions of slavery, felt now that the enemy was unmasked, and pursued their course with a deeper determination and more ex-

alted courage. On the other hand, the opposition
to the government, though on the whole much weakened, was intensified and embittered. The sentiment of distrust and dislike of " radicalism," bred
of long party association with the South when it
dominated the government and controlled the honors and profits of politics, became more sullen and
implacable. The burdens of the war were heavy.
The conscription for the army, harsh enough where
it was honestly made, and rendered often odious by
the corruption to which the provision for filling
state quotas by counties gave rise, spread an angry
suspicion throughout the country, especially in the
larger cities of the East, of which the politicians of
the opposition were quick to avail themselves. The
possibility of foreign complications, and the almost
hopeless difficulty of contending with them if they
should occur, were plain enough to the most sanguine. The confusion in the national councils, and
particularly in Congress, inseparable from the vast-
ness, the stress, and the novelty of the situation, was
obvious. Mr. Lincoln's term was drawing to a
close, and the occurrence of a presidential election
in the midst of civil war, with all its tremendous
possible consequences, was an ordeal which patriotism and faith could face, but as to which wisdom
and experience could give no ray of hope or guidance.

In this situation the work undertaken by Mr.
Curtis was of the highest importance. He proved
from the outset well fitted for it, and, though he

felt profoundly the responsibility imposed by it, this rather steadied and impelled than dismayed him. The work was to be done; the need of it was instant and incessant. His general ideas of the purpose of the war, the policy of the government, the duty of the citizen, were well defined. In their application to the questions of the hour, as they presented themselves, he developed a soundness of judgment, and a capacity for persuasive and convincing argument, that nothing in his previous career had indicated. His editorial style, though with time and practice it was developed, was from the first peculiarly individual, and so entirely unlike any other that at any time for thirty years a stray quotation from "Harper's Weekly" could easily be recognized by an habitual reader. And yet it was curiously unlike Mr. Curtis's style in any other line. It rarely betrayed the eloquence of the orator, the charm of the essayist, or the wit and grace and fancy of the humorist. It was extremely simple, direct, clear, and sometimes even homely. I have spoken of the editor as a talker. Mr. Curtis's editorials are an admirable example of the excellence to which talking of this kind can attain. He seemed to have his reader as clearly in his mind as if he were sitting before him, and he reasoned with him, appealed to him, suggested to him, as he would have done had their eyes met. And the editor did not make the mistake of either overrating or underrating the person to whom he addressed himself. I have sometimes thought that this imaginary companion was conceived by him with a very serious reference to the character of the Weekly as it was when he took charge of it, and that his typical reader was one who primarily liked to look at pictures, and whose interest, thus attracted, was to be directed by the writer. Then Mr. Curtis, with all his unusual gifts, had at heart a deep and wholesome sympathy with men. Separated from the great body of them as he was, and, so far as these gifts were concerned, raised above them, he never betrayed a sign that he felt either separate or superior. The reason and conscience, the patriotism, self-respect, fairness, common sense, to which he appealed, were the qualities of which he was conscious in himself, and which he with perfect sincerity attributed to others.

A familiar form of Mr. Curtis's way of putting things in his editorials was by questions. These he used with good effect. They were not artful, and were not often sarcastic. They seemed to be the natural development of the reasoning that had convinced him, and they served the double purpose of awakening the reader's interest and guiding his mental processes. Fromentin, the keenest and clearest of analysts in his own domain, says of the art of painting that it " is but the art of expressing the invisible by the visible." This subtle definition appears to me to apply to Mr. Curtis's editorial writing. The principles he sought to apply were thought out by him with the utmost care. The particular cases of their application were searchingly studied and maturely considered. He had a sort of personal fondness for the opposite side to his own, and was constantly making a better statement of it than that of his opponents. He brought to the discussion of the public affairs of the hour a wealth of knowledge, historical, contemporary, practical, and a thoroughness of reflection, which are unusual even with writers of the most deliberate and elaborate kind. One has but to read his orations to find the evidence of these qualities, and of the skill with which he could marshal a long array of facts in support of a logical conclusion. In "Harper's Weekly" he gave us the fruit of these capacities, but rarely any sign of them in exercise. The simplest-minded reader could feel the force of his reasoning; only the more highly trained could understand from what deep and widely-fed sources that force was supplied. It is a natural question whether the journal afforded the best field for the use of such powers, and whether they might not better have been directed where their possessor would have been more conspicuously recognized and his achievements more splendid. I shall not undertake to answer the question. I am restrained, at the outset, by my knowledge of the conscientiousness with which Mr. Curtis decided his own course, and of the general soundness of his judgment. I can only say that the influence he exerted in the direction of his aims — and we know how high these were — must have been very great. When from time to time on rare occasions his name came before the country in a way to call out public sentiment, he was overwhelmed with grateful surprise at the depth and extent of the respect, the confidence and the affection he had, all unconsciously, inspired. These would have been a rich capital for him in public life, and I have no doubt that that capital would have increased and multiplied in any place of power and responsibility that could have come to him. But the public feeling toward him was but a faint indication of the influence he really exerted in "Harper's Weekly," for only a very small number of the tens of thousands, often the hundreds of thousands, to whom he spoke week by week for almost thirty years, associated his name with his writing, or had the dimmest knowledge of his personality. The sentiment that at intervals, — sadly few they seem to one who cares to consider fame as a reward for merit — found expression was instilled most largely in the minds of those who knew the writer by the qualities his writing exhibited. But the qualities were the same for those who did not know him. When I recall the history of his country from the issue of the Emancipation Proclamation to the close of Mr. Curtis's life, with the long line of vital questions, which by the growth and evolution of the American nation were submitted to the arbitrament of public opinion, and reflect with what wisdom and fidelity, what courage and unselfishness, he labored for what he believed the right, and what experience has already shown was in the main the right, I cannot but feel that the great share of the labor that was given to the editor's work was richly rewarded, as he would have rated reward.

In 1864 came the presidential election. There was early shown a very pronounced and apparently strong opposition to Mr. Lincoln's renomination. It was manifested most distinctly by what was known as the "radical" element of the Republican party, whose leaders felt that the President had advanced much too slowly toward the destruction of slavery. With these men Mr. Curtis had sympathy so far as their hatred of slavery was involved, and their feeling that it was the source of the rebellion. With their distrust or disapproval of the President he had no sympathy. He felt that Lincoln was perfectly sound in purpose, that his judgment was on the whole safe, that he was entitled to decide since his responsibility was so great, and that he was in a position to know best what, for the whole country, was best. Still more keenly he felt that whatever were the President's possible errors, the risk of any change was appalling. And he had, moreover, a very just perception of the actual condition and tendency of public opinion, and it agreed with the President's estimate of it. He wrote to Mr. Norton (April 7, 1864) : —

" MY DEAR CHARLES, — How grandly the country is speaking for the war and the policy ! Night before last I dined with Colonel Raasloff [1] and

---

[1] The Danish Minister.

Count Piper and Habricht, and I claimed that thus far we had proved that in a republic patriotism was not necessarily subordinated to party spirit. It seems just now as if our true victory were to be greater than even we had supposed.

"I have seen Lincoln *tête-à-tête* since I saw you, and my personal impression of him confirmed my previous feeling. I am sorry that Frémont seems to be placed in a position which can please no real friend of his. Only to-day I have an invitation from the office of 'The New Nation' to meet some friends of all the radical candidates to 'take steps to form a radical national committee, and to secure a radical platform, and a reliable radical man for the presidential campaign about to open.' Last week I went to Baltimore, and supped at the Union Club with a dozen of the most strenuous men there. Every one, when the war began, was a pro-slavery man; now they will have nothing but immediate, uncompensated emancipation. Charles, you and I are superannuated fogies."

Mr. Curtis was chosen as a delegate to the Republican National Convention of 1864 held in Baltimore. He was an ardent and effective supporter of Mr. Lincoln's nomination. A glimpse of his work there is afforded in a letter (June 16, '64), to Mr. Norton : —

"MY DEAR CHARLES, — I hope you like our Baltimore work. The unanimity and enthusiasm were most imposing. I voted against the admission of Tennessee, because I did not want the convention to meddle with the question; and, since she only wanted to come in to help do what we were sure to do without her, I thought that, as the cause was exactly the same for both of us, she should give us forbearance while we gave her sympathy. But it was impossible to resist the torrent, and they all came in. There is no harm done. I cannot but think Sumner wrong. If all New York rebels, I am still a citizen of the United States. That is the simple, obvious, necessary ground.

"The committee of one from each State appointed me to write the official letter to the President, and refused to instruct me. I sent it yesterday, having read it to Mr. Bryant and to Raymond. They were both entirely pleased with everything in it."

In the canvass that followed on the nomination of Mr. Lincoln, and that of General George B. McClellan by the Democrats, Mr. Curtis worked with the utmost vigor, spirit, and patience. His part in the Baltimore Convention had won for him a position of influence in the party, which for him carried with it a full corresponding responsibility. In the columns of "Harper's Weekly," in his constant and wide correspondence and in his speeches, he did all that he could to guide and arouse public opinion. His labors were incessant, and often amid harassing events which, though they could not fail to give him the utmost anxiety, he met with cheerful courage and often with humor. He wrote to Mr. Norton, July 12, 1864, when General Grant's movement toward Petersburg had left the capital

and the Pennsylvania border exposed to possible
raids by Confederate cavalry : —

"And how is Ashfield? I should have written
you there before if I had supposed there was a
post-office at such a height. Do you have to eat
oil more than three times a day to keep warm in
this weather? We don't. But then we live upon
an island in the temperate zone. Or are you warmed
by the news of the isolation of Washington? There
is something comical about it which I cannot escape,
with all the annoyance. The great Dutch Pennsylvania annually sprawling on its back, and bel-
lowing to mankind to come and help it out of the
scrape, is perfectly ludicrous. I hope that this year
all the States will learn that, while they have no
efficient and organized militia, they will be constantly harassed by raids to the end of the war.
We have all kinds of rumors here at every moment,
from which you are free. But the sense of absurdity and humiliation is very universal. These things
weaken the hold of the administration upon the
people; and the only serious peril that I foresee is
the setting in of a reaction which may culminate
in November and defeat Lincoln, as it did Wads-
worth in this State. I wish we had a loyal governor,
and that New York city was virtuous."

In the stress of the deadly struggle for the life
of the nation Mr. Curtis's mind turned frequently
to the study of the hardly less difficult struggles
that attended the foundation of the government.

"Have you thought," he wrote to Mr. Norton,

" what a vindication this war is of Alexander Hamilton? I wish somebody would write his life as it ought to be written, for surely he was one of the greatest of our great men, as Jefferson was the least of the truly great; or am I wrong? Hamilton was generous and sincere. Was Jefferson either? In Franklin's life how the value of temperament shows itself! It was as fortunate for him and for us as his genius."

Another letter to the same friend (August 28th) reports his first degree of LL. D., — a title, by the way, which he never used, or allowed, if he could help it, to be attached to his name, even after he had received the right to it from Harvard, — and also shows the tone of public opinion at that date : —

North Shore, 28th August, '64.

Frank wrote me, or printed rather, in large and remarkable capitals, a letter the other day. I enlivened the tranquil circle here by calling it a Capital letter, — a little work of mine which I dedicate to Jane. Probably you are not aware that I am myself the latest little work of Madison University. Blushes forbid me to write that that discriminating institution has done for the least of your friends what Harvard did for that other celebrated scholar, Andrew Jackson. Yesterday I received a letter with a very large green seal, addressed " G. W. C., LL. D. !" Oh my prophetic soul! I have long called Frank and Zib Doctor.

I say not a word about the war, but did people

ever deserve success at the polls less than the Union party? Two years ago I was the only Lincoln man I knew hereabouts, and I have come round to the same position. Yet he will be elected, or we are dreary humbugs.

. . . .

Good-by, dear boy. I am more cheerful than ever, for within two months we shall see the whole force of treason North and South, and if we sink 't is to see what we shall see! I shall not be able to write on Peace — luckily for you. It will be a good text for J. R. L. Give him my love, if he is with you, and to all the dear ones.

Your friend the doctor sends his benediction.

A week later is an allusion to General Burnside, for whom he had the utmost affection and respect: —

EAST GREENWICH, Monday, 5th September, 1864.

MY DEAR CHARLES, — Burnside is staying with me here at the house of my cousin, Mr. Goddard. Yesterday we sat upon the rocks, and he told me the whole story of the mine and of the Army of the Potomac. It is intensely interesting and perfectly clear. He is the noblest, most magnanimous man I ever saw, and I shall tell you the tale with immense satisfaction some day. On Saturday morning, when the news of Sherman's success came, he was the most unaffectedly delighted man I ever saw. His exultation wound up by his seizing his wife and kissing her.

CHAPTER XIV.

In October Mr. Curtis was nominated for Congress in his home district. Two years before, his friends had pressed his nomination, but, curiously enough, it had been defeated by a prejudice against him as enjoying too much of the confidence of the administration in the matter of appointments, and by the independence and impartiality of his recommendations. The enthusiasm this time "was such," he wrote, "that I quite lost my voice when I came to thank the convention. I shall not be elected," he added, "but the manner of the nomination was better than the matter of the election." Though convinced of the hopelessness of the canvass, Mr. Curtis saw in it an opportunity for the advancement of the general cause, and he entered upon it with the greatest energy. For the next six weeks he spoke almost daily, and sometimes twice a day, and always, as described by a friend, "more for Lincoln than for himself."

The crowded days of those eventful months wore slowly on. While Grant was painfully fighting and forcing his way to cut off Lee's army from the South, and Sheridan laid waste the valley of the Shenandoah from which Lee's supplies had so largely come, Sherman, after the long series of bloody and difficult battles that ended with the capture of Atlanta, had begun the great " March to the Sea," and Mobile had fallen before the fleet of Farragut. The " reaction " was first checked, then dissipated by victory, and on the morrow of the election Mr. Curtis wrote to Mr. Norton : —

HARPER'S WEEKLY, NEW YORK,
9th November, 1864.

MY DEAR CHARLES, — Let us thank God and the people for this crowning mercy. I did not know how my mind and heart were strained until I felt myself sinking in the great waters of this triumph. We knew it ought to be; we knew that, bad as we have been, we did not deserve to be put out like a mean candle in its own refuse ; but it is never day until the dawn. I do not yet know whether Seymour is elected. I hope not, for while he is in power this grand State is a base for rebel operations; and he is put in power, if at all, by those who would make any honorable government impossible. My heart sank as I stood among drunkards and the worst men, yesterday morning, to vote; but it sank deeper when I saw Aaron L., and others like him, voting to give those drunkards the power of the government. I have prepared a very small sermon upon Political Infidelity, for what infidels such men are to themselves and to mankind !

I am defeated, of course, and by a very heavy

majority. In my own county my vote would have been largest of all the Union candidates if my name could have been sent to the soldiers, as the governor's was. As it is, he is some twenty before me. But Fernando Wood and James Brooks are defeated — God be praised! I have never been deceived about myself, but I am forever glad that my name was associated with this most memorable day. Yours most affectionately,

G. W. C.

During the winter that followed, feeling that the triumph of the national cause was now only a question of time, and of brief time, Mr. Curtis devoted the opportunities of the lyceum platform, which no one commanded more completely than he, to the education of the public mind in what he believed to be the lesson of the war. The lecture on "Political Infidelity," alluded to in the last letter, was delivered some fifty times in the season of 1864 and 1865. One has but to remember the interest the addresses of a man like Mr. Curtis aroused in every town, large or small, where he was heard, the intense feeling of the people throughout the North as to all questions related to the war, the eager discussion that followed a lecture of this sort in each community, to understand the scope and the depth of the influence he exerted. The lecture was in effect a fervent plea for perfect freedom of discussion. Slavery had brought the country to civil war, because slavery was the sole

question in our political history as to which discussion had been entirely suppressed in one part of
the land, and avoided, discouraged, and by every
device — political, social, commercial — repressed in
the other. In the darkness that was thus brought
about, the South, on the one hand, had formed a
mistaken notion both of its strength and of the
position assigned to its policy by the intelligent
opinion of the world, while on the other hand the
North mistook the spirit and purpose of the South
and its own rights and duties. The following
passage will indicate Mr. Curtis's treatment of
the first mentioned phase of his subject. Having
quoted Mr. Seward's description of the domination
of the slave power, he referred to Alexander H.
Stephens's retirement from public life in 1859 and
his farewell speech: "Listen to Mr. Stephens in
the summer sunshine six years ago: 'As matters
now stand, so far as the sectional questions are
concerned, I see no cause of danger either to the
Union or to Southern security in it. The former
has been to me, and ought to be to you, subordinate to the latter. There is not now a spot of the
public territory of the United States over which
the national flag floats where slavery is excluded
by the law of Congress, and the highest tribunal of
the land has decided that Congress has no power
to make such a law. At this time there is not a
ripple upon the surface. The country was never
in a profounder quiet.' Do you comprehend the
terrible significance of those words? He stops;

he sits down. The summer sun sets over the fields of Georgia. Good-night, Mr. Stephens — a long good-night. Look out from your window — how calm it is! Upon Missionary Ridge, upon Lookout Mountain, upon the heights of Dalton, upon the spires of Atlanta, silence and solitude; the peace of the Southern Policy of Slavery and Death. But look! Hark! Through the great five years before you a light is shining — a sound is ringing. It is the gleam of Sherman's bayonets, it is the roar of Grant's guns, it is the red daybreak and wild morning music of peace indeed, the peace of National Life and Liberty." The application of the lesson was plain: " Reconstruct, then, as you will. But we are mad if the blood of the war has not anointed our eyes to see that all reconstruction is vain that leaves any question too brittle to handle. Whatever in this country, in its normal condition of peace, is too delicate to discuss is too dangerous to tolerate. Any system, any policy, any institution which may not be debated will overthrow us, if we do not overthrow it."

With the opening days of April came the end of Lee's obstinate resistance. On the 3d the news of the occupation of Richmond by the advance guard of the Army of the Potomac reached New York. Mr. Curtis wrote to Mr. Norton : —

Home, 4th April, 1865.

My dear Charles, — I thought of you all the day yesterday as the news of the crowning mercy came rolling in. The merchants and brokers in

Wall Street came out of their dens and sang Old Hundred and John Brown. From the high windows at the Harpers' where I sat the sky was brilliant and festal with innumerable flags. Fletcher Harper came to me, and said, " How glad I am we did not beat at Bull Run, for then Slavery would not have been abolished, and we should have been worse off than before." My dear boy, who is equal to these things? We hear that the Major Mills who has fallen is your young cousin. Ah me! what heart-breaks salute our triumphs. You will be very sober in your joy.

Almost on the morrow the whole nation was made " sober in its joy," by the loss of Mr. Lincoln. Mr. Curtis resisted, so far as I am aware, all solicitations to address the public, save through his paper, on this signal event. In the Weekly his expressions were marked by deep feeling, but wholly devoid of any tinge of that impulse toward vengeance that was at the time so general. " Tonight," he wrote to a friend, " in the misty spring moonlight, as I think of the man we all loved and honored, laid quietly to rest upon the prairie, I feel that I cannot honor too much, or praise too highly, the people that he so truly represented, and which, like him, has been faithful to the end. So spotless he was, so patient, so tender, — it is a selfish, sad delight to me now, as when I looked upon his coffin, that his patience had made me patient, and that I never doubted his heart, or head, or hand. At the only interview I ever had with him, he shook my hand paternally at parting, and said, ' Don't be troubled. I guess we shall get through.' We *have* got through, at least the fighting, and still I cannot believe it. Here upon the mantel are the portraits of the three boys who went out of this room, my brother, Theodore Winthrop, and Robbie Shaw. They are all dead — the brave darlings — and now I put the head of the dear Chief among them, I feel that every drop of my blood and thought of my mind and affection of my heart is consecrated to securing the work made holy and forever imperative by so untold a sacrifice. May God keep us all as true as they were ! "

Ah well ! to how many of us came this impulse of consecration in that solemn hour. High, indeed, is the fortune of any of us who have remained as steadfast to it as did Mr. Curtis.

In the spring of 1865 Mr. Curtis received, through Mr. Norton, a proposition to take control of a new paper, the purpose of which is sufficiently indicated in the following letter, which I give as disclosing Mr. Curtis's judgment in matters of this sort, and, also, quite explicitly, the peculiar situation he himself held in journalism : —

North Shore, April 26, 1865.

My dear Charles, — Yours of the 24th reaches me this evening. I cannot at once decide upon the proposition which you make, — for I should wish to ask several questions.

I doubt if $50,000 is capital enough to start such a paper as you contemplate, and I am far from sure that it is really needed. It seems to me always best to use existing machinery if possible, and I fear that the influence which would control the new paper would constantly tend to make it outrun the popular sympathy upon whose support it must rely, so far as to defeat its purpose, by limiting its circulation to those who need no conversion. Do not the " Atlantic," the " North American," the " Evening Post," and " Harper's Weekly " — to go no further — address the various parts of the audience that are counted upon for a new paper, and are there not great advantages in having the questions presented in these different forms? The change in public sentiment upon the true democratic idea is so wide and deep, that an organ for special reform in the matter does not seem to be required. It — the reform — has now become the actual point of the political movement of the country ; and the same reasoning which justifies the abandonment of the abolition societies and organs pleads against your project.

If I lay more stress upon the special object of the paper than its projectors intend, then it becomes merely a liberal Weekly of the most advanced kind, and I can see no particular reason for its success.

As for myself, I am perfectly free to say what

I think upon all public questions in "Harper's Weekly" without the least trouble or responsibility for the details of the paper, and with no necessity of even being at the office. The audience is immense. The regular circulation is about one hundred thousand, and on remarkable occasions, as now, more than two hundred thousand. This circulation is among that class which needs exactly the enlightenment you propose, and access is secured to it by the character of the paper as an illustrated sheet. I should want some very persuasive inducement to relinquish the hold I already have upon this audience, for I could not hope to regain it in a paper of a different kind. Of course, "Harper's Weekly" is not altogether such a paper as I should prefer for my own taste ; but it does seem to me as if I could do with it the very work you propose, and upon a much greater scale than in the form you suggest; nor is the pecuniary advantage of your offer such as to shake this conviction.

Now from what I say you will see how I feel. The offer you make is so handsome and honorable that I do not decline it, unless you must have an immediate answer. If the affair can still remain open, will you tell me if the capital is secured — if the paper is to be started *anyhow*, — if there is any person selected for the business editor — whether it is to be a joint-stock association — and what the size, etc., of the paper is intended to be.

If you have the time to inform me upon these

and such points, I will not delay long in giving
you a final answer.

Always your affectionate,

G. W. CURTIS.

Nothing came of the project.

The following note to Mr. James Russell Lowell relates to the " Commemoration Ode : " —

ASHFIELD, MASS., 12th September, 1865.

MY DEAR LOWELL, — I thank you with all my
heart for the noble ode which with all my heart I
have read and enjoyed. Certainly you have done
nothing in a loftier strain, nor has anything more
truly worthy of the great theme been written. If
it be very serious and very sad it is for the same
reason that the sky is blue and the corn yellow.
I have read it aloud to Anna, and read it and
re-read it to myself ; and I am sure it says what
the truest American heart feels and believes. And
if that is not a work worth doing, — if a man *can*
do it, what is ?

The note is signed " Affectionately yours, and
more and more."

Mr. Curtis continued to take an active part,
as well as a strong interest, in politics, and in the
elections of 1866, he was chosen as a delegate-at-
large to the Convention for revising the Constitution of the State of New York. The Legislature
of 1867 elected a Senator of the United States
from New York, and Mr. Curtis's name was pre-

sented in many of the papers of the Republican party. How fitted he was to secure preferment by ordinary political methods is shown in a letter to Mr. Norton, who had written him on the subject.

" The only chance," he writes, " is a bitter deadlock between the three, or two, chiefs. At present (it is a profound secret) the friends of Harris, or his chief managers, expect 42 votes in a caucus of 109, to begin with. The friends of Conkling count upon 50 ; those of Davis upon 20. The friends of the latter proposed to me to make a combination against Conkling, the terms being the election of whichever was stronger now, — Davis or me, — and the pledges of the successful man to support the other two years hence. I declined absolutely."

CHAPTER XV.

As the time approached for him to take up the new duties of the Constitutional Convention he wrote to Mr. Norton May 6, 1867 : —

"You cannot imagine how I grieve over my lost summer — lost before the frosts are gone. But when I was urged to let my name be used, I thought it all over carefully, and concluded that I ought not to decline. It will be a very long and very arduous work, but I shall be deeply interested in much of it, and in all the novelty of a deliberative assembly. I have been reading the debates of the convention of '46. They are endless and mortally dull. All this in dog-days too."

Nor did actual experience cure him of his original distaste. He wrote in July : —

" Ah, if I could run out of this business I think I should feel as if I had had enough of it. I do not perceive an attraction toward public life strong enough to make the tremendous domestic sacrifice which is necessary, and I think that I shall stay at home next winter that I may become acquainted with my family."

Yet Mr. Curtis worked faithfully and intelligently in the convention, and held a prominent place in a body which included many eminent men, — among them Mr. William M. Evarts, afterwards Secretary of State and Senator, and at the time the most brilliant and scholarly lawyer of the State ; Mr. Charles J. Folger, afterwards Chief Justice of the Court of Appeals and Secretary of the Treasury; Mr. William A. Wheeler, subsequently Vice-President ; Mr. Greeley and Mr. S. J. Tilden. He was made Chairman of the Committee on Education and Funds relating thereto, and member of several other committees. His own committee recommended the abolition of the Board of Regents, of which he was a member, and which was at the time almost a perfunctory body, and the creation of the Board of Education, with a single executive officer. This plan was not adopted. He advocated the appointment of the attorney-general and of other state officers, then and still elected, and he maintained that in this way the authority of the people was more rationally and effectually maintained than by the numerous elections in which the voters exercised no real choice. He opposed the prohibition of the sale of liquor and took a very earnest part in the debate on the government of municipalities, supporting the authority of the State over the general police system and condemning the theory of local control. In general his ideas were those that might have been expected from a convinced Democrat with an intellectual sympathy with Hamilton rather than with Jefferson.

On one subject, however, he was very radically democratic. He was the most conspicuous and by far the most competent of the advocates of the suffrage for women, and on his own proposition for an amendment in that sense, he made a speech more elaborate and brilliant than any other of his in the convention. His advocacy was wholly unavailing in affecting the action of the convention, but one can hardly read the debates without feeling that none of his opponents met him on his own ground and that none were able to defend their own ground against his logic, which was never more penetrating and alert. In fact not since his first assault on slavery and its consequences in American politics had Mr. Curtis entered a fight with more complete conviction, with greater ardor, with more careful equipment or a bearing, always within the limit of courtesy, more defiant.

The basis of his argument was the American principle of equality of rights, the principle which he had so ardently adopted in the anti-slavery conflict, and his challenge was to those who with reference to the rights of men held that principle as openly and firmly as he held it, to show with what justice women could be excluded from its advantages. The vote he believed to be the natural and necessary weapon by which the possessors of equal rights could defend them, and the inevitable condition not only to their defense, but to their intelligent and wholesome and safe exercise. But while he maintained this fundamental principle as the ground on which the representatives of all the people of the State must stand in framing the Constitution, he did not shrink from the argument of expediency. And in meeting this argument he sustained a running debate with his opponents, the record of which enlivens the reports of the convention, otherwise "endless and mortally dull" as he found those of 1846 to be. It was not difficult for him to match every objection of mere expediency presented by the other side with instances of classes of males to whom the objection was equally telling if not more so.

The argument that when the great body of women want to vote, as they have gradually come to want the right to their own inherited or acquired property, to an equal authority over their children, and similar rights, they would get that right as they had got these, inspired Mr. Curtis with indignation and scorn, and he hotly resented delay on such a pretext as a stupid wrong to the women who already desired that right. But that argument, or the disposition for which it gave a convenient excuse, prevailed in the convention, as doubtless he expected that it would. He had, however, the consolation of believing that his course in the convention may have served to hasten the day when this to him, absurdly unfair, illogical condition precedent should be complied with. Certainly that considerable body of educated and intelligent women who feel, and who are acknowledged to be, entirely fitted for a share in the political action of the community of which they are honored and useful members must have recognized that no more gallant or accomplished champion ever bore their colors.

The Constitutional Convention came to an end early in 1868, and Mr. Curtis returned to his ordinary pursuits with a sense of profound relief as to the past and with a new vigor, but not without anxiety as to the immediate future. The Republican party was going through its troubles with President Johnson, whose impeachment trial closed in that year. Mr. Curtis fully appreciated the dangers and evils of the stubborn Tennesseean's course, and warmly supported the authority of Congress to determine the policy of the government in the difficult matter of reconstruction, but he was indignant at the wanton abuse visited on the Senators who voted "not guilty," and firmly upheld their fidelity to their oath as they understood it. "Of course," he wrote to his friend Mr. Pinkerton, "if a man thinks that an oath to decide in a specific case according to the evidence is an oath to be bound by party dictation, very well. I differ, but I do not quarrel. So if a man thinks a Senator bought, let him say so, provided he can bring his proof. But to say that a Senator who thinks his oath means what it states and who acts accordingly is infamous, is not criticism; it is an effort to destroy liberty of thought and speech by terrorism." "I think," he added, "as it happens, although I should have voted to convict, that the party is infinitely stronger and surer of success since the fail-

ure of impeachment. I feared a few weeks ago
that we were to be saved by the folly of our foes.
But I see now that we have the conscience as well
as the ardor of youth."

The general action of the strong Republican majority in the Senate during Johnson's term, even
the impeachment plan, had met with Mr. Curtis's
approval; but he watched with the keenest solicitude one phase of the contest, that relating to appointments. The power of the Senate to give or
to refuse its " advice and consent " to nominations
was now used as a weapon against the President,
and in the heat and stress of the struggle, it was
inevitable that serious abuses of that power should
be overlooked, or excused, or even justified. As
a matter of fact the abuses were numerous and
flagrant, and it was during Johnson's term that the
mischievous rule known as the courtesy of the
Senate took a definite form, and by a series of precedents gained an authority that it did not before
have. This rule in substance was that the action
of the Senate should practically be decided by the
Senators (of the majority party) from the State in
which the office to be filled was, or from which the
nominee was selected. At this time the majority
iu the Senate gradually resolved themselves into a
compact and powerful party machine, the avowed
purpose of which was to protect the party from
disintegration through the appointment to Federal
offices of the friends or tools of a hostile President.
Since patronage was the chief weapon of the Presi-

dent, it was natural that his opponents in the Senate should seek to turn it aside, and so far as practicable to wrest it from his hands. This they sought to do by the exercise of the power of confirmation. And since the majority had a common party object, since they felt themselves to be, and actually were, a sort of party executive committee, it was logical for them to apply the methods of such an organization, and give to the members from each State the disposition of matters relating to that State, and to hold them responsible. The situation was novel. Party feeling ran very high. The sentiment of the North as to questions growing out of the war was intense and general, and it was on the side of the Senators. The people believed and most of the Senators themselves believed, that they were fighting for the priceless fruits of the victory won in war at " so untold a sacrifice." For the first time in the history of the party then in power, and for the first time in many years, the Senate and the President were pursuing opposite aims, and the contest necessarily was most bitter, and raged most hotly about the offices, as to which the contestants had joint rights. The tactics and strategy of the Senate were effective, and the " courtesy of the Senate " helped greatly to make them so. But the rule did not lapse with the necessity for it. The power of the Senators of each State under the rule was exercised at first, with a certain sense of responsibility, because the attention of the whole majority in the Senate and of the party was fixed upon them. But when the contest ended with the retirement of Johnson and the accession of General Grant, the Senators did not lay aside their powers nor abandon the particular rule by which these had been distributed. They retained them, and the public attention being relaxed they used them with less and less responsibility and therefore selfishly and to an increasing degree corruptly.

This was an extensive and acute manifestation of that malady of the body politic of the American democracy which has since received the significant and repulsive designation of the "spoils system." Mr. Curtis, as I have said, regarded it with the keenest solicitude, and found in his study of it the first strong impulse toward that long struggle for the purification of politics which was gradually to become the absorbing interest and occupation of his life. Unlike many reformers he was thoroughly acquainted not only with the evil he contended against, but with the system of which it formed a part, and with the good as well as the bad in that system. He was not a closet politician. He had for years steadily and punctually performed the detailed duties of a party man in his own home ; had attended all primary meetings, done duty on party committees and in conventions, and had taken his share of trouble and responsibility in the distribution of offices. Of the party "workers" who insisted that a party organization could not be kept up, or the labor of party contests be secured, were

not the offices used as rewards and incentives, there
were very few who had given to their party the
time and effort given by him, and certainly there
was not one of them who had given more with no
reward whatever, and no desire for any, beyond the
sense of duty done.   Nor was he in the least blind
to the need of parties or to their value, nor ignorant that they were not composed of saints and could
not be.   He was not even without strong party
spirit, that is to say, that intent sympathy with those
who are working to a common end, pride in achievement, and the "delight of battle."   If there was
ever a "loyal" Republican, as the phrase goes, he
was one.   He was as far from being a mere theo-
rist or fanatic in politics as he was from being
a self-seeker.   He was in fact a party leader of
shrewdness and tact and knowledge of men, their
prejudices and weaknesses as well as their virtues.
He saw in the system that based party power on
patronage not only its vileness and its corrupting
tendency, but its stupidity.   His faith in human
nature and his observation and experience proved
to him that this system was an unsound basis that
must crumble from the rottenness of its material.

In 1868 Mr. Curtis was an elector on the Republican ticket, and cast his vote for General Grant, in
whom he had much confidence.   During the next
spring and summer he delivered lectures at Cornell
University, in which he felt a keen interest.   Of
one of these lectures he writes: —

"I have written a lecture upon American Literature to the effect that what we have belongs to the great English stock, as Ovid was a Roman, though upon the Euxine, and Theocritus a Greek, though a Sicilian. The undertone is friendliness for England."

In 1869, on the death of Henry J. Raymond, the founder of the New York "Times," Mr. Curtis received a proposition to take Mr. Raymond's place. He felt that the offer was "flattering," — which it was not exactly, since Mr. Curtis's reputation was on a level, at least, as high as that of the paper, — and he felt also that it was an opportunity for a more direct if not more extended influence on public opinion. But he declined, and wisely. The conditions of his work on "Harper's Weekly" were, as I have said, peculiarly happy. It would have been difficult, if not impracticable, to establish the same in a paper like the "Times."

About this time, certain articles by Mr. Samuel Bowles, in the Springfield "Republican," having excited the sharp disapproval of the party press, Mr. Curtis wrote, in the Weekly: "The more deeply an independent journal sympathizes with the principles and purposes of a party, the more strenuously will it censure its follies and errors, the more bravely will it criticise its candidates and leaders for the purpose of keeping the principle pure and of making the success of the party a real blessing." This was a doctrine which he had already had to apply, and which he maintained to the end.

In September, 1869, Mr. Curtis was nominated

for the office of Secretary of State by the Convention of the Republican party. He declined the nomination. It does not come within the plan of this Life to follow in detail the political course of Mr. Curtis, but the following letter to Mr. Norton seems to me to be of peculiar interest, and I give it nearly entire : —

"I have been nominated by acclamation for Secretary of State of New York, by the Republican Convention, to which I did not know that my name was to be presented. I opened the paper, and I confess the tears were very near my eyes at such a spontaneous summons from one of the best conventions we have had, and whose platform was without evasion, and noble. But upon every account it was impossible for me to think of accepting. I could not add the official duties to my present without breaking down, and I could not reduce my present duties without injustice to my family and to myself; and really I have no doubt I am of more service as I am than I should be in that office. So we hurried down to South Deerfield and I telegraphed the inclosed note to the "Tribune" and the "Times," and "Sun," in which for *candidly* read *cordially*, — a mistake of the telegraph. I was for many reasons very sorry to decline. There is a doubt of our success and I knew that I should be said to fear a defeat. Then I knew that for any candidate, and especially the head of the ticket to decline, would cloud the prospects of the party. And I found that some of the others — say Hillhouse, the best of the ticket — had accepted upon condition of my running. My position was very difficult, but my duty was perfectly clear. It happened as I apprehended. The reception of my name, even as far as Illinois, was really enthusiastic ; I was amazed; I think no man ever had so much favor for so small desert. . . . The consequences of my declining were in proportion. I have had most powerful private and public remonstrances. The Washington " Star " said that it is the most remarkable case of inconsistency ; that I have always insisted that every man should do his share, etc. The Albany " Evening Journal " insisted that there were imperative public reasons that demanded my reconsidering my decision. The Boston " Advertiser " said that I had not hitherto shown myself afraid of leading a forlorn hope. The Democratic papers said that I naturally did not wish to be slaughtered. Dorsheimer of Buffalo, who had most warmly supported me in the Convention, wrote me a truly pathetic appeal. But to all my correspondents I replied that I had not changed, that I had done and was still doing my share of political duty, that while a man ought to make many sacrifices, in the present condition of our politics, to accept so authoritative and honorable a call, yet there were some that he had no right to make, and that the confidence in his judgment which led his friends to nominate him ought to justify to them his decision ; that it is a mistake for an editor to take executive office ; but as for the forlorn hope, if I had only been sure of being beaten I would gladly have accepted. In the midst Hillhouse declined as I had feared, and then General Robinson, the next in importance. The Democrats laughed at the rats running from the sinking ship, and at length the new nominations were made. General Sigel was put in my place and Horace Greeley (!) in that of Hillhouse. Horace wrote a long letter in accepting, and rapped me on the knuckles, in saying that he hoped that it would be said of him that he never asked his party for an office and never declined any honorable service to which it called him. I should rather have it said of *me* that I never declined any such service that I could honorably perform. Of course the party, as a party, must be vexed with me in increasing the perils of the canvass — and unfortunately no future convention will like to nominate the best of men without consulting them previously. But still, much as I regret the event, it was inevitable, and my conduct was right. It spoils, probably, my political *career* in the ordinary sense. It seems to me not impossible from the reception of my nomination that whether successful or not, I might have been nominated for governor next year. But at the bottom of my heart I don't want to be. I could n't enter upon public official life, and devote myself to a political career of that kind, with so much pleasure to myself or profit to the country or to the cause, as in other ways. So what seems the loss of a great opportunity to many of my friends, and to all politicians, is not a loss to me but a gain."

Mr. Curtis was to have his experience with conventions as to the governorship the next year, which he also describes in a letter to Mr. Norton. The reaction which he expected followed the decisive Republican successes of 1868, and the party was defeated in New York in 1869. Meanwhile there had grown up in the State and particularly in the city of New York two powerful machines; one, the Republican, with the Federal offices as its base of operations, and a hitherto unbroken hold of the Legislature; the other, the Democratic, of which Tammany was in control, with its base in the city offices. There was a certain ill-concealed connection between the two, growing out of these common methods. It was not avowed, nor did it extend to all the Republican leaders, but there was already in existence the class of politicians known as "Tammany-Republicans," and they largely controlled the organization of the party in the city.

Mr. Curtis wrote to Mr. Norton from Ashfield, September 17, 1870, a very full account of the convention of that year. He had declined to go to the convention as a delegate, having special family cares at that time which engrossed his attention. While at Ashfield, he was urged by the "administration" leaders to attend and act as chairman. Feeling that possibly the result in the presidential election of 1872 might depend on the course of the convention, and knowing that the party was torn by the factional disputes of Senators Fenton and

Conkling, and that he was personally wholly independent of both, in the hope that he might help to unite and concentrate the party, he reluctantly accepted. He was chosen chairman by a very heavy majority, and his speech was received with great enthusiasm. Thereupon one of the Conkling managers came to him and asked him to accept the nomination for governor. He replied that he would not decline it, if the convention offered it, though he did not wish it, and he insisted that his name should be fairly and honorably presented, if at all. His name was presented, but by a local politician of New York city, a Tammany Republican of very disagreeable associations. The Conkling vote was not given him and General Woodford was nominated, Mr. Greeley being the third candidate. Apparently, the manager referred to had simply used Mr. Curtis to defeat Mr. Greeley. That gentleman believed that this purpose was known to Mr. Curtis and was indignant accordingly. Mr. Curtis was bitterly hurt, for he had consented to the use of his name in good faith, not, certainly, without legitimate ambition, but with the sincere belief that his nomination would be the strongest that could be made, and, therefore, the best for the party and the cause to which he was devoted. It was the first and last time that he trusted his name to politicians for use in a convention. I doubt if he ever quite understood the exact trick that had had been played upon him. It was not easy for him to believe others capable of what was morally impossible for him. But the trick was not so hurtful to him as it was unworthy in its authors. It left him more firmly established in his editorial chair and free for the work of reform that was just opening before him. Had he been nominated and elected governor of New York, he would have given up his editor's chair — both the "Easy," and the other — and the current of his life would have been turned, not, I think, more fortunately.

I turn back a little in my narrative to pick up a few letters to James Russell Lowell. Here is one apropos of an invitation to a dinner in his honor conveyed by Lowell and Mr. Emerson and Dr. Holmes as a " committee " and in a severely formal manner : —

NORTH SHORE, STATEN ISLAND, 15th April, 1869.

MY DEAR LOWELL, — As I had received and answered Emerson's letter I treated yours as a strictly private one, viewing you in the light of a friend and not of a committee-man. In that view I confide to you that the *possibility* of a speech, or remarks, or a few observations, or a brief and pertinent rejoinder, or a felicitous off-hand, etc. etc., fills me with dismay, and already affects my appetite. But you are too civilized for all that, I know. What if I bring two or three old lectures to prepare for any contingency?

Yours always in speechless sympathy,

G. W. C.

The following refers to a few days spent with Lowell at Cornell University: —

NORTH SHORE, STATEN ISLAND, N. Y.,
10th June, 1869.

MY DEAR JAMIE, — Your note and book and that masterly account current with its balance, came safely yesterday; and I have the photos of Ithaca which I knew you would leave behind, and which I will send to you by E. or by somebody going your way.

After you left came also Mr. Spencer with a dozen of those grim cards for you to autograph, and with a view in the Enfield ravine for you. I have been homesick for you ever since we parted, for you were Ithaca to me; and I am amused by hearing people say, "O my! I had no idea it was such a pleasant place." Already I look back upon it with the feeling that I have for the dearest old Italian days. I was an unhappy wanderer after you left, that Friday morning; and when the cook came to the surface to say "God bless you," and the little Mary stood half crying, and the Reverend Phœnix presented arms, as it were, at the door, and they all said, "How good you and Mr. Lowell are," — I was so glad to have my name mingled affectionately with yours, that I waved my lily hand to them like a conqueror.

Good-by, my dearest Jamie, and with the sin-cerest regards to your wife, I am

Affectionately yours,

G. W. C.

And here is one acknowledging a Christmas gift of "The Cathedral" from its author. The "big house" referred to was the residence of the Shaws next to his own home on Staten Island : —

NORTH SHORE, STATEN ISLAND,
29th December, 1869.

MY DEAR JAMES, — It is a fortunate man who can give to his friends as a Christmas box a Cathedral of his own building, — I had already begun to know it. On the last night at the "big house" we all passed through it, I leading, and it left us all in the best and noblest of Christmas tempers, as it will for many and for many, when you and I hear Christmas bells no more. I had just read Tennyson's "Holy Grail," and I said "it is afternoon with him." But with you, my dear James, it is a richer morning hour than ever.

They have left the big house. They have laughingly cut the throat of one of the most beautiful homes, consecrated and endeared by all that makes home precious, where the girls were all married and their first children all born, from which Rob [1] and Charlie [2] went to be killed — in which we have all been so happy and so sad, — and

---

[1] Robert Gould Shaw, brother of Mrs. Curtis, Colonel of the Fifty-fourth Massachusetts (colored) Regiment, killed at the assault on Fort Wagner, S. C., on July 18, 1863.

[2] Charles Russell Lowell, Colonel of the Second Massachusetts Cavalry Regiment, brother-in-law of Mrs. Curtis, and nephew of Mr. Lowell, wounded October 19, 1864, at the battle of Cedar Creek, died October 20.

all this to have a little smaller house and to look upon the water! Of course it is wholly a matter of temperament, of sentiment. But that is only to say that it concerns what most enriches life. I look over and pity the great, silent, gloomy, deserted house. Why should it be treated so?

We are all well and send you our truest love, and I am always

Your most affectionate,

G. W. C.

In a note to Mr. Norton, he refers to the winter of 1869 and 1870, the first one devoted to the advocacy of civil service reform in the Lyceum: —

North Shore, May 3, '70.

My winter was very busy indeed, but very pleasant. James Sturgis is in Mt. Vernon Street in Boston and I began with a month with him. I had only Saturday evening and Sunday for friendship. I dined at the Club, at Sebastian Schlesinger's (with Music), at Judge Gray's; and Tom Appleton gave me one of the most perfect conceivable dinners, Agassiz, Longfellow, Lowell, and Richard Dana, Jr., the guests. How I wanted you! I heard some of the good concerts, every day wagged the pen and every night the tongue, going as far as Portland. My lecture was the Civil Service paper that I wrote for the Social Science meeting, and although a grave and earnest plea, was, I think, very acceptable, although as half of the Lyceum audience are women there could not be the universal interest which is, after all, essential to a lecture. I delivered it in Baltimore — a city that I detest ever since the slaughter of 1861, and to an immense audience in the Philadelphia Academy of Music.

And here is a glimpse of his reception at Vassar College, whither he went with some misgivings : —

"Since my lectures ended, I have written an address for the young women of Vassar College, where I went on Friday last, and to one of the most unique occasions of my whole life. The building is like the Tuileries. There are about four hundred students ; and an aspect of healthfulness, intelligence and refinement, with the elegance and comfort of the college appointments and accommodations, leaves the most delightful and cheerful impression. As you know, the spirit of the College is far from that of the ' Woman's Rights ' movement, at least among the trustees and many of the professors, but I pleaded for perfect equality of opportunity and liberty of choice, and I was never so cordially thanked, even by those, like the President, who I thought might regret my coming.

Maria Mitchell, the astronomer, was most ardent in her expressions. Several noble looking girls, who would not tell their names, came up to me at the reception afterwards, and asked to take my hand. I felt more than ever how deeply the best women are becoming interested. Next week I am to speak at the Anniversary of the Woman's Suffrage Association, and that, I believe, is my last public appearance for the present."

The following notes from letters to Mr. Norton give some of Mr. Curtis's personal impressions of the current phases of politics : —

June 26, 1870.

I think the warmest friends of Grant feel that he has failed terribly as president — not from want of honesty or desire, but from want of tact and great ignorance. It is a political position, and he knew nothing of politics — and rather despised them. Then the crisis was most compound. The special ends of the party were achieved. The reaction was inevitable and should have been expected and encountered. But we have drifted into it without care. Upon no single subject have we been agreed. We have had no policy, have raised no issues. Grant has been headstrong about San Domingo, and the Cuban matter has been unskillfully managed, although the position was correct. In losing Hoar we lose by far the ablest man in the administration. Nobody that I see knows why he went. The Senate would not make him Judge of the Supreme Court, as if such men were to be had for the asking, and his place in the Cabinet is taken by an unknown ex-rebel from Georgia. Is it "vindictive" not to ask Mr. Toombs to be Secretary of War? Why is it that the good men have n't the courage of their convictions. Perfunctory statesmanship is my abhorrence.

July 20, 1870.

At the last moment Congress refused to allow the American registry of foreign ships for carrying during the (Franco-German) war as the President requested. This is to me very significant, for it shows that there is something stronger than party cohesion, even under such circumstances as the war and the pressing request of the party president. Protection must now be considered a vital issue and immediate, not merely possible and postponable.

There is a curious presentiment here of a force that was ultimately to divide the Republican party, and to produce a rearrangement of politics, in which, though not upon that issue, Mr. Curtis was to find himself acting with the Democrats.

NEW YORK, March 4, '71.

It is the very ebb tide upon our side, but Grant will be renominated, if he makes no signal blunder this year, and it is best that he should be. He intended for some time (as I knew) to send me to England, but relinquished it because he did not personally know me — and I had been hostile to San Domingo. I was greatly relieved, for I should have been sorely perplexed. Oh! for an hour of hot sherry sangaree and you!! How our tongues would rattle!

CHAPTER XVI.

THE day that the last-cited letter was written,
Mr. Curtis received from President Grant a nomination as to which he was in no wise "perplexed,"
and from the acceptance of which he had no desire
to be "relieved." It was the nomination to the
commission which, under a clause of the Sundry
Civil Appropriation Act of March 3, 1871, the
President was authorized to appoint, to inquire
what rules and regulations for admission to the
public service, which the President could enforce
under existing laws, would best promote its efficiency. The commission, of which Mr. Curtis was
at once made chairman, consisted of seven members, of whom the others were Messrs. Alexander
G. Cattell, Joseph Medill, Dawson A. Walker, E.
B. Elliott, Joseph H. Blackfan, and David C. Cox.
Mr. Medill and Mr. Curtis were the only members
without experience in the service, the others being
actually or formerly connected with the various executive departments. They were entirely agreed
as to the evils to be remedied, and substantially so
as to the remedy to be adopted; but the heaviest
labor of the commission fell upon Mr. Curtis, who,

however, received valuable assistance from the other members.

The first report of the commission was submitted to the President December 18, 1871, after ten months of most careful and systematic investigation and study. The commissioners were greatly indebted to the committee of which Hon. Thomas A. Jenckes, of Rhode Island, had been chairman, and which had made two very extended and well-elaborated reports, the first January 31, 1867, and the second May 14, 1868. Mr. Jenckes's committee had embodied in these reports not only the opinions and testimony of a large number of officials in the service of the United States, but detailed descriptions and discussion of the systems of Great Britain, Germany, Prussia, France, and China. One of the reports of the English commission was included complete, with an historical sketch, instructions to candidates, and specimen examination papers. Edouard Laboulaye's exhaustive essay on " Education and the Administrative System of Probation in Germany " was translated for Mr. Jenckes's first report, and our accomplished consul at Paris, Mr. John Bigelow, supplied an account of the French service. In the two reports, therefore, covering some three hundred closely printed pages, the new commission had ready at their hands a rich supply of material for the comparative study of our own methods in the civil service and those of other countries, varying in their resemblance or contrast to our own.

Mr. Jenckes had, moreover, made a considerable study of both the views and the practice of the early Presidents and their chief executive officers, which was of great use as showing how widely these had been departed from.

But the aim of Mr. Jenckes had been legislation, and legislation of a very radical character. Two features of the bill offered with his report were, first, that the candidate standing highest in a competitive examination and probation must be selected, and, second, that the Civil Service Commissioners provided for in the bill should make rules for suspension and dismissal from the service after trial by themselves on charges. No such sweeping legislation could be obtained, even had it been desirable, and the Curtis commission was limited to such a system as could be enforced by the President under existing laws. But while the work of the commission was thus limited, and was ostensibly only the promotion of the efficiency of the civil administration, it is safe to say that Mr. Curtis would not have been called to undertake it, and would not have undertaken it, had the need of it not been much more urgent and its object much wider than was indicated by the terms of the appropriation bill under which the commission acted. The real purpose which enlisted him was the restriction and ultimate abolition of the "spoils system," that is to say, the system by which offices were given as the rewards or incentives for service rendered to a party or to its leaders or managers.

"In obedience to this system," he declared in his report, "the whole machinery of the government is pulled to pieces every four years. Political caucuses, primary meetings, and conventions are controlled by the promise and expectation of patronage. Political candidates for the lowest or highest positions are directly or indirectly pledged. The pledge is the price of the nomination, and, when the election is determined, the pledges must be redeemed. The business of the nation, the legislation of Congress, the duties of the departments, are all subordinated to the distribution of what is well called the 'spoils.' No one escapes. President, secretaries, senators, representatives, are pertinaciously dogged and besought on the one hand to appoint and on the other to retain subordinates. The great officers of the government are constrained to become mere office-brokers. Meantime they may have their own hopes, ambitions, and designs. They may strive to make their patronage secure their private aims. The spectacle is as familiar as it is painful and humiliating. We accuse no individual. We appeal only to universal and deplorable experience.

"The evil results of the practice may be seen, first, in its perversion of the nature of the election itself. In a free country an election is intended to be, and of right should be, the choice of differing policies of administration by the people at the polls. It is properly the judgment of the popular intelligence upon the case which has been submitted to it during the canvass by the ablest and most eloquent advocates. But the evil system under which the country suffers tends to change the election from a choice of policies into a contest for personal advantage. It is becoming a desperate conflict to obtain all the offices, with all their lawful salaries and all their unlawful chances. The consequences are unavoidable. The moral tone of the country is debased, the national character deteriorates. No country or government can safely tolerate such a surely increasing demoralization."

Here, then, was the real aim of Mr. Curtis's work, to drive politics out of the civil service and to drive patronage out of politics. It was a fight for a new emancipation that he had taken up. As has been said, the immediate scope of the commission's work was limited to what could be done by the President under existing laws. The first restriction imposed by these laws was defined by the opinion of the then attorney-general, — that, while a class might be determined from whom an appointee should be selected, appointment could not be confined to the single person standing highest in a competitive examination. This was in effect exactly the ground taken by Mr. Curtis from the start. The rules were framed to require the appointment from the three persons standing highest on the eligible list. The second point of importance presented was that of removals. Here the difficulty was not so much what the law allowed, — though there was some difference of opinion as to that,—but the best mode of exercising the power of removal. Many advocates of reform thought that tenure for good conduct should be the rule and, to secure this, that removals should be made only for cause ascertained by a trial and declared by an independent tribunal. Mr. Curtis's report recognized the evil for which this remedy was proposed, but, it declared, "such fixity of tenure tends to great perplexity and inconvenience in administration, and the responsible head of a branch of the public service may justly complain if he has no immediate control of his subordinates. The details of official conduct which most perplex a smooth and satisfactory administration are always obvious to the competent and responsible chief, but are not always, or indeed often, of a kind to be proved in a court. A discretion of removal in such cases, if so guarded in its exercise that it is not liable to be abused, is most desirable in every office." The cause of the trouble was political pressure, under which changes were constantly made simply to give a new band of political workers their "turn."

"Nothing could be more fatal to a sound service. Yet it is not unreasonable that, under a system founded upon party patronage, such practices should prevail. After Mr. Marcy had said that 'to the victors belong the spoils of the enemy,' he remarked, 'but I never said that the victor should plunder his own camp.' Yet that was the logic of his principle. The hardest fighter should have the most spoils. There is no logic in equal division between him who merely wishes well to the cause and him who fights the battle. If influence is to appoint, the lesser influence must yield to the greater; and when a man has not been appointed by reason of his fitness, he must not ask that he be retained on account of his merit. The doctrine of rotation in office implies that merit should not be considered. It treats the public service as a huge soup-house, in which needy citizens are to take turns at the tables, and they must not grumble when they are told to move on. Plainly, if this political pressure for the appointment of a particular person could be baffled, the present uncertainty of tenure would be corrected. The head of a department who should fill the various offices under him not with the favorites of certain men, but with those who are found qualified, would then have none but legitimate reasons for the removal of a faithful and efficient officer. Conspiracy and slander against any individual would then have no especial inducement or opportunity, and capacity character, and efficiency would secure the same tenure as in all other spheres of duty.

"It seems to us, therefore, more desirable to afford this reasonable security of permanence in office, by depriving the head of illegitimate motives for removal, rather than by providing a fixed tenure to be disturbed only upon conviction after formal accusation and trial. There is, indeed, no reason for such a tenure, unless it can be shown from the nature of the system that the power of removal is likely to be abused."

These two points being determined, the rules as proposed to the President provided "for the competitive examination of all applicants, for the appointment of those found to be best qualified, for entrance at the lowest grade of offices in which grading is practicable, for probation, and for promotion." Great importance was attached by Mr. Curtis to the required probation of six months; and, as the most general objection to the reform system came from those who said that capacity could not be found out by questioning, it is worth while to quote the report on this point: "A competitive examination in general and special knowledge, although it would show certain attainments which are indispensable to the proper discharge of certain duties, would not necessarily prove the faculty of skillfully adapting that knowledge to the public service. It is a common remark, that a man could answer all the book questions, as they are called, and yet prove to be an inefficient officer, while one who knew nothing of books might be very serviceable. This may sometimes be true; but there are intelligent persons enough who have also swift, accurate, and thorough business aptitude. In a general examination this can be little more than inferred; nothing but practice tests this kind of efficiency; and we therefore provide that, when an applicant has satisfied all other examinations, his skill in applying his knowledge to the duties of the office shall be proved by a practice of **six** months, and that he shall finally be appointed only when he has satisfied this test. Probation, indeed, is nothing but the test of those essential qualities of an officer which it is often asserted cannot be ascertained by examination."

The rules thus framed were to be applied, it may be said in a general way, to all subordinates in the service above the grade of laborers, and below those appointed with the advice and consent of the Senate, excepting postmasters and certain persons holding places of trust for whom the appointing officer was especially responsible. " In submitting these suggestions with the rules which we have framed," said the report, "**we** feel that it is not so much we who **do it** as the intelligent public opinion of the country. There has **long** been a profound conviction that the system of appointments to the civil service, upon political consideration only, is one which reason and experience equally show to be fatal to economy of administration and to republican institutions. 'All I claim upon the subject of your resources,' said Edmund Burke a century ago, pleading for reform in England, 'is this, that they are not likely to be increased by wasting them.' But our system of the civil service courts waste. It violates the fundamental principles of thrift and economy; it fosters personal and political corruption; it paralyzes legislative honor and vigilance; it weakens and degrades official conduct; it tempts dangerous ambition; and, by poisoning the springs of moral action, it vitiates the character of the people, and endangers the national prosperity and permanence.

"We would not exaggerate the importance of the peril, but the constant exposure of official dishonesty, the vast system of political corruption the disclosure of which has produced a peaceful revolution in the city of New York, should suggest to every good citizen the possibility of a similar revolution which might not be peaceful. If by that great and organized corruption it had been possible — and such a contingency is not improbable — to decide a presidential election, and in a manner universally believed to be fraudulent, the consequences would probably have been civil war. If such corruption be not stayed, the result is only postponed; and nothing so surely fosters it as a system which makes the civil service a party prize, and convulses the country every four years with a desperate strife for office."

The President approved the rules submitted in December, 1871, and the commission, now known as the "Advisory Board," took up the work of preparing the detailed regulations, and the grouping of places in the departments at Washington and the federal offices at New York. This work was completed, and the rules and regulations were formally promulgated April 16, 1872. There was some friction at first, but from that time until March, 1875, the working of the system was constantly more satisfactory, and the official reports of all the departments successively recognized that fact. For a long time under the old system the work of the service had practically and necessarily been done by a relatively small proportion of the employees who had escaped the mischievous influence of political pressure because their experience, ability, knowledge, and fidelity were absolutely indispensable. No responsible appointing officer dared to include them in a "clean sweep," for outraged public sentiment would have deprived his party of the power to confer or continue political patronage. This class took kindly to the new system so soon as it was well understood; and it is a proof both of the soundness of the merit system, and of a certain curious virtue in the "average" American, that, during the three years that the Curtis rules were in force, a very large amount of careful and arduous work in enforcing them was done by men in the service who received no pay and little credit therefor. I shall take up later the fate of this first attempt at reform, and return now to the current of Mr. Curtis's life apart from this task.

CHAPTER XVII.

THE GREELEY CANVASS.

As President Grant's first term drew to a close, the country began to show definite signs of the breaking up of that strong and fervent party spirit which had sustained the Republican candidate in the election of 1868. "The party issues of the last few years," Mr. Curtis had said in closing the Civil Service Commission's report to President Grant, "are gradually disappearing. The perilous questions of fundamental policy have been determined, and the paramount interests of the country are now those of administration. Honesty and efficiency of administration of the settled national policy will now be the chief demand of every party." This was true of public sentiment, but far from true not only of "every party," but of any. It cannot be said that the Republican party, which had the power and therefore the responsibility, had met the demands of public opinion. After the firm hand of the President had repressed the violent reaction in the South manifested in what were known as the "Ku-Klux" disorders, the various state governments in that region had fallen into the hands of Republicans, supported by the negro vote, and had, almost without exception, been badly and corruptly conducted. It was plain that the chief effort of the leaders of the majority in Congress was, not to secure peace, order, and prosperity in the South, but to strengthen the hold of the party on the national government. With this purpose General Grant had little sympathy, and with the means employed to carry it out he had none. But he was without experience, and without trained capacity in civil affairs. His hands were tied by the insidious and half-secret bonds which the Senate had woven about the executive during the term of Mr. Johnson. Within the field where he possessed or asserted independence, he was sadly at a loss. His judgment of men, so swift and unerring in the choice of his subordinates in the army, was curiously defective in the selection of civil appointees. His Cabinet, after he had got rid of Judge Hoar, the attorney-general, and General Cox, of the Interior Department, was, with the exception of Mr. Hamilton Fish, the secretary of state, singularly feeble. Then he had given office to many of his military associates, who had won his confidence and affection by courage, energy, and soldierly loyalty, but who were not to be trusted in civil life, and who almost openly held that they had a right in peace to get as they could a rich reward for service rendered in war. His administration had given occasion for many small and some serious scandals, and there was a well-founded though not very definitely formulated opinion that the political tone of the Federal government was being steadily lowered. Besides all this, the President's scheme for the annexation of San Domingo, and his treatment of Mr. Motley and of Senator Sumner, had produced a feeling of deep resentment among some of the most able leaders of the Republican party.

In this situation what was known as the Liberal Republican movement was started. Mr. Curtis was keenly sensitive to the unfortunate tendencies against which this movement was ostensibly, and for the most part sincerely, an organized protest; but he had a deep distrust of some who were engaged in it, and great doubt of the practical measures to which it would or could lead. He had, also, much confidence in the personal purity and good faith of the President, and in the essential honesty and soundness of the great body of voters who made up the Republican party. He used the agencies at his command — and they were extremely effective — to expose what he was sure was wrong in the conduct of public affairs, and to arouse the conscience and intelligence of the country to correct it. But he knew the power for good as well as for ill of party organization and party sentiment; he despised and dreaded the most pronounced and apparently the controlling tendencies of the Democratic party of the day, which was still the party of sympathy with secession, of hatred of the negro, of financial repudiation, and, in his own State, the party of Tammany and of Tweed; and, though anxious and even disheartened at times, he could not bring himself to cut adrift from the Republican party. When the Liberal Republican Convention in Cincinnati failed to name, as had been hoped, Mr. Charles Francis Adams, — who at the last moment had scornfully repudiated a policy of "truck and dicker," and had bid his friends "draw him out of that crowd," — and had nominated Horace Greeley for the Presidency, he wrote to Mr. Norton, June 30, 1872 : —

"The political situation is described by saying that the Democratic Convention will probably nominate Horace Greeley by acclamation!! The contest will be Grant against the field ; Grant with all his faults, — and they are not great, — against every kind of Democratic, rebellious, Ku-Klux, discontented, hopeful, and unreasonable feeling. The best sentiment of the opposition is, that both parties must be destroyed, and Greeley's election is the way to destroy them. This is Schurz's ground, who likes Greeley as little as any of us. The argument seems to be, first chaos, then cosmos. The 'Nation' and the 'Evening Post' in this dilemma take Grant as the least of evils. He has been foully slandered, and Sumner's speech was unpardonable. He was bitterly indignant with me, — said that my course was inexplicable and inconsistent, and that I was bringing unspeakable woe upon my country. I could only reply, 'Sumner, you must learn that other men are as honest as you.' This election is the last hope of the Democratic party to recover power. The South is wild for Greeley, but only because his name now means a possible Democratic triumph. He excused secession, he tried to negotiate at Niagara, he tried to bully Mr. Lincoln into buying a peace, he bailed Jeff Davis, and the worst Northern Copperheads support him. That is enough for the South; it ought to be enough for the country."

Early in September he wrote again from Ashfield (where he had now bought a house and land separated by one field only from the house of Mr. Norton) : —

"The reaction against Greeley is already evident. Poor Sumner has been forced to fly. I am not surprised. I thought and said that the struggle of joining the enemies of all that he has ever pursued or done might be overwhelming, and in Washington he was old and sad and weary. It is to me a very melancholy campaign; but, like all others, it is very important. I have for myself less and less inclination to position. We shall reëlect Grant, and with the dissolution of the Democratic party new combinations will arise."

The campaign practically culminated with the decisive successes of the Republicans in the States (Pennsylvania, Ohio, and Indiana) which then had elections in October, and closed with the overwhelming defeat of the Democratic candidate in November. In the last days of November Mr. Greeley died. Mr. Curtis wrote to Mr. Norton December 2d : —

"Now comes Greeley's death, one of the most mournfully tragic of events, — heart-break and insanity; and a great gush of sentimental twaddle from all the newspapers; and, that nothing may be wanting to the grotesque pathos, the 'Tribune' proposes that the Greeley electors shall vote for Grant!

"You will have seen how nobly the President stood fast against Cameron in the Philadelphia post-office matter. I suppose that there must be some fight upon the subject in Congress, and I know nobody there, unless it be George Hoar, who will conduct our side as it should be managed. Garfield is timid, Willard is not strong, and no one that I know upon the floor is master of the subject. The Cabinet is not friendly, but fortunately Grant is tenacious and resolved upon the spirit which should govern appointments. I suppose, however, that he may not see why *good* party men should not be taken."

However "tenacious and resolved upon the spirit which should govern appointments" the President was in December, early in the next year a case arose in the New York custom-house in which Mr. Curtis thought that that spirit was so far violated that he felt that he could not retain the part of chairman of the commission. It was in no sense a question of personal or official dignity. It was a question of departing so seriously from the standard which he had publicly adopted as to compromise the cause of reform and impair if not destroy his ability to promote it. He resigned from the commission

March 27, 1874. After he had reached this decision, but before he had acted upon it, he was stricken with a serious illness. Within the five previous years he had added to his ordinary work, which was by no means light, and to the very trying and exposing lecturing tours, first the labors of the Constitutional Convention, and then those of the Civil Service Commission. He wrote to Mr. Norton, then in Europe : —

March 12, 1873.

MY DEAR CHARLES, — Anna holds the pen for me to thank you for your thoughtful and affectionate letter. It comes from your sick-bed to mine, for I have put the last feather on my patient camel's back, and he is broken down. About four weeks ago I came home from a short, hard trip to the West, worn out and ill. For a week I fought a fever which threatened several bad things, but all the bad symptoms have left me except a pudding-head and general prostration. I lie on the couch most all day, and am ordered to rest absolutely for six months. So you will find me when you return what you first knew me, — a gentleman of elegant and boundless leisure. It is a sorry story, and I know you will be pained to hear it. I shall have to work much more moderately hereafter, and am profoundly mortified to have brought myself to this pause. When I am able to move I shall perhaps go for a month to John Field's, at Newport, who most affectionately urges me.

It makes me better to think of your all coming
home again; and with most unchanging love to all
of you, I am your always affectionate,

                                    G. W. C.

The half year of rest, if not of absolute rest,
was taken, and restored him to nearly his usual
vigor and elasticity.   The following winter he gave
up his lectures.   He wrote: —

                                    28 December, 1873.

It is my first winter at home for nearly twenty
years, and, as I am not very busy, except with
reading, it is in every way delightful.   It is pleasant to have my say upon public affairs with perfect independence, and to feel, as I have occasion
to know, that it is not without result.   I am often
very sorry for the P [resident,] seldom angry with
him, and must smile when I reflect that Reid,
Jennings, Marble, and young Bennett are the great
and awful "morning press" of New York!

The situation in public affairs was extremely
confused.   "In '21," he remarked, "the next step
could be seen, but now it is wholly hidden."   He
saw, however, what it might ultimately require,
and he wrote to a correspondent: "The right
and duty, upon proper occasion, to bolt, are the
right and duty of being honest.   The way to secure
the nomination of honest men is to refuse to vote
for those who are not honest."

Commenting on the financial legislation in the

direction of inflation of the currency, he remarked: "The Republican party, in unquestioned possession of the government, has no policy upon any of the most pressing questions before the country."

He received the veto by President Grant of the Inflation Bill as an act of the highest civic courage, and one which saved the country from the utter demoralization with which the dominant party threatened it, but he condemned with plainness the failure of the President to follow, in his administration of the civil service outside of the rules of the commission, the principle declared and embodied in the rules. The election of a Democratic majority in the House of Representatives was not unexpected by him. He wrote to Mr. Norton on the morrow of the election: —

November 9, '74.

Well, my dearest Charles, I am no more surprised than you. For two years the storm has been in the air. How I wish it could have been averted! The result is another of the constant proofs of the impracticability of "political men," and of the wisdom of babes and sucklings. It was meant, and will be interpreted by many, as an admonition. It is that, and will be of great service. But I do not feel sure of the end. I am disposed to think that a party which has been adjudged unequal to the situation will hardly be called to deal with it again until the other party has been tried

And as the other party has so great a proportion of the dangerous elements of the country in it, I feel, not surprised nor disappointed nor regretful, for it was inevitable, but I do feel very sober.

Early in 1874 Charles Sumner died. It is evidence of the esteem in which Mr. Curtis was held that, though a firm and convinced opponent of the political movement of which Mr. Sumner was in his last years one of the most prominent leaders, he was invited by the Legislature of Massachusetts to deliver a eulogy upon the Senator, which he did (June 9, 1874). It was a very noble address, and may be said to mark the opening of a new phase of the career of Mr. Curtis as an orator. He had now practically abandoned the lectures which he had taken up nearly twenty years previous, and pursued with a steadfast and self-denying energy, upon an object that suggests the labors of Walter Scott in his old age. By these, and by his political speeches, he was known and greatly esteemed. He was now to undertake a much higher and more difficult class of oratory, by which in the next twenty years his reputation was greatly to be extended, and, as I think, established on a lasting foundation. I select from this address a few brief passages fairly indicative of the tone of the whole, but having an added interest from the light they throw on Mr. Curtis's own character and his subsequent course : —

" Mr. Sumner knew, as every intelligent man

knows, that from the day when Themistocles led the educated Athenians at Salamis to that when Von Moltke marshaled the educated Germans against France, the sure foundations of states are laid in knowledge, not in ignorance, and that every sneer at education, at culture, at book-learning, which is the recorded wisdom of the experience of mankind, is the demagogue's sneer at intelligent liberty, inviting national degeneration and ruin. . . .

" While great political results are to be gained by means of great parties, he knew that a party which is too blind to see, or too cowardly to acknowledge, the real issue, — which pursues its ends, however noble, by ignoble means, which tolerates corruption, which trusts unworthy men, which suffers the public service to be prostituted to personal ends, — defies reason and conscience, and summons all honest men to oppose it. . . .

" During all that tremendous time, on the one hand enthusiastically trusted, on the other contemptuously scorned and hated, his heart was that of a little child. He said no unworthy word, he did no unmanly deed; dishonor fled his face ; and to-day those who so long and so naturally, but so wrongfully, believed him their enemy, strew rosemary for remembrance upon his grave. . . .

" This is the great victory, the great lesson, the great legacy of his life, that the fidelity of a public man to conscience, not to party, is rewarded with the sincerest popular love and confidence. What an inspiration to every youth, longing with generous ambition **to enter the** great arena of the state, that he must heed first and always the divine voice in his own soul, if he would be sure of the living voices of good fame! Living, how Sumner served us! and, dying at this moment, how he serves us still! In a time when politics seem peculiarly mean and selfish and corrupt, **when there is a** general vague apprehension that the very **moral foundations of** the national character **are** loosened, when good men are painfully anxious to **know** whether the heart of the people is hardened, **Charles Sumner** dies; and **the** universality and sincerity **of sorrow,** such as the **death of** no man **left** living among us could awaken, **show how true,** how sound, how generous, is still **the heart of the American** people. This is the dying service of Charles Sumner, **a revelation which** inspires every **American to bind his** shining example as a frontlet between the eyes, and never again to despair of **the highest and more glorious destiny of** his country."

CHAPTER XVIII.

In the autumn of 1874 Mr. Curtis wrote to Mr. Norton: " I am invited to deliver the Centennial Oration at Concord on the 19th, and I shall accept." The Concord celebration was the first of the long series commemorating the events of the Revolution, and it was Mr. Curtis's peculiar fortune not only to open the series at Concord, but to close it with the address at the unveiling of the Washington Statue at New York in 1883. The Concord oration is noteworthy for the spirited review of the story of the day, for its masterly tribute to Samuel Adams, and for the succinct and impressive statement of the conditions surrounding the birth of the Revolution. It was inevitable that Mr. Curtis should close by applying the lesson of the earlier day to the problems of the later. But in doing this he could not conceal the grave anxiety by which he was possessed. His spirit was hopeful and courageous, but in the presence of the President, whose iron determination and honest purpose, sustained by a hold on the affections of the people only surpassed by that of Lincoln and Washington, had palpably failed to turn back or

seriously to stem the tide of political demoralization with which Mr. Curtis was himself struggling,
the orator's native hope and courage could point to
no assurance of near progress. The closing words
of the address were of high and impassioned exhortation, but they were distinctly sad.

For in the spring of 1875 it had become plain
that General Grant had surrendered, and was not
prepared for the fight which must be made if the
reform of the civil service was even to be maintained within the scope of the rules. He submitted to Congress, at the opening of the short
session in December, a recommendation for the
continuance of the appropriation, but in a tone
that clearly implied that he would abandon the
plan if the appropriation were withheld.   It was
refused, and on March 27th the rules were suspended, and the work of the commissioners came
to an end.   It was, of course, a severe blow to the
hopes of Mr. Curtis, but it did not shake his in-
domitable devotion.   Very much had been gained.
The principle of appointment for proved merit had
been embodied in a definite, working system; and
the system had stood admirably the test, not
merely of experience, but of experience with the
most bitter and unscrupulous opposition from men
of influence in public life, with inefficient and ill-
trained subordinate officers, and with all the difficulties growing from the looseness and low morals
of the service. No one could deny that it had
worked well in exact proportion to the fidelity

with which it had been applied. It had been proved beyond all cavil that it would secure for the government competent persons of a high average character. The provision for probation had been an entire protection against the possible defects of competitive examinations, and these defects had been found to be insignificant. In practice the appointees standing highest in the examinations had, with very few and slight exceptions, passed with equal success the test of probation, and had steadily improved in efficiency after entering the service. The testimony of the officers in authority in the various departments was entirely favorable, and for the most part heartily favorable, as to the effect of the system on the service. On the other hand the immense advantage to them of the relief from worry and waste of time in dealing with the office-seekers was generally recognized. It was shown beyond all doubt that the honest enforcement of the system excluded party politics from the service to the great gain of both. In short, the three years from 1872 to 1875 had established the entire soundness of the reform, and its complete certainty, when honorably applied, to do all that its authors had predicted, promised, or even hoped.

It is a natural question, why it was not persisted in. The answer may be given in the words of Mr. Curtis twelve years later: "It was once my duty to say to President Grant that the adverse pressure of the Republican party would overpower

his purpose of reform. He replied with a smile
that he was used to pressure. He smiled incredu-
lously, but he presently abandoned the reform."
The "adverse pressure of the Republican party"
was of a kind to which General Grant was in no
wise used. The pressure of a hostile force upon
the lines he could meet, for he could have no possible desire to yield to it or escape from it. The
pressure of civilians, when he was in military
command, he could also resist, for his authority
was complete, his responsibility was definite and
exacting, and he knew perfectly what must be the
consequences if he gave way. He knew, too, that
if he did not give way the civilians must. But
the pressure of political friends high in the party
leadership was a wholly different force. It was at
once powerful, subtle, unceasing, and indirect. It
enveloped him like an atmosphere, and was often
most potent when he was not conscious of it. The
men who brought this pressure to bear were far
too shrewd to let him understand their real object,
or to arouse in him anything like antagonism.
They came to him as to the titular head of the
party ; they made him feel that the success of the
party depended on strong and prudent organization, that this could be effected only by a proper
distribution of the offices, and that distribution of
offices by "schoolmasters' examinations" would
tend to weaken and demoralize the party. They
presented the party to him in the light of analogy
to an army, of which he was the chief, they were

the generals, and the place-holders were the subordinate officers. At every step they showed him ease, popularity, success, honor, on the one hand, and on the other the barren results of a futile effort to carry out a visionary scheme, the only practical outcome of which would be to give aid and comfort to the enemy. And I do not at all deny that many of those through whom this pressure was exerted were entirely sincere in their views, while some of them were unselfish and patriotic in their motives. They were veterans of hard-won victories for the Republican cause in a struggle where offices had been freely used to build up and maintain the organization, and they were convinced that to give up the offices was so plainly injurious as to be party treason. The questions of the war were settled. The people were no longer sharply divided by distinct issues. The opponents of the Republican party were steadily gaining strength. These men felt, and to some extent they made President Grant feel, that in such a strait, with a doubtful or at least a very difficult national campaign coming on, it would be folly to reject any resources within reach of the party. They could not see, nor could he, that the use of the Federal offices as "patronage" or "spoils," as the reward and incentive of political effort, was in reality throwing away that supreme resource, the confidence of intelligent men in the honesty and unselfishness of the purposes of a party. Mr. Curtis's view was opposed to theirs, and a few brief months was to verify it. "History teaches," he said, "no lesson more distinctly than that nothing is so practical as principle, nothing so little visionary as honesty. Political movements, like all other good causes, are constantly betrayed by the ignorance which thinks itself smartness, and the contempt of ideas which is practical common sense."

The next year was one of relative quiet for Mr. Curtis. He turned to his work on "Harper's Weekly" with a sense of relief, on the one hand, from the pressure of official responsibility, and on the other with renewed determination to educate, arouse, and direct public opinion toward the reform which had become the chief object of his life in public affairs. He enjoyed his tranquil home and the fairly settled round of professional duties with a deep content. A glimpse of the family life is afforded in the following note to Mr. Lowell, referring to the ode read by the author at Concord at the Centennial Celebration:

WEST NEW BRIGHTON, STATEN ISLAND, N. Y.,
17th May, 1875.

MY DEAR JAMES, — I read and then re-read your ode last evening to the assembled family, and I cannot tell you how fine, how superb, it seems to all of us. It is full of the noblest thought, — of the loftiest melody. The dance of a thousand rills is in it, and the murmur of old woods. If you have ever done anything more satisfactory I don't know it.

This line is only to say that I can't say anything but to tell you that all who love liberty will love it and you the more for this glorious strain.

We are all well, and all send you our love.

Your most affectionate

G. W. C.

In a letter to Mr. Norton, alluding to a week in Washington, there is a note of the really momentous election that was approaching : —

28th February, 1876.

I returned Friday from Washington, where I had passed a week with the Bancrofts. Nothing could surpass their kindness. From the moment I came until that which saw me off, I was passed along from one interest and pleasure to another, seeing and hearing all that is most desirable in Washington. I think the most extraordinary thing I learned was that, a little while ago, Sam Ward (California and lobby Sam) had the whole Supreme Court of the United States — Chief Justice and all — to dine with him at Welcker's on a Sunday afternoon!

I dined at the secretary of state's with Fernando Wood, handing out Mrs. Fish to dinner.

All that I saw and heard of Bristow, whom I knew four years ago in Washington, was good and satisfactory. I asked Jewell, at the attorney-general's table, whom the *party* — not the managers — would make the candidate, and he answered instantly, " Bristow."

Mr. Benjamin H. Bristow, as secretary of the treasury, had won the esteem and confidence of the best men of the Republican party by the energy and simple fidelity with which he had undertaken to prosecute extensive frauds on the internal revenue, known as the "whiskey frauds." He was a native of Kentucky, had served honorably in the Union army, and had taken an earnest interest in the reform of the civil service. In the following summer Mr. Curtis was elected a delegate to the Republican National Convention, and supported the nomination of Mr. Bristow, though he finally voted for that of Mr. Rutherford B. Hayes, leading the opposition to Senator Conkling, who then represented the administration element in the party in the State of New York. It is not necessary here to recite the situation in which the election left the country. It is sufficient to say that the electoral votes of South Carolina, Florida, and Louisiana, and a part of those of Oregon, were in dispute; that a single one of these votes given to Mr. Tilden, the Democratic candidate, would have been sufficient to elect him; that there were two sets of electoral votes from these States sent to Washington; that the House of Representatives had a Democratic majority, the Senate a Republican majority; that the votes were to be opened by the President of the Senate and counted in the presence of both houses. The Republican claim was, that the President of the Senate could decide which votes should be opened and submitted; the

Democratic claim was, that all votes must opened and submitted, and the choice made as to disputed votes by each house, the assent of both being necessary to an election. The former course would have given the election to Mr. Hayes, the latter to Mr. Tilden. The country was in a state of the deepest confusion. Party feeling ran very high. The passions of the war were reawakened, and the dread possibility of civil strife was oppressing or exciting the minds of all.

At the very height of the struggle, and before any peaceful solution of it had been even plausibly argued, Mr. Curtis was called upon to speak at the dinner of the New England Society of New York on the 22d of December. He had chosen as his toast "The Puritan Principle: Liberty under the Law." His speech was a brief one, and it was so complete an example of the spirit in which he met every occasion, and plucked from its heart the deepest meaning, that I shall quote (from the society's report) the latter half of it: —

"Do you ask me, then, what is this Puritan principle? Do you ask me whether it is as good for to-day as for yesterday; whether it is good for every national emergency; whether it is good for the situation of this hour? I think we need neither doubt nor fear. The Puritan principle in its essence is simply individual freedom. From that spring religious liberty and political equality. The free state, the free church, the free school, — these are the triple armor of American nationality, of American security. But the Pilgrims, while they have stood above all men for this idea of liberty, have always asserted liberty *under law,* and never separated it from law. John Robinson, in the letter that he wrote the Pilgrims when they sailed, said these words, that well, sir, might be written in gold around the cornice of that future banqueting hall to which you have alluded : 'You know that the image of the Lord's dignity and authority which the magistry beareth is honorable in how mean person soever.' (Applause.) This is the Puritan principle. Those men stood for liberty *under the law.* They had tossed long upon a wintry sea ; their minds were full of images derived from their voyage ; they knew that the will of the people alone is but a gale smiting a rudderless and sailless ship, and hurling it, a mass of wreck, upon the rocks. But the will of the people subject to law is the same gale filling the trim canvas of a ship that minds the helm, bearing it over yawning and awful abysses of ocean safely to port. (Loud applause.)

"Now, gentlemen, in this country the Puritan principle has advanced to this point, that it provides a lawful remedy for every emergency that may arise. I stand here as a son of New England. In every fibre of my being, I am a child of the Pilgrim. The most knightly of all the gentlemen at Elizabeth's court said to the young poet, when he would write an immortal song, 'Look into thy heart and write.' And I, sirs and brothers, if, looking into my own heart at this moment, I might dare to think that what I find written there is written also upon the heart of my mother, clad in her snows at home, her voice in this hour would be a message spoken from the land of the Pilgrims to the capital of this nation, — a message like that which Patrick Henry sent from Virginia to Massachusetts when he heard of Concord and Lexington: 'I am not a Virginian, I am an American.' (Great applause.) And so, gentlemen, at this hour we are not Republicans, we are not Democrats, we are Americans. (Tremendous applause.)

" The voice of New England, I believe, going to the capital, would be this, that neither is the Republican Senate to insist upon its exclusive partisan way, nor is the Democratic House to insist upon its exclusive partisan way; but Senate and House, representing the American people and the American people only, in the light of the Constitution and by the authority of the law, are to provide a way over which a President, be he Republican or be he Democrat, shall pass unchallenged to his chair. (Vociferous applause, the company rising to their feet.) Ah, gentlemen (renewed applause), — think not, Mr. President, that I am forgetting the occasion or its amenities. (Cries of ' No, no,' and ' Go on.') I am remembering the Puritans; I am remembering Plymouth Rock and the virtues that made it illustrious. (A voice — 'Justice.') But we, gentlemen, are to imitate those virtues, as our toast says, only by being greater than the men who stood upon that rock. As this gay and luxurious banquet to their scant and severe fare, so must our virtues, to be worthy of them, be greater and richer than theirs. And as we are three centuries older, so we should be three centuries wiser than they. Sons of the Pilgrims, you are not to level forests, you are not to war with savage men and savage beasts, you are not to tame a continent nor even found a state. Our task is nobler, is diviner. Our task, sir, is to reconcile a nation. It is to curb the fury of party spirit. It is to introduce a loftier and manlier spirit everywhere into our political life. It is to educate every boy and every girl, and then to leave them perfectly free to go from any school to any church. Above all, sir, it is to protect absolutely the equal rights of the poorest and the richest, of the most ignorant and most intelligent citizen ; and it is to stand forth, brethren, as a triple wall of brass around our native land against the mad blows of violence or the fatal dry-rot of fraud. (Loud applause.) And at this moment, sir, the grave and austere shades of the forefathers whom we invoke bend above us in benediction as they call us to this sublime task. This, brothers and friends, this is to imitate the virtues of our forefathers ; this is to make our day as glorious as theirs." (Great applause, followed by three cheers for the speaker.)

I have quoted this speech from the New England Society's report, and I have included notes of the applause, because they give the reader an impression of the effect of the speech upon an audience, which, even after dinner, as those familiar with it will concede, is more easily amused than stirred. There can be no doubt that the influence of the speech was considerable in determining the acceptance of the plan of a commission, and of the decision of the commission, when reached on the eve of the inauguration. It is not easy at this distance to conceive the real peril of the situation. As I have said, it was the passions of the war that were reawakened and intensified. Many Republicans believed that Mr. Tilden's accession to the Presidency meant the loss of all that had been gained by the war. Many Democrats, especially in the South, believed that Mr. Hayes's accession meant the extension to the national government of the corruption and greed of the " carpet-bag " régime in the South. In the absence of an arbitration agreed to by both sides, either party would have been furious at facing such dangers and wrongs as they believed involved, and no President with a title depending on a disputed and technical interpretation of an obscure statute could have faced such fury without grave risks. To have contributed in an appreciable degree to the dissipation of the storm thus threatened is no slight claim to the grateful admiration of the country. This Mr. Curtis did in a speech of but a few minutes. The speech is interesting also because, though it was

not unpremeditated, it bears marks of being wholly
unprepared.   In the quiet of his study Mr. Curtis
would not have written out the slightly confused
metaphors which, in the fervor of the occasion,
rushed one upon another, for he was singularly
careful in the construction of his periods when he
took time to construct them in advance.   These
traits of the speech, however, only deepen the impression of the power of the speaker whose un-
marshaled utterances so deeply moved his hearers,
and, twenty years later, must still move the reader.

CHAPTER XIX.

THE PARTING OF THE WAYS.

AT the outset of Mr. Hayes's administration, he sought diligently to connect with it men whose names would give it the prestige which his own modest career did not supply, and which the circumstances of his election tended to make difficult. Among others he turned to Mr. Curtis, who wrote as follows to Mr. Norton: —

19th May, 1877.

When the President was here during the last week, Mr. Evarts offered me my choice of the chief missions, evidently expecting that I would choose the English.

Putting myself out of the question, would it not be equally serviceable to the good cause and the administration if it were openly offered to me, and declined by me in a way to give the administration the credit, and upon the ground, not of shirking the public service, but of my preference for my present public duty? That is, could not all the public advantage be gained by the offer, and would not the advantage be greater than the injury to the administration of turning to a second choice? If the administration are not willing to have the offer known unless I accept, ought I to insist?

Tell me briefly what you think, and whether you think, in any case, that a man absolutely without legal training of any kind could be a proper minister. I know that you love me, but I confide in your perfect candor. Please say nothing of it to any one.

It will be seen that Mr. Curtis was not insensible to the attractions of this offer, nor, at first, decided to put it aside. But finally he did so, and unquestionably chiefly from the motive ascribed in Lowell's lines : —

> " At courts, in senates, who so fit to serve ?
> And both invited, but you would not swerve,
> All meaner prizes waiving that you might
> In civic duty spend your heat and light,
> Unpaid, untrammeled, with a sweet disdain
> Refusing posts men grovel to attain."

This is the poet's way of putting it. I do not think that there was in Mr. Curtis's mind a trace of " disdain," even of " sweet disdain," for the post of representative of his country at a foreign court, and particularly at the court of St. James. On the contrary, however he might regard the motives of some who sought such places, he understood clearly enough the honor they brought to those who honorably filled them. His doubt, as his note to Mr. Norton shows, was as to his own fitness. He might have dismissed that, had his modesty permitted him to remember Irving in Spain, Bancroft in Germany, Motley in England, Marsh in Italy. And, since it is Lowell's view I am talking of, I cannot but picture to myself the impression our English friends would have had of the American representative, and particularly of the American " occasional " speaker, had they been permitted to hear and know first Curtis and then Lowell. It is a pleasing fancy, but it is not necessary to develop it. Mr. Curtis saw his " civic duty " at home, and felt that here better than elsewhere he could do what was worth trying to do. He wrote to Mr. Norton (May 28, 1877), who had sought to change his decision : —

" I am truly obliged to you for your letter. I knew it would be hard to satisfy (fortify ?) myself against it, but I have done so, and I shall show you that I do wisely and therefore right in declining."

And in July he wrote to Mr. Lowell, just appointed minister to Spain : —

ASHFIELD, July 9, 1877.

MY DEAR JAMES, — I must not let you go without a word of love and farewell, although I have meant to write you a letter. I told Charles that on every ground, except that you go away, I am delighted that you are going. With me the case is very different. I happen to be just in the position where I can be of infinitely greater service to the good old cause, and to the administration that is meaning and trying to advance it, than I could possibly be abroad. Evarts wrote me that he felt just as I did about it. But, unless there was some overpowering private reason, you could not escape going, and nothing has done this administration more good, nor rejoiced so many hearts, as your appointment. You will be blown on to your castles in Spain by a whirlwind of benedictions.

Anna sends her love, and I beg my most friendly remembrance to your wife, and I am always most

Affectionately yours,

G. W. C.

Mr. Curtis recognized the sincere purpose of the President to do all that he could to raise the level of the civil service, and with it the level of American politics. A new Civil Service Commission was appointed, with Mr. Dorman B. Eaton at its head; and the rules formulated under Mr. Curtis were applied with a measure of thoroughness at Washington, especially in the Department of the Interior under the Hon. Carl Schurz, in the custom-house in New York, and in the post-office, then placed in charge of Hon. Thomas L. James. Mr. Curtis rejoiced at these evidences of progress in the reform, and warmly supported Mr. Hayes. The President needed support. He had deeply offended the Republican leaders, who had been in practically unrestrained power under President Grant, by the very policy which won for him the confidence and respect of Mr. Curtis. He had made a definite stand, which, if it was not absolutely unyielding, was, in all the circumstances, a very firm and honorable one, against the spoils system, and necessarily against the claims of the Senators, whose political influence was almost wholly due to their control of the distribution of the spoils. Chief among these was Senator Roscoe Conkling, of New York, with whom, as the political leader in his own State, Mr. Curtis had been intimately, though by no means always amicably, related. At the approach of the fall election, Mr. Curtis was a delegate to the Republican State Convention, which was in the control of the Conkling faction. He supported in the convention a resolution approving the course of the administration, and particularly its course with reference to the civil service. From the point of view of the most ordinary political sagacity, the resolution was not only just but proper. To refuse to adopt it was to discredit the party in the approaching contest, and to commit the most unpardonable sin in the partisan decalogue, — that of placing a weapon in the hands of " the enemy." Had the resolution been untruthful, had it approved efforts at reform that had never been made, and " recognized " a virtue in the national administration that did not exist, it would have encountered no opposition from the Conkling side. As it was, Mr. Conkling not only opposed it, but he indulged in a curiously bitter and vulgar attack on Mr. Curtis personally. Replying to a note from Mr. Norton, regarding this incident, Mr. Curtis wrote : —

ASHFIELD, 30th September, 77.

MY DEAREST CHARLES, — Your note is here, and it is lucky that you are not, for I should do no work. It was the saddest sight I ever knew, that man glaring at me in a fury of hate, and storming out his foolish blackguardism. I was all pity. I had not thought him great, but I had not suspected how small he was. His friends, the best, were confounded. One of them said to me next day, "It was not amazement that I felt, but consternation." I spoke offhand, and the report is horrible. The agent of the Associated Press came to me and apologized. Conkling's speech was carefully written out, and therefore you do not get all the venom, and no one can imagine the Mephistophelean leer and spite. I have many letters. Oh dear! how much I prefer these quiet hills, and how I am driven out on the stormy seas!

Mr. Curtis was indeed constantly "driven out on the stormy seas," but the force that drove him was from within, not from without. He went where there was danger to the cause of good government, following Sidney's exhortation to a younger brother: "Whenever you hear of a good war, go to it." I quote here some passages from his address in this same year to the students of Union College on "The Public Duty of Educated Men." They will show by what principles he believed himself to be guided, and will throw light on his subsequent course : —

"By the words 'public duty' I do not necessarily mean official duty, though it may include that. I mean simply that constant and active practical participation in the details of politics without which, upon the part of the most intelligent citizens, the conduct of public affairs falls under the control of selfish and ignorant or crafty and venal men. I mean that personal attention which, as it must be incessant, is often wearisome and even repulsive, to the details of politics — attendance upon meetings, service upon committees, care and trouble and expense of many kinds, patient endurance of rebuffs, chagrins, ridicules, disappointment, defeats ; in a word, all those duties and services which, when selfishly and meanly performed, stigmatize a man as a mere politician, but whose constant, honorable, intelligent, and vigilant performance is the gradual building, stone by stone and layer by layer, of that great temple of self-restrained liberty which all generous souls mean that our government shall be. . . .

" Undoubtedly a practical and active interest in politics will lead you to party association and coöperation. Great public results — the repeal of the corn laws in England, the abolition of slavery in America — are due to that organization of effort, that concentration of aim, which arouse, instruct, and inspire the popular heart and will. This is the spring of party, and those who seek practical results instinctively turn to this agency of united action. But in this tendency, useful in the state as the fire upon the household hearth, lurks, as in that fire, the deadliest peril. Here is our republic: it is a ship, with towering canvas spread,

sweeping before a prosperous gale over a foaming
and sparkling sea; it is a lightning train darting
with awful speed along the edges of dizzy abysses
and across bridges that quiver over unsounded
gulfs.   Because we are Americans we have no
peculiar charm, no magic spell, to stay the eternal
laws.   Our safety lies alone in cool self-possession,
directing the forces of wind and wave and fire.   If
once the madness to which the excitement tends
escapes control, the catastrophe is inevitable.   And
so deep is the conviction that sooner or later this
madness must seize every republic, that the most
plausible suspicion of the permanence of the American government is founded in the belief that party
spirit cannot be restrained.   It is, indeed, a master
passion, but its control is the true conservatism of
the republic, and of happy human progress; and
it is men made familiar by education with the
history of its ghastly catastrophes, men with the
proud courage of independence, who are to temper,
by lofty action born of that knowledge, the ferocity of party spirit.

"This spirit adds moral coercion to sophistry.
It denounces as a traitor him who protests against
party tyranny, and it makes unflinching adherence
to what is called regular party action the condition
of the gratification of honorable political ambition.
Because a man who sympathizes with the party
aims refuses to vote for a thief, this spirit scorns
him as a 'rat' and a renegade.   Because he holds
to principle and law against party expediency and

dictation, he is proclaimed as the betrayer of his country, justice, and humanity. Because he tranquilly insists upon deciding for himself when he must dissent from his party, he is reviled as a popinjay and a visionary fool. Seeking with honest purpose only the welfare of his country, the hot air around him teems with the cry of the ' grand old party,' ' the traditions of the party,' ' loyalty to the party,' ' future of the party,' ' servant of the party ; ' and he sees and hears the gorged and portly money-changers in the temple usurping the very divinity of the God. Young hearts ! be not dismayed. If ever one of you shall be the man so denounced, do not forget that your own individual convictions are the whip of small cords which God has put into your hands to expel the blasphemers."

Mr. Curtis was approaching the parting of the ways. There was no doubt, when the time came, as to what guide he would follow.

CHAPTER XX.

On the 17th of October, 1877, Mr. Curtis delivered the oration at Schuylerville, Saratoga County, New York, on the hundredth anniversary of the surrender of Burgoyne. As he said: "The drama of the Revolution opened in New England, culminated in New York, and closed in Virginia." It was the culmination that was celebrated on the battle-field where, for the first time in the long and fluctuating struggle, the American forces met and defeated in the open field the disciplined army of a brave and capable English commander. The story of the battle, and of the events that led up to it, is admirably told in Mr. Curtis's oration. I cite the closing passages, as giving the spirit in which Mr. Curtis was wont to apply to the present the lessons of the past: —

"It is the story of a hundred years ago. It has been ceaselessly told by sire to son along this valley and through this land. The later attempt of the same foe, and the bright day of victory at Plattsburg, renewed and confirmed the old hostility. Alienation of feeling between the parent country and the child became traditional, and on both sides of the sea a narrow prejudice survives, and still sometimes seeks to kindle the embers of that wasted fire. But here and now we stand upon the grave of old enmities. Hostile breast-work and redoubt are softly hidden under grass and grain; shot and shell and every deadly missile are long since buried beneath our feet; and from the mouldering dust of mingled foemen springs all the verdure that makes this scene so fair. While nature tenderly and swiftly repairs the ravages of war, we suffer no hostility to linger in our hearts. Two months ago the British Governor-General of Canada was invited to meet the President of the United States at Bennington, in happy commemoration, not of a British defeat, but of a triumph of English liberty. So, upon this famous and decisive field, let every unworthy feeling perish! Here to the England that we fought let us now, grown great and strong with a hundred years, hold out the hand of fellowship and peace. Here, where the English Burgoyne, in the very moment of his bitter humiliation, generously pledged George Washington, let us, in our high hour of triumph, of power, of hope, pledge the Queen! Here in the grave of brave and unknown foemen may mutual jealousies and doubts and animosities lie buried forever! Henceforth, revering their common glorious traditions, may England and America press always forward side by side in noble and aspiring rivalry to promote the welfare of man!

" Fellow-citizens, with the glory of Burgoyne's

surrender, the Revolutionary glory of the State of
New York still fresh in our memories, amid these
thousands of her sons and daughters whose hearts
glow with lofty pride, I am glad that the hallowed
spot on which we stand compels us to remember
not only the imperial State, but the national commonwealth whose young hands here together struck
the blow, and on whose older head descends the
ample benediction of the victory. On yonder
height, a hundred years ago, Virginia lay encamped.
Beyond, and further to the north, watched New
Hampshire and Vermont. Here in the wooded
uplands of the south stood New Jersey and New
York ; while across the river to the east, Connecticut and Massachusetts closed the triumphal line.
Here was the symbol of the Revolution, a common
cause, a common strife, a common triumph ; the
cause, not of a class, but of human nature ; the
triumph, not of a colony, but of United America.
And we who stand here proudly remembering, we
who have seen Virginia and New York — the
North and the South — more bitterly hostile than
the armies whose battles shook this ground, we
who have mutually proved in deadlier conflict the
constancy and the courage of all the States, which,
proud to be peers, yet own no master but their
united selves, — we renew our hearts in imperish-
able devotion to the common American faith, the
common American pride, the common American
glory ! Here Americans stood and triumphed.
Here Americans stand and bless their memory.

And here, for a thousand years, may grateful generations of Americans come to rehearse the glorious story, and to rejoice in a supreme and benignant American nationality!"

When, in the summer of 1878, at the age of fourscore years and four, William Cullen Byrant died, Mr. Curtis was invited by the New York Historical Society to deliver a commemorative address, which he did on December 30 before an assembly of very unusual distinction, including the President, Mr. Hayes, and members of his Cabinet. The address is in curious harmony with the subject and the author, and, with the exception of that on Lowell, is perhaps the most notable of the series delivered by Mr. Curtis. Its spirit is peculiarly calm, and its style quiet, sustained, and of rare purity and simplicity. I think that it remains the most satisfactory tribute to the noble and gifted and yet not popular character of Mr. Bryant. It gives, moreover, very interesting indications of the scholar's nature in Mr. Curtis. "Undoubtedly," he says, "the grandeur and solemnity of Wordsworth, as Bryant told Dana, had stirred his soul with sympathy. But not the false simplicity that sometimes betrays Wordsworth, nor the lurid melodrama of Byron, nor the aerial fervor of Shelley, nor the luxuriant beauty of Keats, — in whose line the Greek marble is sometimes suffused with a splendor of Venetian color, — nor in his later years the felicity and richness of Tennyson, who has revealed the flexibility and picturesqueness of the English language in lines which a line of Keats describes, —

  " 'Like lucent sirups tinct with cinnamon,' —

not all these varying and entrancing strains, which captivated the public of the hour, touched in the least the verse of Bryant. His last considerable poem, 'The Flood of Years,' but echoes in its meditative flow the solemn cadences of 'Thanatopsis.' The child was father of the man. The genius of Bryant, not profuse and imperial, neither intense with dramatic passion nor throbbing with lyrical fervor, but calm, meditative, pure, has its true symbol among his native hills, a mountain spring untainted by mineral or slime of earth or reptile venom, cool, limpid, and serene. His verse is the virile expression of the healthy communion of a strong, sound man with the familiar aspects of nature, and its broad, clear, open-air quality has a certain Homeric suggestiveness."

It was, however, Bryant the editor, the steadfast and faithful worker in the field where right opinion is cultivated, that elicited from Mr. Curtis the most eloquent tribute. " It is the lesson of this editorial life that public service the most resplendent and the most justly renowned on sea or shore, in Cabinet or Congress, however great, however beneficent, is not a truer service than that of the private citizen like Bryant, who for half a century, with conscience and knowledge, with power and unquailing courage, did his part in holding the hand and heart of his country true to her now glorious ideal." And again, in still more emphatic strain : —

" It is by no official title, by no mere literary fame, by no signal or single service or work, no marvelous Lear or Transfiguration, no stroke of statecraft calling to political life a new world to redress the balance of the old, no resounding Austerlitz or triumphant Trafalgar, that Bryant is commemorated. There may have been, in his long lifetime, genius more affluent and creative, greater renown, abilities more commanding, careers more dazzling and romantic, but no man, no American, living or dead, has more truly or amply illustrated the scope and the fidelity of republican citizenship."

If in these brief quotations I seem to have traced in Mr. Curtis's portrait of Bryant some of the features of Mr. Curtis's character, it is because of the sympathy of aim that inspired both. It is not seldom that the literary artist, like the artist in portraiture, reveals himself in what he sees in his subject.

Shortly after the delivery of this address, Mr. Curtis wrote to Mr. Norton (January 11, 1879): —

" I think my view of Bryant is not unjust, perhaps a generous one, but true to the chief aspects of the man. The occasion was magnificent, for it was unquestionably the most distinguished audience ever assembled in New York. The President accepted, he said, solely to honor me, and Evarts impressed the same truth upon me. After his return the President wrote me a warm little note, offering me the German mission. I was touched, for I saw his wish; but I told him that I had carefully considered the whole subject on a former occasion, and, not without some surrender of hopes and ambitions, I had decided that it was not wise for me to change the order of my life. I had had no misgivings and had none now.

" It does not seem to me at fifty-five probable that I shall greatly vary the order of that life hereafter."

The " order of his life " was, indeed, not to be changed, but the principle that directed it was to lead him into new and constantly more trying contests. In the following year, the Republican party in the State of New York nominated for governor Mr. Alonzo B. Cornell, a former prominent office-holder in the Federal service, an active manager of the party machinery based on the distribution of the patronage, and a conspicuous representative of the group of politicians who had set themselves again to nominate General Grant for the Presidency in 1880, and to renew that domination of the " spoils system " which had followed the breakdown of the first attempt at civil service reform. The nomination was accomplished by the extreme methods of party manipulation that go with the spoils idea, and aroused an intense and indignant opposition in the Republican party, which took the form of refusal to vote for the candidate for governor while voting for other candidates, —

in the technical language of politics, " scratching "
the name of Mr. Cornell. An organization was
formed under the title of " Independent Republicans," commonly referred to, however, as " Scratchers," to promote this plan of protest. It was so
far successful that twenty thousand adherents were
enrolled throughout the State. Mr. Cornell was
elected by the opposition of Tammany Hall, in
New York city, to the Democratic candidate, but
the influence of the independent movement was
very great and lasting.

"Among the mortally wounded," wrote Mr.
Curtis, November 6, " is Conkling. Everybody
here feels that it is he who has ' engineered ' the
ridiculous result of a Republican governor elected
by Tammany Hall in pursuance of a plan to show
that New York will be a Republican State next
year. Tilden goes with him, and, it seems to me,
Sherman likewise. Evarts was, like Disraeli, unspeakable."

The organization of Independent Republicans,
with this distinct moral advantage to their credit,
was continued for the presidential year 1880. It
was plain that they held the " balance of power "
in the State of New York, and might easily decide not merely the Republican candidacy, but the
Presidency. On May 20, 1880, Mr. Curtis, who
had warmly supported the movement, addressed
the organization at a crowded meeting in Chicker-
ing Hall.

"I accepted your invitation," he said, " with

great pleasure, as that of Republicans who know that the Republican party was founded in freedom and for freedom, and who are resolved to keep yourselves free. Your action last autumn, as citizens interested in politics, but without personal or mercenary ends, determined not to sacrifice party principles to party organization, and quietly holding your ground against every form of ridicule and hostility, was a public service deserving the public gratitude, and full of good augury for the future. You were told that you were voting in the air, but you knew that such air-guns as yours had done great execution; and if your twenty thousand airy shots were noiseless, they hit the mark at which they were aimed. The man who is proud never to have voted anything but the whole regular party ticket shows the servility of soul that makes despotism possible.

"It is true that party action becomes impossible if every member insists upon having his own way. There must be, undoubtedly, general concession and sacrifice of mere personal preference, but every member must decide for himself how far this may go and where it must end. No Republican has a right to appeal to me as a Republican to stand by the party who does not do what he can to make the party worth standing by. A party is made efficient only through men. It is necessarily judged by its candidates; and if its members support unworthy candidates to-day for the sake of the party, they make it all the easier to support unworthier candidates to-morrow. If I agree to vote for Jeremy Diddler to-day because he is the regularly selected standard-bearer of the grand old party of honesty and reform, I cannot refuse to vote for Benedict Arnold to-morrow because *he* is the standard-bearer of the grand old party of independence and political glory. If the reply be that no one pretends that we ought to vote for candidates of bad character, I answer that a candidate who for any reason discredits the party, and thereby imperils its success and consequently its object, is, from the party point of view, a bad man, and fidelity to the party demands the rejection of the candidate."

The address had for its subject " Machine Politics and the Remedy." Mr. Curtis's conception of machine politics was party management based on the spoils of office. His remedy was for the individual voter's " scratching " machine candidates ; but the general and thorough and lasting remedy was the reform of the civil service, and the abolition of the use of the offices as spoils. More and more this idea was forced upon him as the one of chiefest and most urgent importance in the public affairs of the nation.

The movement to nominate General Grant for a third term was led by Senator Conkling, the general having become a resident of New York. It was strongly resisted in that State and finally failed, General James A. Garfield, of Ohio, receiving the Republican nomination, and General W. S.

Hancock that of the Democrats. Garfield was elected, and the civil service reformers, as well as the advocates of a more liberal tariff, took heart of hope.

The President was undoubtedly in sympathy with the idea of both classes. In his long congressional experience he had learned the evils of the spoils system, and had denounced them often in a manner at once emphatic and intelligent. He had, however, shown neither the firmness nor the courage essential to carry out an effectual reform by the use of the executive authority, adequate as that would have been in the hands of a determined and independent President. The reformers, however, found an unexpected ally in Senator George H. Pendleton, of Ohio, who introduced a radical though ill-digested bill in Congress. Mr. Pendleton was a Democrat, of very pronounced party feeling, and had immediately after the war been associated with the extreme wing of his party, especially on financial questions. But he was a man of culture, of personal probity, of considerable ability, and his accession to the cause of the reform was valuable. In 1880 the " New York Civil Service Reform Association " was formed, taking the place of one that had dissolved early in the administration of Mr. Hayes, and Mr. Curtis was elected its president, a post which he held until his death. The first work of the new association was directed toward legislation, and the bill of Mr. Pendleton was taken as the basis. Little progress was made, however, at Washington, though kindred associations were formed in various parts of the country, until, in the summer of 1881, the murderous assault upon President Garfield by a half-insane office-seeker startled the country to an alarmed sense of what the envenomed struggle for place might at any time involve. In August the National Civil Service Reform League was formed at Newport, R. I. "Of the league," says Mr. William Potts, who became its secretary, and whose intelligent and untiring labors in that office were of the greatest value, "Mr. Curtis was the inevitable president by common consent, and none who heard his words at the close of the meeting then doubted more than he the end of the work thus entered upon: 'We have laid our hands on the barbaric palace of patronage, and begun to write on its walls *Mene, mene!* Nor, I believe, will the work end till they are laid in the dust.'"

The assassination of President Garfield in 1881 aroused a powerful public sentiment against the spoils system, for the assassin was recognized as an abnormal and yet logical product of that system. Craving for spoils, and hatred of the man who failed to satisfy it, were the immediate motives of his disordered mind. Mr. Chester A. Arthur, who as Vice-President succeeded to the duties of the President's office, brought the subject of reform to the attention of Congress, and "urgently recommended" an appropriation of $25,000 to renew the work of the United States Civil Service Commission which had been dropped in 1873. Congress was, however, as yet deaf to the voice of public opinion, and only $15,000 was granted, and that on the motion of an opposition member.

The refusal of President Garfield to "recognize" the senators from New York, in the distribution of Federal patronage in that State, had resulted in a violent and open quarrel in the Republican party in New York. The resignation of Mr. Blaine as secretary of state had greatly embittered the faction led by the senators. When, in the fall of 1882, Mr. Charles J. Folger, then secretary of the treasury, had been nominated for governor by the Republican party, he encountered determined opposition. For the most part this was probably factional. The leaders in the State who took part in it, and who were in close relations with Mr. Blaine, were politicians of much the same character and methods as those who secured the nomination of Mr. Folger. But, on the other hand, there was a profound sentiment of disapproval and disgust among those who saw in the nomination an instance of the control of party action by the federal administration through the abuse of the offices. This sentiment was strong among the Independent Republicans, or "Scratchers," whose movement three years previously had elicited the hearty support of Mr. Curtis, and he was in complete sympathy with them still. When the nomination was made, he was at his country home in Ashfield. By one of those curious blunders to which editorial offices are liable in the absence of the responsible head, an article by Mr. Curtis was modified to commit the paper to the support of the candidate. On the 27th of September he wrote to Mr. Norton : —

"MY DEAREST CHARLES, — I have resigned the editorship of 'Harper's Weekly.' My article upon Folger's nomination, despite my request, was perverted and made to misrepresent my views, and to make me absolutely ridiculous. The blow to me and to the good cause is very great and not exactly retrievable. To-day I am thought by every reader of the paper to be a futile fool. The thing is so atrocious as to be comical."

It is unnecessary here to trace the source of the unfortunate mistake. It was promptly and in the most manly manner disavowed by the house of Harper & Bros. Mr. Curtis published a letter setting himself right with those who had been astonished at the appearance of the article, and withdrew his resignation. The accidental interruption of the relations of publishers and editor, which had been maintained so honorably on both sides for nearly twenty years, had no effect but to strengthen mutual confidence and respect.

In the election of 1882 the Democratic candidate, Grover Cleveland, was elected by a majority of nearly two hundred thousand votes, and this was accompanied by severe checks and reverses for the Republicans in other States. The first effect of these checks and reverses was to awaken in the representatives of the Republican party at Wash-

ington an entirely new conception of what civil
service reform was, and of popular opinion regarding it — and themselves. The Pendleton bill was
referred to a committee of which Senator Hawley,
of Connecticut, was chairman, and under his zealous
and intelligent guidance, assisted by representatives of the National League, the bill was steadily
pressed. It received the signature of President
Arthur on the 16th of January, 1883, and went
into final operation on the 16th of July, after which
date no appointment to the civil service was legal
unless made in accordance with the provisions of the
law — that is, in compliance with the rules promulgated by the authority of the law, unless expressly
exempted from them. The system adopted was in
substance the same as that framed by the commission of which Mr. Curtis was chairman in 1871.
It aimed gradually to apply the principle of appointments for fitness attested by competition and
probation. The essential control of the President
as the chief appointing officer of the government
was recognized. A commission was to frame the
rules which, when he approved them, he was to
promulgate, and which the commission was then to
administer. The law expressly forbade contributions for political purposes by any person in the
service to be paid to any person in the service, and
prohibited all solicitation of such contributions
within the government offices. The rules were to
apply to the departmental service at Washington
above the grade of laborers, and below appoint-

ments made with the advice and consent of the
Senate, with certain exceptions, and they were to
apply also to any federal officer outside of Washington having fifty or more employees. The heads
of departments were required to classify the employees under them within six months, and thus
the part of the service to which the rules apply
came to be generally designated as the "classified
service." Examinations were to be held under the
direction of the commission, and those attaining
in these examinations a certain minimum standard
were placed on an eligible list in the order of their
standing for each department or office. When a
vacancy occurred, the three names highest on the
list were to be certified to the appointing officer,
who chose the appointee from these. There was
also provision for promotion by competition.

It will be seen that the rules, honestly and intelligently administered, practically excluded politics
from the service wherever they applied. The power
of removal from office was left untouched, and dismissals for party reasons were not prohibited. It
was expected, however, by the friends and authors
of the law, that such dismissals would gradually
cease as the temptation to make them was destroyed.
The history of the service shows that removals from
office are almost uniformly made for one of two purposes, — either to punish refusal of political as-
sessments, or to make room for party appointments.
The law and the rules forbade the former, and
made the latter extremely difficult. The system

as a whole was sound in principle, and capable of great good, but it was far from radical. It was set in operation by President Arthur in good faith, under a commission of which **Mr. Dorman B. Eaton** was the most active member, bringing to it a thorough study of the work and marked ability with untiring zeal. The provisions made by law for the operation of the reform were, however, ludicrously and shamefully inadequate, and represented the half-concealed hostility of the legislators toward it. The appropriation barely covered the small salaries of the commission, traveling expenses, and office expenses. The examinations had to be made by clerks detailed from the service, who received no pay for their work, which was added to their regular duties. But it was the happy quality of the reform to excite the most generous devotion in all honest persons who had to do with it, and it immediately entered upon a career of practical success that has steadily gained with every passing year.

CHAPTER XXI.

" The party issues of the last few years are gradually disappearing. The perilous questions of fundamental policy have been determined, and the paramount interests of the country are now those of administration. Honesty and efficiency of administration of the settled national policy will now be the chief demand of every party." These were the words which, in the closing months of 1871, Mr. Curtis had addressed to President Grant in submitting his report on the reform of the civil service. Their general prediction was sound. It had not come about that " every party " had demanded " honesty and efficiency of administration," for the demands of parties are often framed by men curiously ignorant either of the general requirements of public opinion, or of the requirements of that body of voters who are bound by no party, and who from time to time dismiss one and call another to the control of the government. But, during the thirteen years that had passed since Mr. Curtis had defined the situation in the words above quoted, there had beyond any doubt grown up in the country a sentiment steadily stronger and more definite that "honesty and efficiency of administration" was the imperative and dominant need of the time. The year 1884 was to see the Republican party, after nearly a quarter of a century of unbroken possession of the presidential office, displaced in obedience to this sentiment.

The presidential contest of 1876 may be said to be the last in which the Republican party had made its stand almost exclusively on the issues growing out of the war. Mr. Hayes, on taking office, had made, if not a formal, an unmistakable proclamation that these questions could never again be controlling. He had withdrawn the Federal hand from the States of Louisiana and South Carolina, and he had invited a Southern man to a prominent place in his Cabinet. During his term of office he made every effort, with the approval of a large number of his party leaders, to expel the "Southern question" from politics, and his efforts won general sympathy among the people. In the canvass of 1880, Mr. Garfield, though he was a veteran of the War for the Union, was opposed by General Hancock, a much more conspicuous Union veteran; and the chief issue of the contest, so far as national policy was involved, was the tariff. Mr. Arthur, to whom by the death of the President it fell to send the first message to the Congress elected in 1880, for the first time since the close of the Civil War transmitted one in which no question arising out of the war received any serious comment. The "gradual" disappearance of the party questions to which Mr. Curtis had alluded in 1871 was now completed.

By the ordinary course of political development, the issue of 1884 should have been the tariff, on which parties had been most clearly divided four years before, and on which the policy of the opposition had been most definitely shaped. And though, by the tariff act of 1883, a certain measure of reduction in protective duties had been made, in pursuance of recommendations far more advanced by the commission of 1882, a majority of whom were of the Protectionist party, it is probable that the tariff would have been the controlling question had the party in power nominated almost any of its prominent leaders other than Mr. James G. Blaine. That nomination made the decisive fact in the canvass the opinion of the country as to the personal character of the candidate, and this opinion on the whole was adverse. The decisive fact was not, of course, the only one, nor, in a sense, was it the chief one. The great body of each party was doubtless guided by that powerful and complex and not clearly defined force which we know as party feeling, and was not seriously affected by the known or inferred character of either candidate. And there was a certain influence exerted independent of party association by other causes, such as the race sentiment elicited among voters of Irish birth or descent in behalf of Mr. Blaine, and the counteracting influence of the religious sentiment aroused by the fact that the Catholic priesthood

was reported — on no specific evidence - - to be enlisted in his behalf.   Again, there was the effect
of the association of a considerable number of men
formerly active in the Democratic party with the
highly protected interests dependent on the tariff.
But the outcome of the forces on either side was
so nearly equal to that of those on the other side,
that it remains probable that, had the question
of Mr. Blaine's character been eliminated from
the canvass, the decision would have been in his
favor.

But this decisive element was not a simple one.
If Mr. Blaine failed in the election because of the
adverse opinion of a considerable body of voters
as to his character, it was because the defects attributed to him were of public interest and not of
a private nature, and he was regarded as a representative of a class whose power it was right and
necessary to curb.   The particular fault that his
opponents dwelt most upon was the use of public
office for private advantage, and there was a deep-
seated conviction that that was the most serious,
general, and threatening evil of the times.   Mr.
Curtis, in an address on Staten Island on the Centennial Anniversary of Independence, eight years
previously, had invited his fellow-citizens to this
pledge : " That we will try public and private men
by precisely the same moral standard, and that
no man who directly or indirectly connives at corruption or coercion to acquire office or retain it,
or who prostitutes any opportunity or position of

public service to his own or another's advantage, shall have our countenance or our vote." There was evidence, which many of Mr. Blaine's fellow Republicans found conclusive, that in one distinct instance he had been willing to prostitute an opportunity and position of public service to his own advantage, and there was nothing in his public career to contradict the inference. There was much to confirm it. He had been in public life for a quarter of a century, and had attained a position of great influence and power in his party. His ability as a political leader was eminent, while his popularity was probably more extended than that of any man since Clay. But his rare gifts and great power had certainly not been devoted to promoting the purity or raising the general level of public life or of party action. He was intimately identified, on the contrary, with the tendency, so obvious since the close of the Civil War, in the opposite direction. Republicans who had faithfully, unselfishly, and from the sincerest conviction, labored to construct and maintain their party because it was to them the best instrument for promoting the best interests of the country, sought in vain in Mr. Blaine's record the evidence that his real aims were theirs, and reluctantly came to regard him as the typical opponent of those aims. He had shown no efficient sympathy with the reform movement which sought to exclude party politics from the public service. On the contrary he owed very much of his power in his own party to the unscrupulous use of offices, and the violent disruption of his party in the State of New York in 1882 had been promoted by his friends largely because of resentment at their failure to receive the share they wished in patronage.

There was another phase of Mr. Blaine's career which bore upon his willingness to prostitute the opportunities of public service to his own advantage, and which furnished evidence not so clear and conclusive, but indicating even more dangerous proclivities. He had long been recognized as the leader of the sentiment in favor of a "vigorous" foreign policy, and that recognition was a potent element in the gratification of his ambition. During the brief time that he had been in the Cabinet of President Garfield, he had shown what was his conception of a vigorous foreign policy. He had in two cases undertaken to impose the influence of the United States government upon a friendly foreign government — once upon Chili and once upon Mexico — in a manner unwarranted by international law, and opposed to the traditional impartiality of our policy in dealing with other nations. In both instances his failure had been complete and humiliating. In one he had incurred serious peril of a quarrel; in the other he had been subjected to contemptuous neglect. His course had produced a profound feeling of distrust among intelligent and conservative observers, who saw in it a reckless attempt to cultivate a dangerous popularity at the cost of the interests and honor of his country.

On the anniversary of Washington's birthday in 1884, a dinner was given by the Young Men's Republican Club of Brooklyn, a very powerful and intelligent organization with a large number of very independent members, — at which a number of leading men spoke, all of them urging strongly the need of the Republican party for a candidate of sound character. Mr. Curtis did not attend the dinner, but wrote a letter in full sympathy with the speakers. On the 24th of February a conference of Republicans was held in the city of New York, at which Mr. Curtis was present, with Republicans from many parts of the country, and particularly from New England, at which a resolution was adopted declaring the imperative necessity of Republican candidates who would "warrant confidence in their readiness to defend the advance already made toward divorcing the public service from party politics, and to continue these advances till the separation has been made final and complete." An organization was formed to promote the purpose of the conference and an "Independent Republican Committee" named, of which General Francis C. Barlow was president, and Mr. Joseph W. Harper treasurer.

The Republican National Convention was held early in June in the city of Chicago, where, twenty-four years before, Mr. Lincoln, the first successful candidate of the Republican party, had been nominated. Mr. Curtis was chosen as a delegate

from the county of Richmond (Staten Island),
where he resided. His first choice, like that of
most of the Republicans who were in sympathy
with him, for the nomination, was Senator George
F. Edmunds, of Vermont, a man of high character
and great ability, who had up to that time given
many evidences of his independence of party dictation. When the convention met, it was apparent
that it was unevenly divided between the supporters of Blaine, Arthur, and Edmunds, the first-
named having the greatest number, but not a
majority of the convention. The very unusual situation and the condition of party sentiment were
recognized when, on the 4th of June, before the
convention had decided to proceed to vote for
nominees, a resolution was introduced declaring
that every delegate who took part in the convention was "bound in honor to support the nominee."
Mr. Curtis promptly protested against its adoption.
"A Republican and a free man," he declared, "I
came to this convention, and by the grace of God
a Republican and a free man will I go out of it."
The resolution was finally withdrawn.

When the balloting was begun, it was evident
that Mr. Blaine was to secure the nomination unless the supporters of Arthur and Edmunds could
combine upon one or the other of these two. Such
a combination was impossible. The two men represented in the convention totally different and
opposite ideas of the question which had divided
the party. That question had been clearly de-

fined by the Independent Republican conference in February. It was the divorce of the public service from party politics. Mr. Arthur, though he had enforced the civil service law within the narrow limits of the rules, was not only a believer in the spoils doctrine, but one of the most conspicuous and experienced and least scrupulous of the leaders who had put it in practice and profited by doing so. He owed very much of the strength he was able to show in the convention to the use of Federal patronage. He had won a certain degree of confidence in the country by his dignified and conservative management of foreign affairs, by his liberal views as to the tariff, and his entire soundness on questions of finance; but while, as to these matters, he compared favorably with Mr. Blaine, none of them was of controlling importance. The supporters of Mr. Edmunds could not give their votes to him without openly defeating their chief purpose. His supporters could not give their votes to Mr. Edmunds without abandoning the hopes that animated most of them. The combination could not be made, and Mr. Blaine was nominated. The usual motion was offered to "make the nomination unanimous," and was carried. Mr. Curtis did not vote upon it, and refused the urgent appeals to second it. He remained in the convention, taking part in the subsequent proceedings, until its close, this being what he understood to be his duty as a representative.

"Harper's Weekly" promptly condemned the

action of the Republican Convention. When the
Democratic National Convention placed in nomination Mr. Cleveland, then governor of the State of
New York, Mr. Curtis, after careful deliberation,
decided to advocate his election. He was immediately recognized as the representative of the Republican defection. With Mr. Carl Schurz, he
took the leadership of that movement; his own
position differing from that of Mr. Schurz in this,
that, while their view of the duty of the hour was
the same, Mr. Schurz, by his support of Horace
Greeley in 1872, had broken that association with
his party which with Mr. Curtis had been uninter-
rupted.

Mr. Curtis's decision, though painful, was inevitable. The Republican party had, in his sober
judgment, ceased to pursue the aims which he
had so long sought through it. It had nominated
a candidate whose election he believed would defeat those aims. The course of the party had been
taken in opposition to every possible effort on his
part to prevent it. He had labored with all his
energy and influence to convince his party of the
error and danger toward which it was tending.
Nor had he failed, repeatedly, definitely, and emphatically, to declare the principles of party allegiance by which he had consistently been guided.
He had openly advocated Republican effort to defeat bad Republican candidates in his own State,
in Massachusetts, in Pennsylvania. He had done
so avowedly for the purpose of saving the party

from the control of those who made bad candidates possible; and he had never concealed his conviction that, if this purpose failed in the national organization, the same principle would demand the same action.

He wrote, immediately after the convention, to a very old friend : —

June 10, 1884.

MY DEAR S., — I am very sorry indeed that our sense of duty differs so widely. I cannot urge anybody to support for the presidency a man who has trafficked in his official place for his private gain, and still less upon the ground that the party that nominated him is a better party than the other. There would never be any better party, or indeed any party but that to which we belong, if everything that it did and everybody that it nominated should be sustained because it was not so bad as another party. I did not support Cornell in 1879, because of his ring associations and methods. I did not support Folger in 1882, because of the forgery and fraud which secured his nomination. But I had no personal objection to the men. It is not Blaine's " brilliancy," it is the low and venal system of his politics, of which we had the latest and monstrous evidence at Chicago, that shall not master the Republican party if I can help it. When the only argument is that we are not so bad as the other fellows, it is time to call a halt.

My dear boy, I should be recreant to my conscience, and I should bitterly disappoint all those

who are accustomed to look to me, if, after all that
I have said about political morality, I should now
support for the presidency the one man who is
most repugnant to the political conscience of young
Republicans.   I am in hearty agreement with the
Harpers, who are unanimous upon the point that
such a course would be disastrous, and you can
hardly imagine how deep and strong the feeling of
outrage is.

I wish with all my heart that we agreed about
the matter, and with all the old affection I am always yours.

Mr. Curtis felt keenly the accusation brought
against him of personal bad faith in taking part in
a convention and then refusing to accept its candidate. His conscience was entirely clear, but he
knew that many who had long respected and trusted
him and followed his leadership, many whom he believed to be as sincere as he was himself, and even
some old and cherished friends, thought his course
dishonorable, and the knowledge was exceedingly
hard to bear.   Yet it is clear that no other course
was open to him.   " No honorable man," he wrote
in an open letter to a critic of his action, June 25,
1884, " in a convention or out of it, would allow a
majority to bind him to a course which he morally
disapproved."   In the autumn of 1885 he wrote
to a correspondent who had raised this question a
letter which I find so explicit and compact that I
give it as the best statement of his view : —

" I have received your note, and have time only for a brief reply. The action of a convention is merely a recommendation, and its authority is merely that of a majority. Now, a majority cannot morally or honorably bind a participant in any consultation to support its action if he morally disapproves of it. The fact that he is there to prevent such action is certainly not a reason for him to support it if taken, because that conclusion would make the man who actively endeavors to prevent it more bound by it than one who stays at home and takes no part. As a delegate, the member of a convention votes and does his delegated duty to the best of his ability. Having discharged that special duty, his general duty as a citizen recurs, and he is to weigh the action of the convention like every other citizen, and vote only as his conscience directs.

" There are perhaps five millions of party voters on each side; a convention is composed of about 800 members of the party. The majority would be 401; and to say that the remaining 399 who have opposed the decision are honorably bound by it if they conscientiously disapprove, while all the other millions and thousands of members are not bound, is simply folly."

I have given this statement of Mr. Curtis's views on this matter because, at the time and long after, though it did not disturb, it saddened him. For my own part, it seems to me to have given occasion for much political casuistry, as to which prejudice and interest and unreflecting sentiment have wrought confusion, but as to which the verdict of justice and common sense is beyond all mistake. If the doctrine of Mr. Curtis's critics were to prevail, self-respecting men would not act as delegates to political conventions, and party rule would rapidly and inevitably become corrupt. The independence he asserted is the indispensable condition precedent to rational and decent politics. Unfortunately human nature does not always develop reason or decency under the influence of strenuous party passion. Though the criticism to which I have referred was that which affected Mr. Curtis most, it was by no means all he had to bear. It is simply impossible to give any idea of the abuse, the insult, the scurrility, that were heaped upon him in the public press, and in letters, usually anonymous, addressed to him. It was a startling revelation to him of the vulgarity and brutality of a large number of the men with whom and for whom he had so faithfully and unselfishly labored. Necessarily it only confirmed him in the course he had taken. It was conclusive proof, if any were needed, of the extent to which the evil against which he had revolted had spread in the Republican party. The vile spirit shown, because an honorable and conscientious leader had found himself forced into opposition, was a spirit that would have been no less vile, and infinitely more dangerous, had he submitted to the party dictation and the party had won. Mr. Curtis's service to his country while he acted with the Republican party was in my judgment very great. It was completed and exceeded by the service he rendered when he left the party, and pursued through another party the same high purpose.

CHAPTER XXII.

DURING the remaining years of his life, Mr. Curtis's relation to public affairs was strictly that of an independent critic, and his chief object was the promotion of civil service reform, of which he was now the acknowledged leader and representative. In " Harper's Weekly," of course, his criticism embraced a wide field, and several important and interesting questions — the tariff, the currency, foreign matters, the relation of the President to Congress, which came up within this period — received a fair share of attention, and were discussed candidly, and in the main intelligently. But none of them interested him as did the reform. To the latter, also, he devoted a great deal of personal labor and study. His offices as president of the National Civil Service Reform League and of the New York Civil Service Reform Association gave him an opportunity for effective work which he embraced with the utmost ardor, and pursued with unwearied energy. No important step was taken anywhere without his approval, and very much that was done was due to his initiative. His correspondence was, on this subject alone, enough to tax the patience and strength of any man, but it was never neglected and rarely deferred. His attendance at all committees was faithful, and his part in their work a marvel of patience, vigilance, sound judgment, and inspiring zeal. It was my fortune to be associated with him in a considerable part of these labors, mostly in those of a relatively routine nature, conducted quietly and with none of the excitement of public efforts. He early made upon me the impression of extraordinary practical force. He was devoid of the vanity, the fussiness, the obstinacy and narrowness, that are so unpleasantly obvious in many able and sincere men devoted to reform movements. With great singleness of purpose, he was peculiarly open-minded, as eager to learn as to teach, as ready to follow as to lead. His tact was unfailing, because it was the natural expression of his sympathetic and considerate nature. No one who came into active relations with him in this peculiar work but was unconsciously encouraged to do his best. Even the bores — and Heaven knows that they were not wanting — forgot to betray their full tediousness under the influence of his gentle and firm guidance. He seemed so unaffectedly to expect from every one the fullest measure of unselfish and modest service that it was impossible to refuse it.

The reform enlisted many able men from different parts of the Union. The lawyers naturally were the most numerous, but there were representatives of all professions and occupations, many

of them of national repute. I think it is not an
exaggeration to say that the leadership of Mr. Curtis, never asserted and equally never concealed,
was universally conceded. This, of course, was in
some degree due to the fact that no one else gave
to the work the same amount of time and study.
In his own mind, I should say that it was the opportunity presented, and the responsibility imposed,
by this leadership that chiefly impressed him, and
these were met with a courage, assiduity, and minute and constant care, such as few men give save
under the spur of interest or ambition.

The feature of greatest public interest in Mr.
Curtis's reform work was his annual address at the
meeting of the National League. This was delivered each year on the first evening of the two-day
meeting, and consisted primarily of a review of the
course of the reform for the year just closed, a statement of what remained to be done, indications of
the next steps feasible, and always included an argument and an appeal for the general cause. These
addresses, with some earlier ones and Mr. Curtis's
report as chairman of the Civil Service Commission
made to President Grant in 1871, form the second
volume of the "Orations and Addresses" published after his death. This volume is in some respects the most valuable of the published writings
of Mr. Curtis. In it will be found the substance
of what he had to say on the phase of public affairs
that engrossed the most of his thought, energy,
and time during the last twenty years of his life.

Here is his explanation of what it was in our politics that needed reform; of what the consequences would be if the reform were not brought about; of what would be the immediate and the progressive benefits, should the reform succeed, of the general principles and the specific aims and methods of reform. It was by no means a simple or narrow cause in which he had enlisted. Its most apparent scope — the improvement of the civil service, making it efficient, clean, reasonably economical, and an honorable career for honorable men — was certainly not unimportant, and it was never ignored or underestimated by Mr. Curtis, who in this as in other matters was sensible and practical. But in comparison with the wider and ultimate effect sought upon the politics of the country, upon its public life, the character of the government, and the public conscience, this primary effect of the reform was, in his mind, subordinate and incidental. Had the reform been confined to its attainment, we may be sure that he would have given to it, as he did to numberless movements of minor and relatively passing interest, a cordial advocacy proportioned to its real merit, but nothing more. He never would have surrendered to it the days and nights of steady labor, the deep and anxious study, the patient attention to detail, that he gave gladly to civil service reform. Nor could it have inspired him to any of the more important of these addresses, which are, in their kind, among the best that remain from Mr. Curtis, and among the best that the history of political life in the United States affords.

The struggle for reform was in fact to Mr. Curtis, as I have already suggested, another struggle for popular freedom, for the assertion of the national conscience, for the gradual repression and the final abolition of a tyranny not differing in essence from that of the slave power. He found this tyranny — and he had no difficulty in demonstrating the fact — as unjust and as debasing within its limits as the one that fell with the triumph of the Union armies. And in some regards it was more dangerous, because less obvious, more insidious and obscure, and less easily arousing the indignant revolt of the moral sense of the people. It was the consciousness of this truth that awakened and kept alive in him for so many years that fervent and unflagging zeal, that generous and firm devotion, of which these addresses are the witness.

Any one who will read the volume will not fail to be impressed by the development of Mr. Curtis's conception of the range of the reform, and of his manner of discussing it. The substance of all the chief arguments is, indeed, to be found in the earliest addresses, and in the report to President Grant in 1871. But with the progress of the reform, with the unfolding of the way in which it impressed both its friends and its foes, with the changed conditions of politics and the varying policy of successive administrations, there comes a very striking extension of Mr. Curtis's treatment of the subject.

Probably the address at the eleventh annual meeting of the National League in Baltimore in 1892, in the spring of the year in which he died, may be accepted as the fullest and most impressive statement of the whole matter. I am not aware that Mr. Curtis had at that time any serious concern as to his health; but he was in his sixty-ninth year, he had had some of the warnings which age brings of the limit of human energy and endurance. Looking over the large circle of his associates, many of them affectionate friends, all of them admiring and trusting followers, he must have missed some who twenty years before had stood by his side. He saw very few who had reached his age, and, I think, none that had given to the cause the long years of wearing labor that he had given. Possibly there was a half-recognized sense that he was nearing the end. Assuredly the address was such as he might have made had he known that it was the final legacy to the beloved cause, the farewell words of instruction and guidance and inspiration.

In this address he made the clearest and most complete statement of the underlying principle of the reform. When he came to publish it, he gave it the title, " Party and Patronage." Its subject was the need of curbing the encroachment of executive power lodged in party and maintained by patronage. He traced the resistance of the English Parliament to the pretensions of the royal prerogative, and the resistance of the colonies to the pretensions of the English Parliament, and he described the action of the framers of the Constitution with the purpose of limiting the use of the appointing power: —

"The people had assumed their own government, but, as they could not administer it directly, it was administered by agents selected by party, or the organized majority, but under such restrictions as the whole body of the voters, or the people, might impose. The crown had vanished. There was no king or permanent executive. There were a President and legislature elected by the people for limited terms. But the practical agency of the government was party, and, whoever might be elected President, party remained in the administration permanent as a king, and with the same control of the executive power. But the executive power, whether in the hands of a king or party, does not change its nature. It seeks its own aggrandizement and cannot safely be trusted. Buckle says that no man is wise enough and strong enough to be vested with absolute authority. It fires his brain and maddens him. But this, which is true of an individual, is not less true of an aggregate of individuals or of a party. A party or a majority needs watching as much as a king. Indeed, that such distrust is the safeguard of democracy against despotism is a truth as old as Demosthenes. Like a sleuth-hound, distrust must follow executive power, however it may double and whatever form it may assume. It is as much the safeguard of popular right against the will of a party as against the prerogative of a king. Distrust is in fact the instinct of enlightened political sagacity, which sees that the peril of popular institutions lies in the abuse of the forms of popular government. The great commonplace of our political speech, ' Eternal vigilance is the price of liberty,' is fundamentally true. It is a scripture essential to political salvation. The demand for civil service reform is the cry of that eternal vigilance for still further restriction by the people of the delegated executive power.

" Civil service reform, therefore, is but another successive step in the development of liberty under law. It is not eccentric or revolutionary. It is a logical measure of political progress. In the light of a larger experience, and adjusted to the exigencies of a republic in the nineteenth century instead of a monarchy in the thirteenth and seventeenth centuries, in the spirit of the wise jealousy of the Constitution, in the interest of free institutions and of honest government, it proposes still further to restrict the executive power as exercised by party. It is a measure based upon the observation of a century, during which government by party has developed conditions and tendencies and perils which could not have been foreseen in detail, although, at the beginning of party government under the Constitution, Washington said of party spirit: ' It exists under different shapes in all governments, more or less stifled, controlled, or repressed ; but in those of popular form it is seen in its greatest rankness, and is truly their worst enemy.'

" What our fathers could not guess, we can see.
Party, which is properly simply the organization of
citizens who agree in their views of public policy
to secure the enactment of their views in law, has
become what is well called a machine, which con-
trols the political action of millions of citizens who
vote for candidates that the machine selects, and
for measures that the machine dictates or approves.
Servility to party takes the place of individual independence of action. So completely does it con-
sume political manhood, that, like men suddenly
hurried from their warm beds into the night air,
shivering and chattering in the cold, even intelligent citizens who have protested against their
party machine as fraudulent and false, and an organized misrepresentation of the party conviction
and will, declare that if their protest against the
power of fraud and corruption does not avail, and
the party commands them to yield, they will bow
the head and bend the knee in loyalty to fraud and
corruption. The despotism of the machine is so
absolute, and the triumph of the party so supersedes
the reason and purpose of the party, that we have
now reached a point in our political development
when, upon the most vital and pressing public
questions, parties do not even know their own
opinions, and factions of the same party wrangle
fiercely to determine by a majority what the party
thinks and proposes. Meanwhile, so completely
has the conception of a party as merely a convenient but clumsy agency to promote certain public ob-

jects disappeared that one of the chief journals of the country recently remarked with entire gravity that it found 'no fault with conscientious independence in politics,' which was like announcing with lofty forbearance that, as a philosophic moralist, it found no fault with truth-telling or honest dealing.

"But it is by party action, nevertheless, that reform must be secured. Why, then, do we anticipate success? Because party itself is finally subject to public opinion, and, whatever the machine may wish, it is at last obliged to conform to public opinion, as a sailing-ship to the wind. Party machines, truculent and defiant, resist, but like kings they yield at last to, the people. The king, whose arbitrary excesses produce the peremptory popular demand for relief, ordains, however reluctantly, a restriction that limits his power. So the French Bourbon, Louis XVIII., signed the Charter of 1814, and the Prussian Hohenzollern, Frederic William IV., summoned the Constituent Assembly of 1848. They call this surrender *motu proprio*, an act of their sovereign will. But they knew, and the world knows, that it is the will of a greater sovereign than they, the will of the people. Our appeal is now, as it has always been, not to party, but to the people, who are masters of party. As the English barons, in the phrase of an old English writer, cut the claws of John; as the English Parliament taught terribly the English king that not he, but the English people, was the sovereign; as the American colonies taught the

English Parliament in turn that the American people would rule America, — so, by every law and custom demanded by public opinion · which restrains the arbitrary abuse of executive power by party, the American people are constantly teaching American parties that not the parties but the people rule. We cannot expect the king nor the Parliament nor the party to solicit the lesson or to enjoy the discipline. We cannot expect their supple courtiers, either in the palace or in the saloon, to demand that the king or the party shall be bound. But bound nevertheless they are, bound by the people they have been, and bound by the same power they will be. The record of this year, as of the last year and of every year since the League was formed; even the reiterated pledges of platforms, although reiterated only to be largely broken; the most sweet voices of the stump, that sink into barren silence; the bills introduced that gasp and die in committee on the one hand, and on the other the constantly enlarged scope of the reformed system in the public service, — all reveal the ever-stronger public purpose, and the constantly greater achievement of that purpose, to add in civil service reform another golden link to the shining chain of historical precedents which, by wisely restraining executive power, promote the public welfare."

It is plain, from the extracts that I have given not only from his later speeches but from others, that the standard of reform with Mr. Curtis was very high, — that he regarded it as of national importance, and had gradually, after his service on the commission, come to place it above any object professed or pursued by either of the great parties. During the eleven years that he presided over the National Reform League, it was his duty to judge the party in power by this standard. This was not an easy task. In 1884 he spoke in the very height of the bitter and heated contest for the presidency between the party he had repudiated and the one to which he had brought his support, — qualified, indeed, and guarding his perfect independence, but requiring the immediate and absolute choice between the candidate of one and the candidate of the other. From 1885 to 1888 he spoke with Mr. Cleveland in the President's office, and was obliged, applying to the known acts of the administration the standard he had defined, to describe wherein the administration fell short, and how far the President for whom he had voted was responsible for the shortcomings. From 1889 to 1892 he was again forced to survey the course of his old party, to apply to it with equal sincerity and equal fairness the same searching tests. It will be seen that his peculiar and trying function was exercised during each of two national elections, in which, as an editor and a leader of public opinion, he took an active and in one of them a decisive part, and each of which was followed by a change in the party in possession of the presidency. It was practically impossible that what he said should not influence party action, nor did he seek to avoid such an effect. It was equally impossible that he should escape the accusation of partisan prejudice and exaggeration, however anxious he was not to give either justification or excuse for such accusation. I think it is a reasonable judgment on his work that he was singularly fair, not only in intention, but in the labor, study, reflection, and consultation that he devoted to ascertaining the facts, and to determining their real significance and value. I thought so at the time, weighing the addresses as they were delivered from year to year, and I am strongly confirmed in the opinion by a careful review of them. A very significant piece of evidence upon this point is the fact that, among the active workers for civil service reform who were intimately associated with him in the league, and who may be said to have felt a pretty definite though indirect responsibility for his utterances while their association with him lasted, were a number of ardent and convinced Republicans and equally convinced and ardent Democrats, and, so far as I am aware, none of them felt called upon in any degree to free themselves from that responsibility. Friends and advocates of the reform who were supporters of Mr. Blaine, and who condemned unqualifiedly Mr. Curtis's choice in 1884, found his speech of that year without any fault that they felt themselves required to point out. The most resolute Democratic reformers conceded his fairness to Mr. Cleveland.

The most—I cannot say enthusiastic, for I do not recall any—but the most friendly, supporters of Mr. Harrison were ready to make a corresponding concession. Abuse there was, of course, from both sides, and much honest and sincere but ignorant misconception. But the men who followed Mr. Curtis's course most closely, knew it most completely, and could best pass upon its motives, were entirely satisfied of his candor and loyalty.

CHAPTER XXIII.

THE TYPICAL INDEPENDENT.

THE year 1888 presented to those who had refused to support the Republican candidate four years before, and had given their votes to Mr. Cleveland, the not wholly simple question of whether they would return to their former association. The message of President Cleveland in December, 1887, devoted chiefly to the question of taxation forced upon the country by the enormous surplus and accumulation of revenue, made the tariff the chief issue of the presidential campaign. The failure to nominate Mr. Blaine eliminated his personal character as an obvious and unquestioned element in the decision. The manifest tendency of a very large part of the Democratic party towards unsound and dangerous financial legislation, which appeared to command the assent of a majority of that party and to be opposed by a majority of the Republicans, was a matter not lightly to be dismissed. The policy of Mr. Cleveland as to administrative reform had not been consistent, and had been fairly though roughly described as for reform or against it, according as the reform sentiment did or did not control the decisive vote in any given State. In these circumstances a considerable number of the Republicans, who with Mr. Curtis had supported Mr. Cleveland in 1884, now gave their support to the Republican candidate, Gen. Benjamin Harrison. Mr. Curtis decided that his duty was otherwise. His view of the question was explained in some detail in a letter addressed to a correspondent who had written him a letter of friendly disapproval and criticism. I give it, in preference to any public utterance, as being peculiarly characteristic : —

TO A. C. TILDEN, SAN FRANCISCO.

NEW YORK, 12th September, 1888.

MY DEAR SIR, — I am very much obliged to you for your frank and friendly letter of the 4th, and I am very glad to answer it in the same spirit.

My strong anti-slavery feeling made me a Republican, and the original purpose and character and membership of the party seem to me to have been more humane, progressive, and truly American than that of any other party. But as a Republican, after the primary purpose of the party had been attained by the result of the war, I was constantly engaged in withstanding the party tendency to political abuse and corruption. This culminated in 1884 by the nomination to the presidency of a man who, in my judgment, had trafficked in his official place for his personal profit. The election of such a man would have been disgraceful to the party and dishonorable to the country, and this consideration was paramount to all others.

I therefore supported Mr. Cleveland, not because I had renounced *my* Republican principles, but because I held to them, and as the surest way of securing the defeat of Mr. Blaine, and because I believed Mr. Cleveland to be an honest and courageous man who would resist any mischievous tendency of his party. During his term it has been evident that the spirit of Mr. Blaine is that of the Republican party, and that he is at present its true representative. Mr. Cleveland has resisted much in his party, but not as much as I had hoped. But I still regard him as honest and courageous. Now, as the chief issue of the campaign is the method of reducing the revenue, and as I agree with Mr. Cleveland's policy and look upon the Republican policy as very injurious, and as I see that Mr. Blaine is the controlling genius of his party, and that a vote for Mr. Harrison is really a vote for Mr. Blaine, the same principles that made me vote for the Republican candidate formerly induce me to vote for Mr. Cleveland now.

But I am not a Democrat. I shall vote against Mr. Hill, the Democratic candidate for governor in New York, and I think Mr. Cleveland much better than his party. I am an Independent, and I am so for the same reasons that made me a Republican formerly. The purposes that I would promote were then uniformly to be served by supporting that party. But all the circumstances are changed, and now I can serve them best by voting independently of party names.

If my principles had been changed for any unworthy purpose, there would be truly a shade upon my name. But they are the same now that they were when I stumped for Frémont in '56, and supported Lincoln, the greatest of modern Americans, in 1860 and '64. In the sense in which you use the words, I am not an adherent of Mr. Cleveland. I have been disappointed in much that he has done, and have said so plainly and publicly. I think him honest, although often sophisticated, and in the present situation support him as the better alternative. Should Mr. Harrison be elected, I should hope to be equally just in my estimate of his conduct.

I write this long statement because I should be very sorry that a young man, who from what he has heard of me is inclined to wonder regretfully at my course, should lack any explanation which I can give him.

With all good wishes, I am

Very truly yours,
GEORGE WILLIAM CURTIS.

The last literary work of Mr. Curtis, outside of his regular tasks, was the editing of " The Correspondence of John Lothrop Motley."[1] It was a work of much labor and some delicacy, owing to the strong feeling aroused in Mr. Motley and his friends by the circumstances of his resignation of the mission to Austria, and of his retirement from

---

[1] New York: Harper & Bros. 2 vols. 1889.

the English mission. The brief statement made by Mr. Curtis in the preface may well be pondered by editors generally: " In preparing (the letters) for publication, the editor has withheld whatever he believed that the writer's good judgment and thoughtful consideration for others would have omitted. This rule excludes comments upon persons and affairs which, however innocent or playful, might cause needless pain or misapprehension. It excludes, also, much of the repetition which naturally occurs in such letters, and a large part of the domestic and friendly messages and allusions which, although illustrating the writer's generous sympathy and affectionate disposition, are essentially private. If much of such matter is still left, it is because, with all his interest in literary pursuits and in public affairs, Mr. Motley was essentially a domestic man, and a more rigid exclusion could not have been made without injustice to his character. Otherwise the letters are printed as they were written."

The last public address of Mr. Curtis was that on James Russell Lowell, first delivered in Brooklyn, February 22, 1892, and repeated in New York in March. In it he said : —

" Like all citizens of high public ideals, Lowell was inevitably a public critic and censor, but he was much too good a Yankee not to comprehend the practical conditions of political life in this country. No man understood better than he such truth as lies in John Morley's remark : ' Parties

are a field where action is a long second best, and
where the choice constantly lies between two blunders.' He did not therefore conclude that there is no
alternative, 'that nought is everything and everything is nought.' But he did see closely that, while
the government of a republic must be a government
by party, yet independence of party is much more
vitally essential in a republic than fidelity to party.
Party is a servant of the people, but a servant who
is foolishly permitted by his master to assume sovereign airs, like Christopher Sly, the tinker, whom
the lord's attendants obsequiously salute as master: —

> " ' Look how thy servants do attend on thee,
> Each in his office ready at thy beck.'

To a man of the highest public spirit like Lowell,
and of the supreme self-respect which always keeps
faith with itself, no spectacle is sadder than that
of intelligent, superior, honest public men prostrat-
ing themselves before a party, professing what they
do not believe, affecting what they do not feel,
from abject fear of an invisible fetich, a chimera, a
name, to which they alone give reality and force,
as the terrified peasant himself made the spectre
of the Brocken before which he quailed.

" With his lofty patriotism and his extraordinary
public conscience, Lowell was distinctively the Independent in politics. He was an American and a
republican citizen. He acted with parties, as every
citizen must act if he acts at all. But the notion
that a voter is a traitor to one party when he votes

with another was as ludicrous to him as the assertion that it is treason to the White Star Steamers
to take passage on a Cunarder. When he would
know his duty, Lowell turned within, not without.
He listened, not for the roar of the majority in the
street, but for the still small voice in his own
breast. For, while the method of republican government is party, its basis is individual conscience
and common sense. This entire political independence Lowell always illustrated.

"Whatever his party associations and political
sympathies, Lowell was at heart and by temperament conservative, and his patriotic independence
in our politics is the quality which is always unconsciously recognized as the true conservative
element in the country. In the tumultuous excitement of our popular elections, the real appeal on
both sides is, not to the party, which is already
committed, but to those citizens who are still open
to reason, and may yet be persuaded. In the most
recent serious party appeal the orator said : ' Above
all things, political fitness should lead us not to forget that at the end of our plans we must meet face
to face at the polls the voters of the land, with bal-
lots in their hands, demanding as a condition of the
support of our party, fidelity and undivided devotion
to the cause in which we have enlisted them. This
recognizes an independent tribunal which judges
party. It implies that, besides the host who march
under the party color and vote at the party command, there are citizens who may or may not wear

the party uniform, but who vote only at their own individual command, and who give the victory. They may be angrily classified as political Laodiceans; but it is to them that parties appeal, and rightly, because, except for this body of citizens, the despotism of party would be absolute, and the republic would degenerate into a mere oligarchy of bosses."

When, in the letter to the San Francisco correspondent above cited, Mr. Curtis wrote, " I am an Independent," it was the standard of independence described in his characterization of Lowell that he had in mind. He was very faithful to that standard, and the trials of his fidelity were more severe, intimate, and lasting than those of Lowell. " Literature," he said of the latter, " was his pursuit, but patriotism was his passion." Of Curtis it may be said that patriotism was both his passion and his pursuit, to which literature was constantly and with no small sacrifice, nor without pangs of reluctance, but constantly, subordinated. He was not only for thirty years a political journalist, but he was a political speaker, and an active participant in party effort. While his devotion to the purposes of the Republican party was the main-spring of his work in and for that party, his long years of unremitting and systematic activity in it wove about him numberless strong ties of sympathy, association, and memory. These were not easily severed nor severed without pain. He was the most conspicuous instance of his time of the

Independent who, without hope of reward or gain and at such a cost, followed the orders of his conscience. This, as I have said, I regard as his greatest service to his country, and as a service of inestimable value. For the independence of Mr. Curtis was not narrow, or obstinate, or ignorant, or conceited. Of that kind there is no lack. It is, to a certain order of mind, not merely easy but attractive. The conscience which Mr. Curtis obeyed was enlightened and open. He was as careful, painstaking, and critical in seeking to know the right as he was firm and determined in support of what he finally decided was for him the right. And he was, so far as I have been able to see, singularly respectful of the same sort of independence in others. His indignation at hypocrisy and self-seeking in public life was a flame as steady as it was hot; but toward honest difference of judgment — honest in the formation as in the expression — he was not merely tolerant, he was frankly and sincerely respectful. His great gifts, for which he had or made great opportunity, made his career an example of far-reaching and lasting influence; and I think it may with reason and justice be said that the influence was, without qualification, pure and good.

CHAPTER XXIV.

THE work of the Board of Regents of the University of the State of New York, to which Mr. Curtis had been elected in 1864, and of which he had thought so little when he was a member of the Constitutional Convention that he had tried to have the Board abolished, was greatly changed when in 1888 Mr. Melville Dewey, of New York, became its secretary and executive officer with a residence at the state capital. The many and various and sometimes conflicting laws regulating the authority and functions of the regents were codified, rendered consistent, and in some degree modified. The powers, which for the greater part had been either misunderstood or neglected, were now found to be considerable, and with the energetic management of Mr. Dewey, the board became a living organization, with possibilities of great achievement, and with steady and rapid progress in actual accomplishment. The original purpose of the board, when created, was the establishment and conduct of a university that should be the crown of the system of education in the State, towards which all other institutions should be guided,

and the standard of which should be at all stages
kept in mind. To serve this end the regents
were given the right of inspection of all incorporated institutions of learning, with power to issue
certificates based on their own examination. By
the firm and skillful use of these powers, by estab-
lishing a carefully devised standard for the granting of certificates, by an admirable plan of graded
and uniform examinations, by thorough, intelligent,
and systematic inspection and records, the regents'
certificates were given so high a value as to be indispensable. Thus on the one hand all the edu-
cators in the State were made to desire the approval of the regents, and on the other hand
their active and beneficial coöperation was secured.
After a very great amount of labor, performed in
an exceedingly short time, the original purpose of
the board was in the direct way of being accomplished, and its standard was recognized and controlling. In addition to this work of the regents,
its influence upon the professional schools of law
and medicine was steadily strengthened ; the State
Library, which had previously been little more
than a constantly growing heterogeneous mass of
books, was reduced to order, and so classified and
arranged as to admit of indefinite expansion and
of corresponding usefulness ; while, by various
means, its treasures were made available over the
whole State, and local school libraries were multiplied. The scientific collections of the State were
reorganized, brought under one general control,

made mutually more useful, and their development provided for. In all this work Mr. Curtis, who became Chancellor of the University in 1890, took not only the greatest interest, but a large part. Recognizing the special knowledge and gifts of Mr. Dewey, he gave to him the heartiest and most appreciative support; but, while he felt the impulsion of "such a steam engine" (as, in one of his letters, he called the secretary), he was not in the habit of shifting responsibility, and sanctioned only what he carefully understood in principle and in all essential practical features. The tax of this unpaid and inconspicuous though honorable work upon his time and strength was considerable; but he was fortunate to see its results so far achieved, and its methods so firmly established and so effective, as to constitute a satisfying reward. The following notes from Mr. Dewey explain the relation of Mr. Curtis to their work, and to those associated with it : —

"My admiration for Chancellor Curtis grew with every occasion of personal contact. Of his public and private life I can only say that I share in the universal admiration. As chancellor of the University, however, he was known to me as to no one else. From the time he took office, January 30, 1890, his interest in our work, and his faith in the splendid future before it, grew constantly. At our last interview he emphasized this more strongly than ever before, and was looking forward to our immediate future with a confidence which, with all my enthusiasm, came to me as a new inspiration; for I felt, when one so careful and conservative as Mr. Curtis had, after twenty-eight years of service as a regent, looked through our plans and our recent development and felt so fully satisfied as did he as to our future, that we, who were too much at the heart of the work to see it with the perspective of one at a little distance, ought to be well satisfied with the verdict.

" Mr. Curtis was exceedingly conscientious in regard to all his official duties, but was entirely free from that spirit which often, in conscientious men occupying supervisory positions, becomes so embarrassing to administrative officers.   He watched all our work with great care, and criticised or made suggestions with absolute freedom; but he held that those who were giving their lives to this office, and night and day were in its atmosphere and studying its interests, should be trusted as far as practicable with all *details* of administration.   His course was a golden mean between that of those perfunctory officials who sign their name to any kind of a document placed before them by assistants or subordinates, and who take the honor without assuming the responsibility, and that of the similar officials at the other extreme who so often cripple the best work by insisting on projecting their own personal equation into the work of subordinate officers of a totally different type of mind. He seemed always to deal with us as he would like to be dealt with under like circumstances; and

I can recall no case, in these happy years of official association with him, in which he has not recognized to our entire satisfaction our right to shape minor details as we found best in our daily work, though he always faithfully and intelligently insisted on knowing that the general principles and policy of the department were observed. Nothing in my life has been so satisfactory to me as Mr. Curtis's statement last January that he was perfectly satisfied to have his name stand at the head of our publications and stationery, as responsible to the public for the character of the work that we were doing in the University offices. He always seemed to read between the lines, and to understand clearly the spirit in which our work was done, without making it necessary to call his attention to our devotion to duty, or to the unselfish interest in the University work which is so marked a feature of nearly every prominent member of our staff. I need hardly say that in the office each one felt that he had lost a personal friend ; and each one realized how great was the public loss when he was gone who in so unusual a degree at once fully discharged his responsible supervisory duties, and yet left to the working officers that sense of freedom from every unnecessary interference without which the highest and best work is never done."

CHAPTER XXV.

IN writing the life of Mr. Curtis as an "American Man of Letters," I have not forgotten his claim to such a designation, though I have tried to give, as nearly as possible within the limits of the book, the materials for an estimate of his course as a man of public affairs. As has been suggested, had he devoted himself to letters only, or were he known only by his literary work, his reputation in that kind would have been more distinct and might be more lasting. The extent of his writing was great. The Easy Chair alone, were the monthly papers continued for nearly forty years collected, would form some thirty volumes of the size of the present one. His addresses, from which three large volumes have been selected, could easily have supplied at least twice that number. All his work was carefully and conscientiously done, most of it with more trained critical discrimination than was given to the half dozen volumes of essays and travel, and the novels that are commonly accepted as his "works." Of the Easy Chair especially it must be remembered that it was the chief product of Mr. Curtis's pen, was wrought in the pure literary spirit, and was, as much as the work of any prose-writer of his time, literature. It suffers now from the ephemeral form of its publication. Even the collected essays in their dainty form, and with the light device from "The Tatler" with which the author introduces them, "I shall from time to time Report and Consider all Matters of what Kind soever that shall occur to me," still suggest the fleeting interest of a monthly appearance and disappearance. Nor can it be denied that Mr. Curtis himself had little confidence in their permanent interest, and was with difficulty persuaded by his publishers to select those that were put into a volume before his death. I doubt, indeed, whether he would have done so, had he not had access to the collection of his friend, Mr. Pinkerton, who had faithfully gathered and bound them all. But an author is not the most trustworthy critic of his own work, and it is not to be inferred that Mr. Curtis was not from first to last scrupulously attentive, in these essays, to a very high standard. The form in which they were originally given to the public, so far from relaxing his sense of responsibility, rather kept it active. He had a constant and strong impression of the very great number of readers whom he reached, and of the peculiar function performed by the magazine in the American family. He knew that to thousands of these families, with eager, interested, curious minds, with active intellectual impulses, but with scant opportunity or time for what is generally known as culture, the magazine was what its name implied, — their store of literature. His wide and long-continued experience in lecturing, covering as it did all the free States and extending over more than a quarter of a century, brought him intimate knowledge of the classes who composed the readers of the magazine. He knew their needs, their mental appetites, their aspirations; he knew very well also their limitations, and he regarded them as entitled in every way to his best work. His best he certainly gave them. There is something slightly pathetic and wholly beautiful in the spirit of the Easy Chair toward this curious *clientèle*. It is absolutely free from any taint or suspicion of condescension. Through the hundreds of essays there is manifest a simple, loyal, unaffected respect for the readers. There is not even any invidious elimination of subjects that might easily be supposed to be "caviare to the general." Poetry, art, music, letters, the higher politics, take their place freely and naturally beside social satire and reminiscence and anecdote. I have spoken of the writings of Mr. Curtis in "Harper's Weekly" as a kind of talking in which the editor had the air of speaking face to face with his readers. From the Easy Chair there was talking also, and the candor, the high courtesy, the unfailing self-respect that expresses itself in respect for others, which are qualities of the best talking, are manifest. Indeed, no other style could so easily have borne so varied a burden. The writer who sets out to produce a volume on philosophy, literature, morals, history, society, or any defined phase of them, finds his hand subdued to that he works in, and his writing, though satisfying or delighting those interested in his particular topic, may easily repel those who are not, or may weary them, or leave them indifferent. But when a man of rich and highly-trained mind, a wide reader, a vigorous and alert thinker, with a vivid and sustained interest in a great range of differently interesting subjects, permits you to listen as he talks, ripely but with leisure, sometimes profoundly but always genially, you get from him something of his best in whatever direction his thought may turn. This is what one gets of Mr. Curtis in the Easy Chair, and what has made that series of essays, during the long years of their regular production, a unique and charming and very important contribution not only to American literature, but to the development and formation of national opinion and sentiment.

In Mr. Curtis the man of letters and the orator were blended. The more important of the orations were written out and read, though they did not seem to the hearer to be read. Some of them were committed to memory, but the memorizing was complete and the delivery without hesitation, so that in each case the personal impression of the orator was the same, and the impression was very strong. The matter was prepared with the audience constantly in mind, and nothing was neglected which could arouse or hold them ; but the essential thing with the orator was the substance, the thought, which the form must serve. Mr. Curtis's conception of the function of the orator can be gathered from the range of his subjects as described in previous pages, and from the extracts given. It is pleasantly illustrated by the following notes of a conversation with him furnished me by one of his associates in " Harper's Weekly : " —

" When I was in Washington," said Mr. Curtis, " I used to see much of Senator Conkling, and we spent many evenings together. Upon the whole I liked him, in spite of the defects which no one who came into communication with him could overlook. I remember one talk with him about eloquence, in which he naturally considered himself a connoisseur. After we had discussed it abstractly for a while, he asked me for an example of what I called true and high eloquence. I repeated to him the peroration of Emerson's Dartmouth address, which you of course remember, — ' Gentlemen, I have ventured to offer you these considerations upon the scholar's place and hope, because I thought that, standing, as many of you now do, on the threshold of this college, girt and ready to go and assume tasks public and private in your country, you would not be sorry to be admonished of those primary duties of the intellect whereof you will seldom hear from the lips of your new companions. You will hear every day the maxims of a low prudence. You will hear that the first duty is to get land and money, place and name! "What is this Truth you seek? What is this Beauty?" men will ask with derision. If nevertheless God have called any of you to explore truth and beauty, be bold, be firm, be true. When you shall say, "As others do, so will I; I renounce, I am sorry for it, my early visions; I must eat the good of the land, and let learning and romantic expectations go until a more convenient season;" — then dies the man in you; then once more perish the buds of art and poetry and science, as they have died already in a thousand, thousand men. The hour of that choice is the crisis of your history, and see that you hold yourself fast by the intellect.' It did not impress the senator much. He found it too tame and creeping a style, and I naturally challenged him in his turn for an example. He took an attitude, and in his most oratorical manner gave me an exordium that is in the school readers by an orator named Sprague, I think. It begins: 'Not many years ago where we now sit the rank thistle nodded in the wind, and the wild fox dug his hole unscared.' The senator's manner, the evident fervency of his belief in his masterpiece, and the contrast of it with Emerson's, all together were too much for me, and I broke out in a peal of laughter which I could not restrain. I fear Senator Conkling never quite forgave me that laughter."

It is not without significance that in 1870, a quarter of a century after Mr. Curtis's life at Concord and the club evenings in Mr. Emerson's library, the former should have quoted from the latter an example of what he regarded as " true and high eloquence." " We can have him once in three or four seasons " is Mr. Curtis's report of the lecturing committee's view of Emerson. " But really," he adds, " they had him all the time without knowing it. He was the philosopher Proteus, and he spoke through all the more popular mouths." If Mr. Emerson did not speak directly through the mouth of Mr. Curtis, who had too much of his own to say to permit of this, his influence was considerable. Both were optimists, both idealists. That is to say, they believed in the best, that it was possible ultimately to attain it, and imperative always to pursue it. Mr. Curtis brought this belief into fields of work very different from those of Mr. Emerson, who began his speaking in a pulpit, and never quite lost the sense of remoteness that the pulpit impressed upon his intense nature. But Mr. Curtis, when he had fairly found his work, and began to speak, not merely for what he had to say, but for the effect of what he should say, kept an idealism as lofty and an optimism as unflagging as those of Mr. Emerson, and in circumstances that tried them far more severely. From the time of the delivery of the address at the Wesleyan University in 1856 to that of the Lowell address in New York in March, 1892, there was hardly a lecture or oration of Mr. Curtis that was not meant to set forth a high ideal, to apply it to some duty actually pressing, and to stir and strengthen the hearts of his hearers for the task the duty imposed. With this dominant tendency it would have been easy for a man with his unusual gifts as a speaker to become an agitator, with the narrowness and monotony that incessant agitation often brings. From this he was wholly exempt, not only through the variety of his intellectual sympathies and the thoroughness of his training, but by the constancy of his moral impulse. It was the near duty that enlisted him, and with the years ever new duties approached and claimed and received his zealous service. As to each of them the essential rectitude of his nature imposed upon him not merely zealous service, nor yet merely careful preparation for such service, but deliberate judgment as to the duty itself. Zealous he was in the noblest and completest fashion, but never a zealot, not blind nor rash, nor obstinate nor conceited. He was as anxious to be right as he was determined in what, with an open mind, he had decided to be the right. The prevailing characteristic of his oratory became therefore not advocacy, though powerful and brilliant advocacy there was throughout, but persuasion with that foundation of reason and fairness and candor which is essential to real and lasting persuasion.

In the immediate impression made by the oratory of Mr. Curtis his personality counted for much. Not the intellectual and haughty grace of Wendell Phillips' presence, nor the massive features and commanding figure of Charles Sumner, weighted with conscious dignity, corresponded more completely to the style of their utterance than did Mr. Curtis's peculiar beauty to his. His charm was felt the moment he rose. His form was manly, powerfully built, and exquisitely graceful. His head was of noble cast and bearing; his features were well marked, and in his later years almost rugged; finely cut, but of the type that is not blurred or effaced within the range of an audience. His forehead was square, broad, and of vigorous lines; his eyes of blue-gray, large, deep-set under strong and slightly shaggy brows, lighted the shadow as with a flame, now gentle and glancing, now profound and burning. His voice was a most fortunate organ, deep, musical, yielding without effort the happy inflections suited to the thought, clear and bright in the lighter passages, alternately tender and flute-like, ringing like a bugle or vibrating in solemn organ tones that hushed the intense emotion it had aroused. His gestures were very few and simple. There was nothing of the "action" that the trained orator of the old school studied so carefully; no effort to sustain the attention of the audience, as Everett did, with a skill that an actor might envy; none of the restless and irrepressible movement, which in Beecher responded to the rush and torrent of his eloquence. The speaker seemed absorbed by the expression of his thought, unheeding the eyes, seeking the judgment and the heart, of his auditors.

"I see now," wrote Hawthorne in 1851 to Mr.

Curtis on the appearance of the "Nile Notes," "that you are forever an author." And an author Mr. Curtis was to the last. If he did not cling to the usual forms of authorship, he was continually under the spell of the literary spirit; and he gave to all his productions unstintingly and almost unconsciously that which makes books literature, — absolute and loving fidelity to the best thought. His addresses are full of his love of scholarship and of the fruits of that love, and his ideal of the citizen was the citizen who regarded and performed his duties as a scholar should. He was not insensible — on the contrary, he was keenly sensitive — to the charm of form, studied it, delighted in analyzing it, and strove for it with unfailing zest. He was a most delicate and acute critic of literary style, and, though he wrote relatively little on this subject, there was nothing more enjoyable than his discussion of it in conversation, when his talk illustrated, in its rhythmical flow, its vivid and luminous play, some of the rarest attributes of style. But the style he admired, and which he early formed and steadily developed, was that which, according to the Buffon tradition, "is the man." Literature was to him the record of the best, and it was the best that he sought in it; it was the best also that he tried, modestly but with affectionate constancy, to contribute to it. Literature as a source of enjoyment he did not underestimate, but his deepest enjoyment was in its substance and in the inspiration it breathed into his life. For the mere daintinesses of letters he had little taste; and the over-refinement which is, as it always has been, the ambition of small minds or the weakness of larger minds, aroused in him only an amused pity.

His mind, even in its earliest and most fanciful production, was essentially vigorous and sane, of a fibre as firm as it was fine. And this quality was developed by his education, as in a sense it determined it. He was not a college-bred man, but he was severely trained in most that gives college breeding its advantage. He was a careful student in many directions, though an independent one. His knowledge of German, of French, of Italian, — which he rarely betrayed in his writing, — was not only sound but delicate, and on his lips these languages had the graceful ease and certainty of intimate acquaintance. The fact is significant of his intellectual methods, of their thoroughness and system, of which there is no severer test than mastery of tongues not habitually used. His reading was wide, as any reader of his works can see, but he was habitually chary of quotations. He had a sound memory, though not a particularly ready one. His mind was assimilative, and seemed more and more so as time passed. It would not be difficult to trace in literature the wide and varied springs of his thought and style, but they would appear as elements blended and incorporated and made his own.

His place in American scholarship was formally and amply recognized by the degrees conferred upon him, which, seeing that he was not a college graduate, and was enrolled in none of the well-defined professions, and had no specialty in letters, were remarkable in number and character. They were as follows: Hon. A. M., Brown, 1854, Madison, 1861, Rochester, 1862; LL. D., Madison, 1864, Harvard, 1881, Brown, 1882; L. H. D., Columbia, 1887. But with this quadruple right to the highest official literary rank, he remained always, save in the publications of the University of the State of New York after he became its chancellor, the plain editor and citizen.

Mr. Curtis was intimately connected with the study and development of art in New York. He began his newspaper work by reviews of the exhibitions, and, though these do not now rank high as criticism, they were sound and helpful in their day, and based on what was then a very unusual degree of observation and knowledge. He always counted many artists among his friends, and of the truest as artists and as friends. He was one of the earliest members of the Century Association, and used playfully to say that the only office he really aspired to was that of president of the Century. In all gatherings of artists and lovers of art he was welcome and honored. He was for many years a trustee of the Metropolitan Museum of Art, and a trustee in fact as well as name. His taste in art was refined and catholic, not coldly critical; and if he was not, and did not care to be, in the strict sense, a connoisseur, he was in the best sense, as used in the charter of his beloved Century, an amateur.

Mr. Curtis was in his religious sentiments what, for lack of a more definite term, is called a Unitarian. For many years it was his habit, when the Unitarian church on Staten Island was without a pastor, to read of a Sunday, from the pulpit, a sermon to the congregation. He was the vice-president of the American Unitarian Association; he was, at the time of his death, President of the Unitarian National Conference, and he not infrequently spoke, on questions involving the to him religious duty of the citizen, in the church of his friend, the Rev. John W. Chadwick, of Brooklyn. It is needless to say that he was not a sectarian, and that there was no taint in his mind of that narrowness and bigotry which are the peril of a belief rejecting much of what is most generally accepted. His creed remained that expressed in the simple statement written to his brother in early manhood, and quoted in the first chapter: "I believe in God, who is love, that all men are brothers, and that the only essential duty of every man is to be *honest*, by which I understand his absolute following of his conscience when duly enlightened. I do *not* believe that God is anxious that men should believe this or that theory of the Godhead, or of the divine government, but that they should live purely, justly, and lovingly."

A biography of Mr. Curtis, though it may convey to its readers some impression of what he did, and of the influence of his **work and of his life,** must necessarily fail to give any adequate impression of his personality **as it** was known **to** those who had the privilege of his intimacy, -- those to whom love or friendship unlocked the treasures of his delightful nature. The picture which, to use a phrase frequently on his pen, " will be forever in the memory " **of** his friends, was **not** that **of** the orator, or of the leader in great causes, but that **of** the companion and friend.

His **tranquil** and lovely home on Staten Island **and** the home in Ashfield among the remote hills **of** northern Massachusetts, bore **to** the busy and struggling city something **of the** relation that their master in his **home** bore to **the** man as **he was known** in the world **of** affairs in which **he** took so brave **and** strong a part. He **was** of **a** singularly simple and consistent nature. He had not, **as** some have, **a** different character at home and abroad, but **rather a** different manifestation of it. His talk was, on **the** whole, the best I have ever **known.** It was at once free and measured. He had great skill as a narrator, a natural skill, the fruit of keen and sympathetic observation and of hearty enjoyment of re-presentation. He had wit at times caustic, but never cruel or unfair or conceited, and **always** bright in itself and illuminating. He had humor **of a** generous and suave sort; and he was capable, even **in** his latest years, of much of that play with the topic **or** the feeling of the moment which we recognize as " fun," though we cannot define it, and which was almost riotous in his early letters. His love of music was constant, and, as a close friend writes, "his touch on the piano, his voice in singing, had a peculiar quality of sweetness." He smilingly adopted as to Wagner the remark he often quoted as to Emerson, of the Bostonian who "did not understand," but whose "daughter did;" and he took a half-sportive delight in dwelling on the memory of the great singers of the past, of whom Jenny Lind was to him the supreme type; but his tribute to Theodore Thomas, at the farewell banquet to that apostle of Wagner, was a very noble tribute to the master as well. He had a gift in the nature of genius for hospitality and for friendship; and it was a curious evidence of the richness and capacity of his nature that, amid strenuous duties and labors that were crowding, exacting, and must have been often exhausting, he was able, not to find, but to make time for such generous social intercourse. He had the precious advantage of demanding and of giving in such intercourse only the substance and reality; he did not despise, he simply ignored, the artificial requirements. He was at home in all circles, because in all he was unaffectedly true to a nature constantly sincere and kind and simple, but a nature also opulent and varied, sensitive, sympathetic. His enjoyment of society, as of the outdoor world of art, of music, and of books, was a sort of talent which developed to the end, and did not wither or fail, and which he delighted to cultivate. I think one

essential condition of it was his extraordinary unselfishness. The irritation that is bred of vanity,
jealousy, envy, the weariness and distrust that are
the revulsion from the feverishness of unworthy desires, seemed impossible to him. He invited and
won the best, because naturally and without con-
straint he offered the best. It was due to this
quality of his nature that it was possible to say of
him, with reason and without exaggeration, that
he was "the man of all Americans, perhaps the
man in all the world, who was most widely held in
affectionate regard, the most lovable and the most
loved of all." The expressions of this sentiment
after his death, from all parts of the land, from
men of all parties and all classes, overbore even
the expressions of sorrow. "Our tears must fall,"
said his friend, Mr. Norton, to those gathered in
the little church at Ashfield, "that we are to see
him no more; but our hearts must be glad that his
memory belongs to us forever, is part of ourselves,
and will be to us a perpetual help and joy." And
in the sorrowful first meeting of the executive committee of the New York Civil Service Reform
Association, Archdeacon Mackay-Smith closed a
simple review of the character and service of the
dead chief: "We must believe that he who did this
work and lived this life was very near to God."

His last public utterance was in March, 1892,
when he repeated in New York the Brooklyn address on Lowell. Early in June he was taken
seriously ill, and after long and acute suffering, on

the last day of the summer, in the quiet home on Staten Island, he died. A few days before the end, a younger brother on parting asked if there was anything he could do for him. "Nothing," was the answer, "but to continue to love me." The words seem his last message to those who knew him, and to the multitude of those who knew only his work. It has been constantly in my mind.

"What is to be written," said a life-long friend of his when his death brought under discussion the preparation of a biography, "is the story of a character." It is the sense of his character that finally remains most distinctly, most firmly, with the most vital influence, from the contemplation of his life. Charm of many sorts he had, but the supreme and pervading one was the completeness with which he could render the charm of virtue, and the spontaneous and constant proof he gave that he was himself possessed by it. I have alluded many times to this in the course of this volume, because it was manifested in so many phases. In public questions, from the early days when in his boyish letters he anticipated Charles Sumner's challenge to Webster to assume that leadership of the cause of the right which alone could give his genius its full scope, to the last noble and mournful tribute to Lowell as a leader of the conscience as well as the intellect of the nation; in his brief but splendid campaign against slavery; in the trying period of the Civil War; in his long and patient efforts first to keep his party true to its best and then to reclaim it; in the years of advocacy of reform in the civil service as the cause of honest and pure public life; in the unselfish and fruitful championship of political independence to which so much of his closing years was given, — in all these shone the high moral purpose of the man. In his literary work — after the books of travel which were his sole venture in a realm where imagination was sovereign — under a thousand lights, in greatly varying forms, and associated with peculiar beauty of fancy, of construction and style, there was the same moral purpose. His rare gifts he brought, a rich and constant tribute, and laid them at the feet of the conscience which was to him the divinely appointed saviour of the world.

INDEX.